THE LANGUAGE OF SPICE

A NOVEL BY

CAROL PECHLER

MENLO PUBLISHING COMPANY

MENLO PARK, CALIFORNIA, USA

Cover location: Morotai Island, North Maluku, Indonesia

ISBN: 978-0-9896154-4-0

Printed in the United States of America

Menlo Publishing Company

225 McKendry Drive, Menlo Park, California 94025

MenloPublishing.net

DEDICATION

Wonderful fellow traveler, my daughter Robin

ACKNOWLEDGEMENTS

- Our writers' group, essential for our useful deadlines, and especially for supportive criticism: Ruth, Betty, Lynn, Chris, Sandra, Mel, Michael, Frances.

-Editing support from Pat, Angela, Frances, Henk, Sam

-Lee Blevins, for formatting, designing, advice, and first printing.

-My dear Henk, whose loving support includes editing and traveling with me to sites in the story.

- My daughter, Robin, my invaluable, dear, fellow traveler.

- Our cats, who sat beside me during a good share of my writing.

-The silver lining to sheltering in place, making way for full focus on editing.

PROLOGUE

Wind gently rustled the leaves. The leaves hummed a melody and danced on their thin stems and sent sun reflections in all directions. The little flashes distracted her for a moment, to a memory of six years before, when she first experienced a strobe light on a twirling mirrored ball. She and several fellow graduate students danced on the flashing lights to the incredibly loud psychedelic music of Jefferson Airplane at The Fillmore in San Francisco on April 12, 1967. But now, sitting under her clove tree, in Ternate, Indonesia, she felt grateful for the quiet.

TABLE OF CONTENTS

PHILIPPINES, 1968

1. Back to the U.S.A.

"Oh *mahal ko* - my darling, have I hurt you?" Migo propped up his head with his elbow on the pillow, startled out of his reverie of the calm, the release.

Laura had turned away from him and was now sobbing deeply, and then another cycle, unable to keep silent, unable to jump out of bed to the bathroom to muffle her sounds.

Outside, the steady chorus of tenor-pitched horns honking on Roxas Boulevard didn't quite cover up her efforts to hide her grief, her mixed feelings.

She turned toward him and reached for his hands. "We won't... It can't work, Migo!" she sobbed.

"Of course we will," he protested. "I want to be with you always; I've told you!"

"It just can't work. I've got to go back to the U.S. to finish my degree and get a job. I can't stay here. And you have a good job here."

"But I told you, my darling, I'm willing to go with you!"

"You know you can't give up your position on the best newspaper in the entire Philippines, and besides, your family has big hopes for you; they're very proud of you, and they'd much rather have a nice Filipina daughter-in-law from a good family, not a rag-tag, up-from-ashes American, maybe pretty enough, but who might try to entice you to leave them."

"*Oh mahal ko*," he squeezed her hands, "I want us to stay together. Let's find a way. You mean so much to me."

"I've thought a lot about it, Migo, you know. You've been so good to me. Good *for* me, but it just won't work out." She closed her eyes, sobbed again, and wiped her streaming tears.

She managed to quiet herself. *I thought he also figured we were just temporary; didn't know he was getting so serious.* She looked into his eyes, smiled, and said, "I feel a little foolish, crying like this after such a wonderful experience with you. I guess this...ecstatic moment... opened up my emotions when I thought, 'this is the last time...'" and she started sobbing again.

"Oh my dear," and he pulled her into his embrace.

After a short time she gently pulled away and stood up to dress. He followed her example and said, "I'll take you to the airport in the morning."

"Oh, Marilu insisted on taking me. Better if we say goodbye here in the hotel room; we can be by ourselves."

They hugged, sorrowfully.

U.S.A. 1968-1972

2. Writing Up

I'm so fortunate to have this IBM Selectric typewriter, Laura thought, as she carefully sorted her notes for analysis and then typing. *I'm so lucky that my grant paid for it. Faster than manual. Great invention.*

Back in Berkeley, California, Laura had progressed to writing the last part of her Ph.D. dissertation, beyond the "divergence" stage, of reading books, articles, and her field notes, to the "convergence" stage of actually writing. She smiled with readiness to begin her work for the day.

So happy with my new desk: plenty of room for my stuff on top, and for the baby below. She had bought a flat, hollow interior door at Minton Lumber, 30" x 78", and four wooden legs that she had screwed on at home.

Laura checked on her little Charlotte who was asleep on a large cushion on the floor and was covered with a little cream-colored blanket that she had knitted in anticipation of the baby's "coming out." *Good, still sleeping.*

Today Laura worked on her discovery in her fieldwork that surprised her. Many young men in her island village had learned a certain language unlike other Philippine languages. Throughout her year on a tiny island in the southern Philippines, she had discovered that young Muslim men here worked to learn multiple languages. One of these "second" languages showed special value, and that was a Philippine creole language spoken as a first language in the nearest city, Zamboanga, a day's ride away by double-outrigger canoe and inter-village bus. This language, young men had told her, was harder to learn because it was not so close to their Samal (along with all other Philippine languages, it - Samal - was in the Austronesian language family), but this other language was so important that many young men had learned it! They called it Chabacano.

She had tested their proficiency in the languages they claimed to know, and now she compared their Chabacano proficiency with their various jobs. *Amazing, this small village, with so many languages and so many types of jobs!* In contrast, village elders had told her that not so long ago, the only available lines of work were subsistence fishing or farming. Added on now were jobs associated with selling products for cash in the city: fish, copra (from coconuts), woven baskets, and *sari-sari* store ownership. And smuggling from Malaysia and Indonesia to the south had grown in popularity: brought across the open Sulu Sea border were cheaper copra, batik fabrics, and cigarettes. And in the city, the young men needed to use the Chabacano language.

Laura looked out the window to the Berkeley sky. *Fog's burned off; blue sky!* She reflected on her own job search. *These young men have to work hard for the most lucrative jobs, but they have real possibilities. I'm working hard, too, and I had to learn their Samal language, but is there a job here for me? The university positions are drying up.*

She looked down at her little Charlotte. "Hey! Where *is* she?!" she said aloud. The cushion was bare of baby, and the blanket was half off of the cushion, its corner pointing toward the kitchen. Laura, so startled that she wondered if she was having a nightmare, jumped out of her chair and tiptoed toward the kitchen. "Oh! There you are, my darling; you can crawl! You were so quiet!" *And I was so focused!* She knelt on her hands and knees to return Charlotte's beaming smile, face close to face. Laura turned upright to sit on the floor, and Charlotte climbed into her lap. They hugged and laughed. *I've got to finish this dissertation fast. I've got to get a job, for both of us. You're my biggest responsibility, now. I've got to get a job, for **your** sake.*

3. Single Mom

Laura's fellow student Grace came over around eight o'clock in the evening, their usual time to talk after Laura would have put her baby to sleep. The big topic was jobs for each of the dissertation-writing students, that is, those within a year of finishing their graduate studies. This year, postings were very few, and each letter announcing a new faculty opening that arrived at their university department led to a flurry of communication among the students. To see Laura in the evening, fellow students came to her apartment, because Laura wanted to make sure that her baby got optimum sleep.

"Nothing for us again, Laura," Grace announced on arrival. "It's Northwestern, but they want an Africanist." She set her bicycle helmet down, and slumped onto Laura's old, too-soft sofa. "Our classmate David got a response from UCLA! Maybe at least *one* of us will get a job!"

Laura brought two cups of chamomile tea to the sofa. "Let's wish him well, and the rest of us too. To David!" They raised their steaming cups and took careful sips.

After chatting for a while, Grace asked, "Why didn't you want your baby's father to know about her?"

"Because, because, uh, it couldn't work out. I didn't learn I was pregnant until after I'd returned here to the U.S. By then he was an ocean and a continent away. And we hadn't been so serious in our short romance. Of course he hadn't planned the pregnancy either, and you know what we've always heard, that a surprise pregnancy is a single man's nightmare, heard as a threat of marriage. And then, I wanted to raise the child in the U.S. Even if I told the father and he would decide to join me, he would have a very hard time getting work in the U.S., and he would be humiliated to not work.

"How are you so sure?"

"I'm not positive, but chances here would be very low for him. He's a journalist, you know. I mean, I was having a fling. Foolish, careless. Didn't intend this serious consequence."

"So did you consider abortion?"

"Yeah, of course I thought of it. But I couldn't live with the idea; couldn't bear to be a murderer."

"Why not adoption, then?"

"Couldn't manage that either. I thought, if I could get a respectable job, like a faculty position, something I've been *working for*, for years!"- and they both raised their cups, with determined grimace-grins. "And then I could give the child a good life." Turns out that the jobs were much more scarce than I had imagined."

Grace said, "Probably having a child makes it more difficult to get a job, doesn't it? A lot of people would view this as ruining your reputation. Did you have some special reason for keeping the pregnancy? Like manifest destiny? Maybe the Lord wanted you to have this child, for a particular purpose?"

"Didn't occur to me. Still doesn't."

"Would you ever change your mind, and contact the father?"

"After excluding him for almost two years already? How could he handle that kindly?"

"Why don't you find out?"

"Uh, uh, little Charlotte and I are doing fine by ourselves, thank you."

"How about another father, a stepfather?"

Laura embraced her cup with both hands and looked down into the brew. "I've learned that having a child scares men away. It appears I chose to have her rather than another man, though I didn't know it when I made my decision to stay with the pregnancy."

"Wow, you might resent your daughter, by now!"

"No, she's a wonderful companion. Enough."

"Does she resent *you*? Surely, she doesn't now, but will she, later?"

"Hmm, I don't know. Big question, unknown future. Ask me in ten, eleven years, after her puberty is under way."

"Have you been looking for other kinds of jobs, projects, here in the States?"

"You wouldn't believe how hard I've been trying. I mean, I could work typing dissertations for other people if the work would pay me enough to support the two of us. But it wouldn't. If I were alone, I might even continue in school to get a Spanish bilingual teaching credential. – It'd take another full-time year of classes. But it'd be very hard to support the two of us: I'd have to get like a waitress job, and with homework and classes, it'd be hard to get sleep, and when would I ever see my daughter? And who would take care of *her?* That'd cost, too."

She sighed. "Do you really want to hear about my job search, Grace?"

"Sure."

"Okay, here goes.

"Studying Chabacano is so specialized that it's a long shot for getting a faculty position. More promising would be machine translation (MT). It's a part of this exciting new field called Artificial Intelligence. Those engineers thought MT would be easy; but now they've had to hire linguists. But I think the

engineers will take over that field, and I don't know anything
about engineering.

"I didn't do something sensible like going into a marketable
field, but just relied on the modeling of our professors, who
have done alright in getting good positions, and earning
enough to support their wives and children. Harder for
women to get good jobs, but universities appear to be
somewhat less biased than private industry on hiring
women. Maybe earning a Ph.D. is seen as "manly" and
elevates me beyond the restrictions on women. Like Golda
Meir in Israel and Sirimavo Bandaranaike in Sri Lanka have
been able to rise to the top, because early on they were seen
as 'different from other women.' Even Laura Nader,
anthropologist in our UCB department, [University of
California, Berkeley, UCB, or 'Cal'] reported that in her
fieldwork in the Sierra Madre of southern Mexico, she was
able to hang out with men, observing their work, because she
had short hair and wore pants and therefore was 'more like a
man.'

"Anyway, that's what I'm hoping."

Laura added, "Slim job market, more difficult for women, and
now, for a single mom."

Both women were silent for a few moments.

"Already 'different', that I'm a single mom. But my cohorts in
this category are seen not as 'elevated,' but rather as 'morally
loose.' I've definitely made it more difficult for myself.

"But maybe linguists and anthropologists understand. After
all, many marry someone from their fieldwork, frequently in
a culture with 'primitive' technology. He brings – *her* – back
to the U.S., and we have a high rate of divorce in our field.
Getting along well in the place where the romance started,
where the local person is the expert, is attractive to him, the
anthropologist. But when the cultural expertise shifts to the

partner when they go to the U.S., the relationship tends to not work out well."

"Yeah, we have examples among our professors."

"But back to jobs: I aspire to a decent, respectable job, which in our fields means a university faculty position. There's no other job for me. But also, I aspire to be with a life partner in a good marriage, maybe another child, and a decent income. Have the jobs com*plete*ly dried up? Do I have to com*plete*ly change fields to find a good position? Or, am I just not clever enough?"

"Laura, we're all so hard on ourselves. It looks like a difficult time to get a university position; they're drying up."

"Oh, Grace, why oh why did I go into this field? I have passion but no particular talent. I didn't know Spanish very well before coming here to graduate study, I don't know Tagalog well, and my memory isn't sterling. I have to work harder than others to memorize. As you know, I'm a little shy, so I really notice when I make mistakes in another language. I care; it inhibits me. There's a good reason for my lack of self-confidence. I don't like to compete. I think I've gotten this far because I can work harder than anybody. And I can multi-task. I guess it does take some confidence to work hard. I know that if I keep at it, I can finish."

"So maybe it's even harder for you than the rest of us as we're finishing up."

"Yeah, the paradox. Having the child without marriage – a taboo here – makes it harder to get a good job. But now that I have her, I'm even more desperate to have a job, to support her."

"But the main thing, Grace, is that I had *no idea* how Charlotte would become my top priority."

"What do you mean, top?"

"Well, I always have been working toward a good job, working hard, like all of us, even though the faculty positions have been disappearing. But now that I have Charlotte, I'm responsible for her, a little one who cannot take care of herself. Before, if worse came to worse, maybe I could sleep on my sister's sofa while job looking, but now, I...
I desperately need to provide respectable living conditions for her."

"Of course."

"As you know, she came into my life by surprise, without planning, and before I had a job. And I immediately decided against abortion, I knew that my status as a single mom would be severely frowned upon by potential employers. And I didn't know how attached I'd become to her. She's my everything now."

"Do you think you'll ever find *the* man in your life?"

"Much more difficult now, and perhaps less important than before. Oh, of course, it'd be good if she had a dad – that is, a stepdad – in her life, but I told you, men don't want to take on 'someone else's' baby. I think that having her has closed out meeting *the right man.* Do you agree?"

"Yeah, maybe I'd be worried about how another man might be reticent about dating a woman with a child. And maybe you're right about both finding a man and finding a job! Oh, my dear Laura! So, while you've been writing your dissertation, hoping that you'd have a job by the time you've finished, you've made it much harder to get that job!"

"Yes. I can't take on any new university study for a more marketable career because I need to support two. I won't be meeting 'the man of my life' because I have a little child. And because she's in my life, I have to return to a developing country in the tropics to get data that would help me apply for the rare university position opening back in this country.

So you see, I don't have a choice; I *have* to go back there, especially because of my dear, dear little child."

4. Languages in Contact

Another evening, baby asleep, Grace sat with legs up and crossed on the sofa with Laura, both holding glasses of Gallo red wine.

Grace asked, "Again, why go back to the Philippines? Why not just work up more analysis of your dissertation data? – It'd be faster, and you wouldn't have to worry about your daughter getting a tropical disease."

Laura thought for a while before responding. "I just think she'll be safe there."

"How about her father? Will he learn that you have returned? What would he do?"

"I just won't tell him we're returning, and I'll be working in a new town far away from him."

"But you have to go clear across the Pacific?"

"No speakers of Chabacano here; I've already tried to find speakers here in the Bay Area. I've put an ad in the paper, and I've asked lots of Filipinos here to help me find someone. None, none.

"Just to remind you, I learned about this contact language, and this is a new exciting field in linguistics!"

"Remind me."

"Sure. Chabacano is a special human language, a creole language, formally called Philippine Spanish Creole. It has mostly Spanish vocabulary but different sounds and very different grammar. I'm so anxious to study it. I'll make a pioneering contribution to linguistics. I'll come back with data and analysis that'll get me a good job in our tiny field.

But Grace, you don't have to deal with a big move, do you, with your study of a Native American language?"

"Nope, the Kiowas are just a couple of states away, in Oklahoma. Easier to get there, but I kind of envy you the adventure of going across the Pacific Ocean to a very different place and culture, even the weather!"

Grace frowned. "I've heard about pidgins and creoles, but you don't hope to find the 'missing link to the origin of human languages,' do you? I've heard that rumor."

Laura answered, "Creoles are found all over the world, mainly around the equator, and studying them is important to learn whether or not they hint as to how humans first got language."

"Hmm. Maybe... I hope for you. But Laura, another problem: you told me last week that you're afraid to be alone at night. And that's here in the U.S. where you're a native! How can you manage so far from home, a newcomer in a strange place with different customs, and with a language you don't understand? Wouldn't you be even more afraid?"

"Yeah, I don't know why I'm afraid." She looked at her glass for a moment, and then asked, "Are you afraid to be alone at night, Grace?"

"No, I'm fine."

"Yeah." She looked at her glass again. "I've asked this question of other women, and I don't know *anyone* else who's afraid like I am."

"So what happens when you're alone: what do you do?"

"I'm hypervigilant, nervous, can hardly sleep. But actually, now, little Charlotte helps me. Doesn't make sense, but maybe it's as if the Lord wouldn't let anyone hurt a little child, so I'm safe as her protector. And before her, you'll remember that I had a dog. He did all the diligent vigilance for me, that is, until he got too old. I learned that a dog can be as good a companion as a human! But he died before I went to the Philippines two years ago."

"Hmm. Whatever works… But how did you manage last time you were in the Philippines? Weren't you scared then?"

"Well, I never slept alone in a house there – always with other people in the house - so I didn't really have to test my fear at night."

"Think you can ever overcome it? Or will you always need your daughter, or a dog? Or a man?!"

"I don't know, Grace. I do hate being dependent on having someone else in the house when I sleep."

"Laura, do you think maybe one motive for women to marry is that they'll be protected by a man at night?!"

"Wow, I'll try to avoid *that* motive! But a dog or a cat can be a real companion, right?"

"And how about overcoming? I mean, do you have PTSD (Post Traumatic Stress Disorder) about some childhood experience?"

"Not that I know of…." She thought for a while. "Funny, isn't it? I'm willing to take risks other people avoid, like coming to this university where everyone else is smarter than I am…"

"Not true!"

"Well…and going to graduate school, something for men, not women…"

"Not true!"

"Grace, can you believe this? When I started graduate school here, I dreamt I was a man! I looked down, and I had a man's anatomy! I woke up scared; I'd had a nightmare."

"Oh, God!" Grace laughed.

"That's what I thought anyway. Remember that I'm the first in my family to go to college. And then I was willing – *wanted* – to go across the Pacific to a strange new place with new languages and cultures. I looked very different from the people there. Certainly there was no clear prospect that this research would lead to a job. So I have been willing to take that big risk, but I'm afraid to be alone at night. Funny, huh?"

"Yeah. And I'm not sure it's the best choice." Grace reached over to pat Laura's shoulder. "But I'll support you all the way, my dear, if that's what you're determined to do."

5. Fascinated with this Language

Grace asked Laura to make a ginger lemon tea, and then she said, "I'm reconsidering; I'm dubious. Tell me more about this language you find so special that you're going to base your whole career search on it!"

"How about if I start at the beginning?"

"Sure, I'd *love* to hear all about it!"

"So back in June of 1968 I had just arrived in the Philippines, and after just a couple of days in Manila I headed directly down, by Fokker prop jet, the 600 miles to Zamboanga. From there I went out into a small community to work on a not-yet-studied language of Filipino Muslims: Samal. Before leaving Zamboanga City, I overheard people talking on the street, and was surprised to discover so many Spanish words jumping into my ears.

"I had learned before going to the Philippines that Spaniards had occupied the country for 300 years before 1902. Then, as part of the Spanish-American War, the Americans had chased out the Spaniards.

"But in 1968, hearing them talk 66 years later, so many Spanish words were such a big part of every utterance! I knew that Tagalog and probably many of the other 200 Philippine languages had borrowed a lot of Spanish vocabulary. My first day in the Philippines, in Manila, I had bought lanzones, little tropical fruits, in a market. I had pointed. The seller said, *"Issaw media kilo, tres pesos."* (One half kilo, three pesos.)

"I had remarked about the counting words to a Filipino who was helping me out, who told me, "Yes, everywhere. Number of items is in Tagalog, weight or volume, and cost, are in Spanish. Two number systems, different tasks.

"But what I was hearing in Zamboanga was different, so much more Spanish. I could recognize so many Spanish words that I could almost understand what people were saying, even when they were talking about me!"

"Like...?"

"Like, '*Mira, Milikano atras,*" or, 'Look, an American behind us.'

"The sounds of both words and intonation were different to my ears than Spanish; they sounded more Philippine. The grammar? – I couldn't catch it. Certainly not Spanish, nor what I knew of Philippine languages."

"Wow. Kind of like trying to learn Portuguese when you already know Spanish?"

"Sort of, but mostly regarding vocabulary. Before embarking on the year's research trip, I had studied a little Tagalog and Cebuano before undertaking the year's research trip. And I already knew a lot of Spanish. I suppose that's one reason I decided to go to the Philippines in the first place: Spaniards had colonized the country for 300 years and had made quite an impact.

"And before I went, I had learned about contact languages, but this was my first experience actually hearing any. Imagine, when starting the study of a language, already knowing a good share of the vocabulary! And what was going on with the sounds and the grammar? I wanted to learn more, and I didn't forget about this Spanish-filled language during my year of study of Samal.

"And then out on Sakol Island and learning their first languages – two of them - I heard teenage boys talk about this language. They told me that they found it hard to learn because it was so different from their first languages or Tagalog, which they studied in school. But I found it *easier* to learn because I knew most of the vocabulary: Spanish!

"So next, I sat with two men who knew Chabacano pretty well, and also some English. They told me that the language had 'not so many words,' and it was very easy to say, 'happened already' and 'will happen in the future.'

"Of course as soon as I came back to California, I read what I could on pidgins and creoles, especially Spanish-based ones."

Grace asked, "Still worth pursuing?"

Laura smiled. "Still an exciting topic! The literature I read also hinted at the earliest developments of human languages. Are contact languages primitive, a link to the evolution of adult human languages? Or were they immature, like babies' acquisition of language? After I started reading, I quickly learned that these languages are only *deceptively* easy and actually can be almost as complex to learn as ordinary languages."

"So, you were busted; still had to work hard to learn it?"

"Sort of, but even so, I wanted to learn more. I wanted to know what happens when a language 'gets pidginized' or 'gets creolized.' I read more about their so-called simplification. In Chabacano, I had learned (in Keith Whinnom's volume published in 1956) that time reckoning was much simpler than in Spanish. "I walked" had a simple past tense marker, 'ya,' as in '*Ya anda yo*.' 'I walk' or 'I'm walking' had become '*ta anda yo*,' and 'I will walk' had become '*di anda yo*.' But I've had hints of subtle complexities."

Grace frowned. "So why didn't Filipinos just learn Spanish from the people who took over their islands?"

Laura said, "Aah! To define creoles, we have to know something about their social history – that is, of the languages. They started out as 'auxiliary' languages. Creoles emerge when people of more power (in this case, the

Spaniards, in 1565 when they first conquered some Philippine islands while competing for the Spice Trade) – when people of more power bring together local people of several languages but with no language in common. So Spanish explorers brought peoples together as workers. The workers learned the high-frequency vocabulary of the explorers, but they 'simplified the grammar,' and also, they retained the speech sounds of their first languages. And the grammar that emerged was unique to this auxiliary language, but, we've learned, amazingly similar to that of pidgins and creoles found around the world, even those from different time periods."

Grace asked, "See if I can summarize: Spanish vocabulary in Chabacano – simple and small quantity of vocabulary, you say – but has sounds more of surrounding Philippine languages."

"Right."

Grace continued. "But Chabacano has a grammar different than any of these "normal" Philippine languages, *but* similar to other contact languages! So how? Maybe the Spaniards brought Chabacano with them? After all, they had already colonized other places, hadn't they? – even in Africa?"

"Yes, you know this, Grace! Spanish sailors, and Portuguese before them, started with voyages around Africa. Portuguese were first, in 1492, to navigate around Africa's Cape of Good Hope into the Indian Ocean, and then Spaniards as well, early in the 16th century."

"Okay, so back to the Portuguese and Spaniards. Then what? These auxiliary languages took over in the Spanish and Portuguese ports?"

"Yeah. What first developed are now called pidgins by linguists. But when the by-now pidgin-speaking workers had children, their children grew up speaking this as their first language. And then, as the languages became more complex, for instance with more vocabulary, linguists distinguished them by calling them creoles."

"Oh, so creoles are 'complex pidgins'?"

"Yeah. Sometimes they've been called 'pidgins gone native.' These languages offer rare opportunities to observe rapid change within one language. Almost undoubtedly the Portuguese sailors who landed in Ternate, Indonesia, in 1512 brought Portuguese pidgin speakers with them, perhaps from Malacca. Then, decades later, when the Spaniards took over, the pidgin/creole relexified to Spanish."

"Hmm, relexified. Because the languages are so closely related?"

"Probably. And with interacting history."

"So by the time these Spaniards took some 200 of their local guards and servants from Ternate, Indonesia, to the Philippines in 1662, the language had long since evolved into a creole language. Our evidence is that Spanish scribes arriving in the Philippines on board ship wrote that it had been the first language of the community of 200 during at least 60 years."

"So, did it have Portuguese, or Spanish vocabulary?"

"Back then, vocabulary of these two European languages overlapped even more than today. And currently, in Chabacano, some Iberian words sound more Portuguese, like 'sabon' instead of 'jabon' for 'soap." One linguistic description of Chabacano estimates that it has around 80% Spanish vocabulary, especially the high frequency words. The additional 20% are mostly Tagalog words. The people in neighboring towns around the Manila Bay are almost entirely Tagalog speakers. And about sounds: if you listen from a distance, vowels and consonants as well as intonation sound more like Tagalog, definitely not like Spanish."

Grace said, "I have more questions, Laura; is that okay?"

"Sure! What next?"

"Hasn't any Filipino studied this language?"

Laura smiled. "A little, but the language has low prestige. People say it has 'no grammar.'"

"And nowadays, does anyone speak it?"

"Well, back in 1662, it developed in five places in the Philippines when the Spaniards took those 200 guards and servants there: two places in the south and three in the Manila area."

"So did Portuguese and Spaniards – sailors, you said - start the pidgins, and these developed into creoles by the local people? I mean, we've heard also of Jamaican Pidgin English and Haitian Creole French. Maybe all contact languages are European based? And if so, why? – Just because of Europeans traveling the seas?"

Laura said, "I've even read that one linguist made a strong case for Old English having evolved into a pidgin and then into a creole and on into Medieval English after the Norman conquest of England in 1066. Why?

- First, 60% of English vocabulary after 1066 came from French

- Second, verb tenses and conjugations simplified considerably from older English and from those of other Germanic languages.

- Third, likewise, declensions almost disappeared. In modern English, only pronouns marked them ("he, his, him" etc.)"

Grace muttered, "Oh, 'der, die, das': so much trouble to learn in German!"

Laura continued. "Two of the strongest arguments against the 'creole' theory for English were:

- First, we have such a large percentage of irregular verbs in English,

- And second, English has had such extensive contact with other languages, and the contacts have led to regularization and simplification of the grammar."

Grace stopped her. "But you haven't answered: did only European languages become creolized? Doesn't seem logical."

"You're right. Linguists first became aware of European-based creoles, but especially lately they have found evidence of the contact phenomena between other language families as well."

Grace put down her no empty wine glass. "Well, Laura, you've convinced me that these languages are fascinating. You've already applied for a grant?"

"Yep, to NSF, (the National Science Foundation.) Submitted it last week. I think I have a decent chance to get one because it's a topic of interest. If I get the grant, it'd pay living expenses for both me and Charlotte."

"I hope, for your sake. When do you expect to hear from them?"

"Six months. I'll be finished with the dissertation and the orals by then."

"I know it's getting late, but can you show me what you've written in your application?"

"Sure." Laura collected a thick manila folder from the dining room table and opened it up on the coffee table. She scooted it over to Grace.

Grace turned some pages. "Oh! You're going to Spain as well? And Chile?"

"Yeah, but mainly to the Philippines and a short trip to Indonesia. To Spain because I want to track down any original sources about this and other Spanish pidgin or creole languages. I have just learned about a certain Jesuit priest, Don Diego de Esquivel, who in 1662 wrote a grammar and dictionary of the creole language spoken on the spice island of Ternate, Indonesia."

"How did you learn about him?"

"Oh, you'll like this, because I'm on a treasure hunt! A hundred years later, a historian cited his work. I want to find Esquivel's work. And I want to learn about him! Who was he, and how did he get to Ternate in 1662? Maybe I'll find documents about him in Ternate!"

"God, I hope you have a chance for a grant, Laura!"

"Yeah, lots of competition for just a few grants, and I know that linguists will be the reviewers of my application. But Professor James advised me to broaden the interest in my proposal by including references to the Spice Trade that had such a big impact on world history. That is, to show that Chabacano developed as part of the Spice Trade."

Laura shuffled to a section of her application and showed it to Grace.

"Europeans had become obsessed, by the 15th century, with the mystical flavors and curative powers of eastern spices. The European prices of cloves and nutmeg bloomed higher as measured by weight than those of gold or diamonds. Portuguese, Spanish, and then Dutch, French, and English – Europeans from all these countries - competed for suitable ships and navigation systems. As a byproduct, a special kind of language developed, especially Portuguese-Spanish pidgins and creoles. We find a trail of them along the sea routes to and from the Spice Islands.

"And these languages might offer new discoveries about how human languages develop."

"Gosh, this sounds exciting, Laura," Grace said. "I think you could make a real contribution, and I sure hope you get the grant."

PHILIPPINES, 1972

6. Finally, Ternate!

Finally, Laura and Charlotte, now four years old, arrived in the Philippines. Laura had her two-year grant for fieldwork, for analysis, and write-up.

Ternate, Cavite Province, Philippines, was their destination for the main part of Laura's research. She had read that in 1662, after several battles against Portuguese and Spaniards, Dutch sailors had closed in on "The Spice Islands," including the clove capital, Ternate. Paleobotanists had determined that the clove tree evolved only on Ternate and a couple of tiny islands nearby, and so that island became the main Portuguese, and a couple of decades later, the main Spanish fort, and third, the Dutch headquarters for European exploitation of Indonesian spices. Ruins of three forts were still standing in 1972 on Ternate, two Portuguese and one Dutch.

Portuguese lost to the Spaniards, and then, Spaniards, losing to the Dutch, retreated to their larger colony, the Philippines. The Spaniards considered Manila Bay the most important bay in all of Southeast Asia. In 1662, Spaniards "rescued" about 200 people whom they had, during the previous decades, converted to Christianity, and who worked for the Spaniards as guards and servants. These people could serve these same roles in the Philippines. And these new settlers in the Philippines were the people who by 1662 spoke a Spanish contact language as their first language.

The Spaniards' first stop was the southern Philippine port of Zamboanga, 400 miles to the north of Ternate, Indonesia. Here they left some of their "refugees." In 1972, the contact language was still thriving there, spoken as a first language by some 50,000 residents and by now called Chabacano. Its use was growing because it had become the *lingua franca* of many Cebuanos who were currently moving down to Zamboanga from their central islands. Muslims were also coming into town from outlying islands, into the Campo Muslim neighborhood, and were also learning Chabacano as the *lingua franca* of the city. So some 200,000 residents of Zamboanga in 1972 spoke Chabacano as their second language. And the number was growing.

Back to 1662: the retreating Spaniards continued their voyage north to Manila, headquarters of the Spanish colony. They deposited a few of the remaining refugees to settle in Ermita, Manila, and a few more in the Spanish fort of Cavite. Laura learned that by 1972 the language was dying out in these two places near Manila, where only people in their 70's and older spoke it, but no one used it regularly.

A small number of Chabacano speakers from Zamboanga much later settled in Cotabato, to the east of Zamboanga, but by 1972, only a few adults spoke the language there.

In 1662, the remainder of the refugees were taken to an uninhabited area 30 miles south of Manila, at the mouth of Manila Bay. They had a job for the refugees: they would become lookouts for any unfriendly ships entering Manila Bay, by building a bonfire on the mountain behind their village to warn Manila. These refugees named their new home after their homeland, Ternate. They had brought with them a three-foot tall image of the Christ child, who had a "war-like" expression. They built a Catholic church and placed this image prominently on the wall behind the altar and facing the congregation. Laura learned that nowadays in January each year, many Filipinos, even from far away, make a pilgrimage to ask the blessing of this Christ child.

This emphasis on the homeland was one reason Laura had decided to make Ternate, Philippines, her main field site. The other reason was that the language was still spoken, as their first language, even by young children, and Laura thought it might be the most likely site for any older vestiges of

Chabacano vocabulary. The modern inhabitants nowadays subsisted by fishing and farming, and though just a two hour bus travel from Manila, the community was mostly independent of the city.

Laura was concerned that even in Ternate, the contact language Chabacano might be doomed. Settling into the town, she had heard both adults and children as well speaking the language, but she also knew that children were learning Tagalog in school. And now that English was being introduced on television – several families had recently acquired televisions - English might further erode the use of Chabacano in Ternate.

Laura already knew of linguists' reports from Africa and the Caribbean that, unlike speakers of other languages, who tend to show strong loyalty for their languages, speakers of pidgins and creoles everywhere tend to share their neighbors' disdain for their "ungrammatical" language. Under these conditions, contact languages tend to die out.

Laura was passionate about recording and analyzing this language, but not only for herself. She also wanted to showcase its importance to Filipinos.

Back, again, to 1662: The Philippines had become a crucial hub for the transport of spices eastward across the Pacific Ocean to the recently discovered New World, Their main port on the west coast was Acapulco, and then the spices were transported overland, eastward, to Mexico City. The crews of the Spanish galleons frequently sojourned for a year, and then traveled overland down to Vera Cruz on the Caribbean and sailed the Atlantic Ocean to Europe.

She wanted to learn more about what seemed a crazy mania for spices. What had attracted the attention of the whole "Old World"? How had a pound of nutmeg in 14th century Europe become more valuable than gold? Fervor for nutmeg and cloves from Eastern Indonesia, and cinnamon and pepper from India, was the main driver for several European nations to compete with each other to conquer the Spice Trade. In the process, they learned how to build ships capable of sailing across open oceans to search for routes to capture these spices, and to get them ahead of their European competitors.

Sailors and the merchants who funded the drives got rich. Empires were established, and the New World had become revealed. The balance of world power shifted. Globally, the modern era was stimulated by the Spice Trade.

Laura had read that the Spice Trade had started long before the Europeans got involved: Indonesian and Indian spices had been traded for centuries by Middle Eastern and North African merchants, who kept their sources secret. Why did people want spices? To flavor and preserve food, to make perfume, to embalm the dead, and to make medicine.

But Europeans also prized the prestige the spices brought. Spices were expensive, bought by royalty and other rich people in Europe. Spices had been transported over the long journey by land – the Silk Road – or by sea and then land, carried on camels across the Sahara to Cairo, and then across the Mediterranean Sea to Venice, and from that hub, out to other destinations in Europe. But now Europeans wanted to cut out the middlemen. Finally, by the late 15th Century, they had developed ships and navigation capable of crossing seas. European kings and queens funded explorations. Christopher Columbus proposed a westward route and accidentally encountered the New World.

Europeans fought during much of the 16th Century, often brutally, over Asian spices and trade routes for them. And the world rushed into the modern era.

Awestruck by her emerging awareness of centuries of history behind her decision, Laura and her little daughter would take up residence in the quiet little town of Ternate at the mouth of the Manila Bay.

7. Why Fish at Night?

Laura and Charlotte reached Ternate by bus in two hours from Manila. The bus had stopped at several towns on the way for unloading and loading of goods and people. The little town sat in front of forest-covered hills from which spilled the Maragondong River. The first Chabacano speakers had settled beside the river on its flat delta, a few hundred feet inland from the Manila Bay, probably for safety from potential marauders. Down at the river's mouth, palm trees bent over white sands toward the sea, and the few houses there were built high on stilts. Just beyond the shore and under water except for low tide, lay a beautiful, pristine coral reef. Beyond the reef sparkled the waters of Manila Bay and farther out, the South China Sea.

The people nowadays in this town earned a little cash from dried coconut meat (copra) and fish. They used the money to buy white rice, fuel for their outboard motors, cigarettes, and western pants, shirts, and fabric for dresses.

In 1972, Laura loved to go out snorkeling in the middle of the day. Why? Because the whole population, maybe 6,000 people, had the sense to take a nap in the shade after lunch. Charlotte napped as well. Laura craved moments alone, moments hard to find here. Both the neighbors and others in the house where she and Charlotte were long-term guests were inquisitive enough to look through her suitcase when she was out. The host children watched her change clothes and brush her hair.

But no one asked her where she was going when she left after lunch to snorkel, as others settled themselves in the house, with a gentle breeze blowing up through the bamboo stripped floor to cool them off, or in the shade under a tree.

The early afternoon sea was her escape into privacy.

Snorkeling, gazing down on coral tables teeming with flora and fauna, she felt she was in a dream state. *This can't be real, these vivid colors, this constant but completely quiet movement of fish, swaying plants, changing water colors and even changing temperatures. Sometimes the fish notice me, even brush against my arms or legs, but mostly they don't care that I'm right next to them. I could so easily reach out to touch! But when I try, they dart away.*

Occasionally she tucked her knees up to her chest and then lifted her legs quickly behind her and out of the water in order to dive down to inspect a clown fish in its sea anemone. But mostly she floated dreamily, gazing down. *This world I've never seen before, hardly knew it existed. And they're completely oblivious to me. It's even more exotic than these people who speak a language I'm just now struggling to learn, and with a lot of culture which I don't understand. These people go about their days not even caring about California! That world doesn't even matter to them. They smile sometimes at strange moments to me, so I'm not sure what some smiles mean. They tease me, and I'm not sure I understand, like that old woman who said to me, 'You have three dresses and I have only one, so you give me one!" How did she know how many I have? And was she just teasing, or does she really expect me to give her one? Like the fish, the mariscos, the plants, the coral reef: SO much to learn about!*

Early on in her fieldwork in Ternate, Laura sat on the beach in the late afternoons to interview fishermen. One day she noticed a fisherman come close behind her, and she thought he might be looking at her head. A couple of days later, he asked *"Tu pelo: possible di servi un bwen senyuelo de pescado!"* (Your hair: it might be a good fish lure!)

Laura looked up to him with suspicion. *"Probablemente no sirve bien."* (Probably wouldn't work.)

"Pwede darme un pedaso?" (Could you give me a piece?)

She pondered. *Probably won't work; it's not shiny in the water, just matted. But what if it **did** work well? He'd be after all my hair! And I sure don't want to cut any off for him. Am I really safe here? But, I'm a little curious too.*

She said, "I have my hairbrush here in my bag. I'll give you the leavings from this morning's brushing... And tell me your name again?"

"Sorbino. Gracias!"

As soon as she provided him the little roll of long hairs that she pulled out of her brush, he took off with the treasure. She watched him hurry along the soft sandy path to his house on stilts under coconut palms, and then she turned back to the other three fishermen who quietly waited for more questions on fish and how to catch them.

The next morning on return from their usual night fishing, Sorbino, followed by two others, came to Laura, who was sitting by herself on the balcony of her guesthouse, to tell her of his disappointment that her hair hadn't attracted any fish.

"No sirve, ma'am."

"No estoy surprendiendo, Sorbino; lastima." (I'm not surprised, Sorbino; sorry.)

She wanted to learn about fishing; she needed to learn the associated language. But fishing was men's work.

She had hired a young local man, Antero, who could read and write some English. She worked intensively with him to learn Chabacano. She asked questions of townspeople and had Antero's help in understanding answers. Then at nighttime, after reading to Charlotte and helping her to sleep, she memorized her new vocabulary and grammar. She read and wrote by the one *kolayet* (lantern) in the house.

One afternoon she asked Antero about fishing. *"Possible di va yo con los pescaderos?"* (Do you think I could go out with the fishermen?) Antero said he'd arrange with his uncle, Rubin, and he, Antero, would accompany her as well.

She knew about lights in the sea at night: simply swishing her feet at the shore, the water sparkled from its phosphorus. But out on the water at night, the little fishing boat elicited much more sparkle, not only from its hull slowly cutting through the dark, but also its outriggers, each of them attached by braces holding them some three meters out.

"Mira las lusas!" (Look at the lights!) she called to Antero. *"Si, y las estrelyas arriba tambien,"* (Yes, and the stars above also) he responded. With no moon, the stars were bright, and the dark sea both reflected the stars and emitted its own lights.

Rubin sat up front holding high a *kolayet*; fish came up to the light, and Juling reached out to catch them in a net. Pepe on the other side held a long spear to try to stab swim-aways. Within an hour the catch flopping around in the hold of the canoe consisted of six or seven two-foot long fish; she couldn't tell what kind, maybe tuna.

Then the net caught on coral! Isiah, who was using the "J-pattern" of rowing on just one side of the canoe, reversed his strokes to stay in place in order to reduce the tearing of the net. Juling prepared to release the net. He grabbed a small knife, and Rubin worked his way back toward mid-boat with his lantern to aid Juling's vision. Juling lowered himself over the side, holding onto one outrigger brace, and then released himself into the dark.

Laura held her wristwatch up to the lantern in order to calculate his time under water.

One minute, 90 seconds...105... and Juling burst out and grabbed the brace over his head. He shook his head once, indicating that he'd have to go down again.

Laura saw her opportunity to help. She quickly rummaged around in her carry-on bag and brought out her waterproof miner's headlamp, a snorkel, a face mask, and fins. "I can offer these." Juling looked, and hesitated, apparently considering. She then gathered the courage to ask, "*O possible ke pwede yo probarlo?*" "Or, would you let me try?"

She did try, and on coming up with the edge of the net, she offered that she'd teach Juling tomorrow how to use the equipment.

8. Best Winds for Fishing?

Laura had had her training session with Juling, and now she sat on the white sand beach with Anuncio, an elderly fisherman with a wrinkled brown face and thin but muscular arms and legs. His son and two other young men, also fishermen, sat beside him. In front of them glistened the calm late afternoon Manila Bay, its light aqua colors turning to deeper turquoise and gray. Behind the little group stretched a sea wall of broken coral, one meter high and two meters wide, on which several little boys, all nude, sat listening to the expertise of the fishermen trying to explain to this pinky, yellow-haired newcomer how they decided when and where to fish.

She struggled to understand new words and concepts, which she wrote down on the notebook in her lap. After a short while, she protested, *"Pero esos no son palabras Chabacanas, suyos nombres de los vientos!"* (But your names of these winds aren't in Chabacano!)

"De verdad. Son palabras de todos los pescaderos en nuestras islas." (That's right, they're the names that all the other fishermen on these islands use.)

Laura wetted her finger in her mouth and held it up to feel the wind. "This wind now is...?"

"Tungara'," answered Rubin.

"De verdad?" - You all agree?" Laura looked around at the other three men, who nodded.

She looked behind her toward their town and the hills behind. *"Tungara'* blows from... from behind our hill?" The men pointed with their lips in the direction of the hill behind and to the left of them, and they nodded once again.

She pulled out her compass and examined it. "It's a northeast wind, then," and she drew a line with arrow and the name on the map that she had crudely drawn. The men leaned slightly forward to examine her map of their little community.

"So, when in the year does *Tungara'* blow?"

"Warm time only, like now," said Juling. He added, "Now for three moons already. When the sun sets on that side of our shore." He pointed to the right as they looked out to the sea.

Laura wrote down *April – June?* on her paper and added *Sunset in June?* on that spot of her roughly drawn map.

She looked at the men and smiled when she saw that they appeared eager for more questions. "So how do you fish during *Tungara'* time, and what kinds of fish do you catch?

"Night fishing, *kolayet,*" said Rubin. "Plenty kinds of coral fish, and some big ones, *Bidbid* and *Dalag-dagat."*

The old man spoke up. "*Tungara'* not good wind for *Dalag-dagat*; best time for *Burara.*" The other two men expressed opinions. Laura wrote very fast, including utterances she couldn't understand. She wrote in her sort of shorthand in IPA (International Phonetic Alphabet), but knew she was missing a lot. For instance, she couldn't be sure how to divide the utterances into words. She planned to ask Antero later to try to reconstruct the discussion for her. She hoped that tomorrow might bring another session with the fishermen in the fading sunlight, long after they'd finished their daily net repairs and long naps, and before their dinner and their nightly sail out into the deep.

Lord, this is fun, she thought. *When the local experts disagree and I get to hear them, that's when I'll really learn about this language and culture.*

9. Little Charlotte Works Too

My work is so much easier now!

Since Laura returned to the Philippines, now four years later, to conduct her fieldwork on Philippine Creole Spanish, she immediately noticed the data gathering was faster, better, deeper. She was more familiar and comfortable with local culture and the language than she had been during her initial fieldwork in the past. *But it must be more than that.* She was a happy returnee, even though she had a new fieldwork site, Ternate in the Philippines. The people came to know her, even the children. She and they laughed together, exclaimed delight, even hugged. Meeting new people, they seemed to know that she was relaxed and happy to meet them. She dressed more like them than she had five years earlier as a newcomer to the country. She now wore clothing that covered her more: loose blouses with sleeves, and skirts that covered the knees. Of course Chabacano speakers were delighted that she soon could speak – somewhat - with them in their language, even though she frequently stumbled. Outsiders in neighboring towns never wanted to learn Chabacano because they disdained it as "bastard Spanish, with no grammar." And, Ternate was surrounded by Tagalog speakers, so Ternatenyos also spoke Tagalog with other outsiders.

My little Charlotte, she's the main reason fieldwork is easier… Well, maybe the people and culture are more familiar to me now as well. People were fascinated with Laura's four-year-old daughter. Most rural people out in the boondocks had seen blond children only in the very occasional magazine – and now even on their neighbors' televisions - and even though little Charlotte was a *mestiza* – of mixed race – her hair was almost blond. People continually exclaimed, using English, "a living doll!" Laura saw that people noticed – what was also to them – her very normal interaction with her daughter. Adults even told her, "You're a parent, like us."

And little Charlotte was very social. Not only was she quite willing to play with children with whom she did not share a language, but she also, within an hour of play, began using a word or two of their language. During play, children might say, *"Ben aka!"* (Come here!) and motion toward their group. Charlotte would hesitate only for a moment, but then come to them. And she'd reciprocate in the play. She'd walk a short distance away, turn around to them, and say *"Ben aka!"* With delight, they'd join her. Laura mumbled to herself, *She's also a talking doll; or if not yet talking much, at least she understands!*

Charlotte – and Laura agreed – would let children invite her into their house, and she'd come out wearing a local girl's clothing, for example hand-woven loose pants and an embroidered blouse. Laura at first was worried that the children wanted Charlotte's American clothing, but before long, Charlotte was back in her own clothing. Girls seemed to want to dress her up, like playing with a doll.

Adults gave her candy. Laura took her to the elementary school, and even looked into classrooms. Once, the teacher invited the two Americans in, pulled up two chairs in front of the class, and then offered seated Charlotte a piece of candy. The classroom of children watched Charlotte eat it, while the teacher and Laura asked questions of each other. After this experience, Laura stopped taking Charlotte into a classroom, because she didn't like Charlotte getting such precious treatment. After this episode, she played with school-age children only after school was out for the day.

One afternoon, Laura was standing near some fishermen who had brought in their catch, when the oldest man in the town, Numeriano Tibayan, said to the others, *"Ke ben la pickaninny,"* (Here comes the little child), referring to Charlotte.

Laura heard him, and she was astounded to hear this word for the first time in her more than a year in this town working on the language. In the literature on contact languages, it was a very special word, one of the few "universals" of European-based contact languages. Laura knew that it was first recorded in the 17th century in a West Indies creole, and that its earlier etymology was apparently Portuguese *pequenonino*, meaning "very little."

Laura reflected, *She didn't **discover** the term, but she **did** elicit it. What a valuable co-researcher, my little Charlotte!*

10. Migo is a *Father?*

"Hey, Migo, you know that *Melikana* (American) you dated a few years ago?" Lety, his sister, had left her slippers at the front door and padded onto the cool hardwood flooring of their Forbes Park mansion. (They spoke in Tagalog.) Migo was working on a feature story for the *Philippine Times* newspaper, one about residents out in the provinces getting electricity and telephones.

"Yeah." He looked at the pen in his hand, halted on the paper, and he tried to stifle his slight annoyance at this interruption.

"Well!" Lety said.

"So?" Migo (his formal name was Miguel) was getting impatient with her dramatic pause.

"My friend Marilu says she's come back here."

"So what? She hasn't contacted *me*. We never wrote. It was all over."

"Well. Marilu saw her at Rustan's market today, talked with her *and* with her little daughter!

"Hmmpf. She's married, then?"

"No! Migo, the child is a four-year-old *mestiza*! (Eurasian girl) And very cute."

Migo sat up and stared straight ahead.

....

The next evening Migo met his friend Andoy (formally Adrian) a fellow journalist, and they played dominoes out on Andoy's parents' veranda. They drank beers. After a while, Migo brought up the topic. "Know what I learned yesterday?"

"Mm."

Migo took another swallow of his beer. "I learned yesterday that I might have a daughter."

They made the usual jokes. Then Andoy asked, "Someone coming after you for child support?"

"No. She never even told me, and now the girl is four years old."

"Was it that Lolita, I mean what was her name, that you, mmm, dated, when you were both kids?"

"No, *naman*! (emphasis). It was the American, Laura; you remember her?"

"Sure... Out of your league! Mmm... How do you know it's yours?"

"I don't know. But I want to find out."

"Why?"

"I don't know yet. But it's pretty important, isn't it, bringing a child into the world? – I mean, being a part of it?!"

11. Are You *Sure?*

Migo met with his friend the following evening, so far, his only confidant in this new revelation. *Sure not gonna let Lety know that I'm investigating!*

They played dominoes again, and their voices were nearly obscured by the racket of slamming down the tiles in play on the marble table in the veranda. *Clatter, clatter!*

Andoy took the initiative: "Moved on from last night's foolishness?" He looked up at Migo.

"As a matter of fact, I contacted our classmate Kennedy. Handy to have a friend who is a family attorney, no?"

"Not if you don't have – or *make* – troubles."

Migo ignored the insult. "So I asked him can I demand a paternity test, and what would be my rights if I'm shown – proven - to be the biological father."

"*Dios*, what rights do you want? – to pay child support? To give the kid inheritance rights to your family's estate?"

"I don't know yet. I just want to find out."

Andoy signaled to Paco, the servant who was hovering just outside of view, to pour more beers.

They raised their glasses with another call of "*provecho*" and took long drinks. Then Andoy sighed and asked, "So what did you learn from Classmate Kennedy?"

"Yeah. He said I start by filing a petition to claim paternity. He said that actually it won't get far because: one, we have these old-fashioned paternity laws in this country that are vestiges of Old Spanish Law, that say that 'illegitimate children' are strangers to the father."

"Case over!"

"Nope. He also said that even under California law, where I suppose the child was born, the 'alleged father' must petition within two years of the child's birth, *and* he 'must set forth facts establishing a reasonable possibility of the requisite sexual contact between the parties.'"

"The little girl is four years old, you said?"

"Yes, and the mother left the Philippines four and a half years ago."

"So even under California law, where the child was born, you cannot start a case, right?"

"Yeah, *but:* Kennedy told me that we *could* serve the petition for a pre-hearing before the case would be thrown out of court, and the hearing date could get delayed, and delayed again. "

"What good would that do you?"

"Well: the "respondent" would be served with a copy of the petition *and* a summons to appear in court for the pre-hearing. And at that time the judge might – *might* – demand that the child submit to a genetic test, probably a blood test."

"Dios. You know how to re-ignite a romance, don't you, Migo!

.....

Migo reported further that Kennedy, who at first advised him against proceeding through the court system, suggested that he instead try to revive the romance.

"How shall I do this; any ideas?" he asked Andoy the following night.

"Do you really want to...to... you'll just stir up trouble!"

"Well, I really missed her when she left. I really wish we could get back together again."

"Complications! Beats me. Ask your sister," Andoy answered.

Next morning Migo managed to be having breakfast in the kitchen when Lety rushed through to grab a banana before going off to work.

"Magandang umaga" (Good morning.)

Lety raised her eyebrows to look at him. *"...Umaga,"* she replied, apparently surprised at his formality.

"Uh, *Ate* " (Sis)...

"Apa, Migo?" (What, Migo?)

"Uh, *Ate*, I have a question to ask you."

"Yeah? It'd better be quick."

"Uh, *Ate*, I've really missed Laura, and now that she's back, I'd love to see her."

"Laura?! Hey, Migo, she's too big a fish for you."

"I sure have been missing her."

"Well, forget her. Did you even write to her? Did she ever write to you?"

"No, but..."

"But! – That's everything!"

"She told me 'goodbye' forever when she left, because she said she'd never be able to afford to come back here. But now that she's back, Lety, can you help me?"

"Huh! What do you want from me?

"Just... just... What do you think is the best way to approach her? – A letter? Or flowers? Have a friend re-introduce the idea of seeing me again? Or just show up on her doorstep?"

"*Kapatid* " (Brother), you've enticed me to think about this. Let's talk this evening, around... umm..." and she pulled her little calendar out of her purse... "at around eight o'clock." Calendar back in her purse, and she was off.

.....

That evening they sat out in their screened-in veranda, tiki-torches lighted outside the perimeter, drinking chilled calamansi juice. Both prefaced their talk by announcing fatigue from hard work at their jobs.

"Any ideas, dear *Ate*?" asked Migo.

"Yeah, I think your best chance is to have Marilu talk to her. I'll ask her."

"Thank you, thank you, *Ate*. I can't wait! I'm so anxious to see her! I just want to hold her in my arms."

.....

Saturday morning, Lety called Marilu for a short meeting, "something to ask you before I go shopping."

Marilu met Lety as she drove into the driveway, and Lety jumped out to give her a hug.

"My brother says he really misses Laura and now that he's heard she's back in the RP (The Republic of the Philippines) he wants to see her."

"Oh?"

"Marilu, do you think you can put in a good word for him?"

Marilu looked up to the sky. "*O Dios*" (Oh God.)

"What, Lety? Do you know anything about her feelings for him? Does he have any chance with her?"

"Probably not. But for you, my dear friend, I'll try."

Marilu waited until after dinner that night. It had to be this night because Laura would be leaving Sunday morning for Indonesia for two weeks, and she'd be leaving Charlotte behind with Marilu and the maids and the nursery school.

After sundown, after refreshing showers and dinner, evening was by far the most peaceful time to reflect, to think, and to talk.

And they'd been talking for a while.

"Oh, God, Marilu, how did he learn I'm back?" moaned Laura.

Marilu sat quietly and listened.

"He never wrote... I mean, I never wrote to him, either.
I really liked him, but..."

"But what?"

"I just didn't see how it could work out. And when I learned I was pregnant... I wanted to have my career in the U.S., not here, and I just didn't see how he could manage there. I guess the relationship just wasn't strong enough to overcome the difficulties."

"...Your feelings, you mean?"

"Yeah, my feelings. I really liked him, but from the beginning, I figured it was temporary. Not for life."

"So, what should I tell Lety? Do you not want to see him?"

"God, what if he learns about Charlotte? What would he do? Maybe he'd worry I'd try to get financial support from him, and I don't want that! I'd have tried before this if I'd wanted his involvement. I guess I was hoping he wouldn't hear that I had returned."

.....

"She won't see me?! Not even to say hello? Damn!

"Kennedy, Can you write a letter to her to demand a paternity analysis? I'll get her a blood test appointment so you can notify her of it in the letter, and if she complies, then I will also deliver my own blood test."

.....

"God, do I really have to meet this appointment, Marilu?"

"Better get a lawyer, my dear."

...

Migo discussed with his friend Andoy, and then with his sister Lety, and even with his parents, that he would like to become an active father to this 4-year-old girl whom he hadn't yet met.

He talked Kennedy into starting a civil court case for half custody. A month later he heard that Laura had gone for two weeks but now still hadn't returned.

"Kennedy, please change my petition to full custody if the mother doesn't return by the time of the court case."

12. To Indonesia

This somewhat obscure language, Chabacano, brought me to the world-changing five-millennia-long Spice Trade! Laura's fascination continued to turn more toward the intersection of the Spice Trade in the Far East and the development of these special languages. She had come to the Philippines to study the living linguistic evidence of the 16th-17th European explorations, and now she wanted to take a look at the actual Spice Islands in eastern Indonesia. These islands are 800 miles south of Manila, and she had put the travel budget into her research grant. Each of several islands in a line, north to south, consisted of a volcanic peak surrounded by a skirt of land. She headed for Ternate. That was the name of both the island and its only town, and the name of its volcanic peak was Mount Gamalama.

She had read that the Spice Islands – in the Moluccas - were beautiful, she thought maybe as beautiful as the Philippines: forest-covered, with many white beaches, white sand from the coral reefs surrounding them. One important difference was that some of the beaches there had black sand from lava. Those islands were geologically young volcanic peaks that had recently risen out of the sea. And even though in 1972 the Moluccas were no longer the focus of international trade, some exports continued of nutmegs, cloves, and lumber. The people and their clothing were beautiful as well: local people wore colorful, flowing clothing, their bodies were slim and muscular, and their faces were attractive. And they still sailed lateen-rigged schooners for often long-distance trade, sailing as far as Singapore, 1000+ miles to the west. For local travel and fishing they used small double outrigger canoes, just as Filipinos did.

The European explorers who first conquered the Spice Islands were Portuguese in the 16th century. Shortly after that, the Spanish arrived and defeated the Portuguese. Each nationality of sailor-explorers set up a fort [*benteng*) on

Ternate: *Benteng Tolukko* in *1512, Benteng Kalamata* in *1540,*
formerly *B. Kayu Merah,* formerly *B. Santa Lucia)*, and
Benteng Oranje, the first headquarters of the Dutch East
Indies Company, from 1609 to 1619, but then they moved to
Jakarta. These forts were still extant – that is, in ruins - in
1972.

Portuguese and then Spaniards had brought the contact
languages with them as they traveled eastward, to Malacca,
Malaysia, then to the north in Macau, China, and then on to
Ternate. By 1662, Dutch sailor-explorers were making
progress in conquering all of the Indonesian archipelago, and
so the Spaniards retreated with their 200 servants and
guards to the Philippines.

Laura quickly learned that she'd have a challenge getting
from Ternate, Philippines, to Ternate, Indonesia. The Spice
Islands had been so important to world history, but they now
seemed forgotten. She couldn't find any commercial
transport by sea. By air, she'd have to start out in Manila, fly
the 850 miles westward to Singapore and then 350 miles
southward to Jakarta. From there, three times a week, a small
plane flew 900 miles back eastward past Makassar [now
Ujung Pandang] to Manado on Northern Sulawesi, next to
the large island of Borneo. In Manado, she would wait for as
long as a week to travel the final 200 miles eastward on a
small inter-island boat to Ternate. *Kind of daunting, slow, and
expensive.*

Marilu told her about her friend Belen whose husband
worked for the American logging firm Weyerhaeuser down
in Davao, 600 miles to the south of Manila. The husband
managed a crew of Filipinos logging on Indonesian islands
near Ternate, and they had a small boat transporting
workers back and forth the 400-mile passage across the
Celebes [now Sulawesi] Sea, from Davao, Philippines to
Ternate, Indonesia. Maybe she could get permission for
Laura on that boat. Laura readily agreed.

A few days later, Marilu came back to Laura waving a telegram with the news that Belen wanted to go visit her husband in Ternate, and so she and Laura would travel together. The boat's captain hadn't wanted to take responsibility for a single woman with a boatload of men, but two women would make them both safer. Belen would return later by air. "Please come next Sunday for departure on Monday," Belen had written. "Thank you, Marilu!" Laura shouted.

INDONESIA, 1972

13. Ternate, Fabled Island of Spice

She couldn't sleep. Out at the bow before dawn, she leaned against the gunwale, experiencing more than she could take in all at once. Their small inboard motorboat chug-chugged southward, but they seemed to be surrounded by a quiet calm. The glassy, softly rippled sea surface reflected rapidly changing colors from the east, from dark blue-gray, to deep maroon, then peach, and finally bright yellow as the sun peeped over the horizon. A few sea birds flew over the boat, cawing.

Port and starboard, the boat passed small but high islands, several of them displaying one or more volcanic cones towering above their forest trees. *No coconut palms here, therefore probably no human habitation, because they are almost always planted by people,* Laura thought.

She slapped her cheek at the buzz of a mosquito.

The sea water smells clean and... tropical, like in the southern Philippines. But what makes it smell like that? Maybe the marine life beneath us? But maybe also because we're passing by islands, so the air holds the fragrance of their trees and flowers.

The cool night air rapidly warmed as the sun climbed into full view. Always heavy, loaded with moisture, it embraced her. The little hairs on her forearms softly waved in the breeze generated by the boat's forward chugging.

I wonder if I'll recognize the real Ternate from the 16th century drawings and the 20th century photos? But we're coming from the north, and all of the drawings are made from the east, looking straight at Mount Gamalama from the harbor.

These islands, like in the southern Philippines, they're so quiet even from our short distance. Like they're sleeping.

I wonder if I'll be overwhelmed, like when I first went to the California Bay Area when I was 17 and took the Bay Bridge from Berkeley over to San Francisco? Just couldn't believe my eyes at the wonder!

My first trip to the Philippines, I was overwhelmed by the tropical smell when the plane door opened, as if I'd be knocked down. I was struck by the heavy fragrance of flowers, sweet, but also... sweet moldy. Decadent. Safe? Certainly exotic! I was excited, attracted, but awestruck because air came so heavy and fast into the plane, it seemed almost like a liquid wave.

.....

"Oh, Belen, Ternate looks just like the pictures!" Belen had hurried to join Laura at the bow. "The motor slowed down and that woke me up."

Knowing that their estimated arrival time was eight o'clock and it was now at 7:30, they were alert. Ternate's cone shape was a perfect right-angle triangle, and at first, they could barely discern it from the other islands, but the boat had slowed down and chug-chugged directly toward it. A quarter hour later, the captain cut the motor and the boat silently glided to the dock.

On board and on shore, workers hustled into position, preparing for the docking. Lines were secured. Belen scanned people waiting on the dock and suddenly excitedly waved her arm high to her husband as she nudged Laura.

Filipino loggers on board had gathered their small bags and lined up to walk the narrow plank to the dock. Laura followed Belen toward her husband who had come to the side of the boat. Belen and he briefly hugged. Belen then introduced Laura to her Steve.

"Where are you staying, Laura? Do you have a place yet?" he asked, and before she could answer, he pointed to a *rumah makan dan tidur* (house for eating and sleeping) not far down the road paralleling the shore. "I've heard that that's a good place. Tomorrow we can take you around if you like; here's my card, and you'll find a telephone in there to call me at work. I'll pick Belen up at home and we'll come get you." The two women hugged and murmured "Good trip; happy to share it with you." And "Thank you, Belen!"

Laura walked toward the sign *rumah makan dan tidur* and entered the white concrete block one-story house. She came into a dimly lit, small dining room painted light blue and infused with the fragrance of several spices cooking, the fragrance stirred by two oscillating table fans on side tables. Five little metal tables were each surrounded by four metal folding chairs. As she entered, an interior curtain – of many long-beaded strings – was pulled aside, and a woman with a broad smile emerged from the kitchen. *Big very white-toothed friendly smile like in the Philippines!* Laura immediately felt welcomed, even without a common language.

She said something that Laura couldn't understand, and then she pulled a chair from a table and gestured for Laura to sit. Laura remained standing, looked down at her bag and then up to the woman, and held her clasped hands next to her head which she leaned to the side toward them. The woman smiled and motioned for her to follow between two cloth curtains into a small, neat bedroom.

The woman said *"Saya Taman"* and then gestured with the back of her open hand to Laura. Laura guessed this was a sharing of names. Belen had told her to give respectful titles: to men, *Tuan*, and to women *Ibu*. So Laura gestured toward her and said "Ibu Taman," and then touched her chest, and responded "La-u-ra." Ibu Taman replied "Ibu La-u-da." She pulled open a door down the hall to show Laura a toilet. Then she returned to the kitchen.

Laura set her bag down, used the toilet, and then flushed it in the same way she had learned in rural Philippines – if there were toilets. A faucet came out of the side wall, and hanging from the pipe was a pair of pliers. Under the faucet stood a half-filled plastic three-gallon utility pail, and floating in the water was a partially filled one-liter can that had previously held motor oil. Laura knew that dipping the can into the water and pouring it into the toilet was the way to flush it. She then turned on the faucet with the pliers to wash her hands and to refill the pail. The next step was to turn the faucet off and re-hang the pliers. She then dried her hands on the outside thigh areas of her skirt. She quickly brushed her hair, picked up her small bag with wallet out of her duffle, and entered the dining room, where Ibu Taman had set out a breakfast for her: a fried egg (*Is that a duck egg? – Very pale-yellow yolk – too pale!*), a fried piece of dried fish, and a little mound of succulent light-green seaweed.

Ibu Taman sat at a nearby table and watched Laura eat. The food was familiar to Laura, like food she had eaten regularly in rural Southern Philippines. She was hungry and ate eagerly.

She prepared for her mission: she wanted to see the ruins of the Portuguese and the Dutch forts which she had heard were still standing.

She showed Ibu Taman a picture of the Portuguese Fort Tolukko and asked, "Where is it?" The woman pointed out the door to the road going northward. She then "walked" with her fingers, showing Laura that she could walk there. *Gotta learn this language,* Laura grumbled to herself.

Outside again, she walked less than a quarter of a mile on the dirt shoulder of the asphalt road. To her left, set far back from the road, in a field, stood a tall, white concrete house – *well, a western-like mansion* - with double steps leading to a roofed porch with pillars. At the start of the long driveway was a sign written in Arabic letters and below it, in Roman letters, the word *Sultan....I'll try to visit there later.*

Another hundred meters along the road and to her right, she saw a little hill on a cape jutting out into the Molucca Sea. On this cape, some 30 feet above the water looked to be her destination: a stone building, some 20 feet high. She walked in and looked around. No one was at Fort Tolukko. Walls standing, no roof. Stones, some moss-covered. No sign of recent activity. *It's here, it's open, I'll come back.*

Returning to her *rumah makan dan tidur,* she sat to drink water and agreed to a mid-day meal. A white man sat at another table, who offered a brief, formal smile. She sat quietly, water in hand, to cool down from the bright sun. After a short time he greeted her. "Hello, surprising to see another European here. I'm Willem Cornelissen," and he held out his hand.

"Laura Rhodes." They talked. He learned that she would be staying here in the *rumah tidur*.

"Here just two weeks?"

She learned that Willem was in Ternate for four months from the Netherlands, also for fieldwork, and that this was his second stay in eastern Indonesia. By the finish of their short talk, she had agreed to go in the afternoon for tea on the terrace of the house where he was a guest of another Dutchman named Clifford.

She felt concern about accepting Willem's offer. *Safe up there? But just for afternoon tea.*

14. The Tree Botanist, the Linguist

By two days later, Clifford had readily agreed with Willem to invite Laura to stay in a room in his expansive villa, rather than her tiny curtained-off alcove in a *rumah tidur* in "town." "Tell her that she can lock the guest bedroom here from the inside." After dinner and almost at dusk, the three sat outside.

Clifford had provided them *Bintang* ("Star") beer brought up from a discreet restaurant in the town, selling "under the table" because Muslims are forbidden in the Koran from drinking alcohol. In that restaurant, they served take-out beer in white plastic water jugs in order to conceal the drink from other customers.

They sat on Adirondack chairs with cold glasses in their hands, looking out over the little town of Ternate and beyond, to the Molucca Sea, the island of Tidore to their right, and in the distance ahead, the much larger island of Halmahera. The late afternoon sun turning orange behind them caused their long shadows to reach out beyond the edge of the garden, spilling over its plateau, reaching down toward the town and the water.

Clifford leaned toward Laura with a smile. "So what brings you to Ternate, my dear?"

"I'm working in the Philippines on a creole Spanish language, in a town called Ternate, named after this town in Indonesia. I'm a linguist."

"Oh? You know many languages?"

"That's a polyglot. A linguist studies the science of languages."

Clifford smiled. "Oh, we have a Dutch creole language. It's in South Africa."

"Yes, Afrikaans."

"Oh, of course you would know. But a town of Ternate in the Philippines? I didn't know."

"Yes, Spanish missionaries, and now town members, have kept records. In 1662, some 200 people were taken from here by Spanish colonizers to protect them from the encroaching Dutch, who as you know were in the process of conquering all of Indonesia, for the spices here. So I've come to look at this place our Filipino Ternatenyos call their original homeland."

"Aah, our miraculous trees." Willem leaned back into his chair.

Laura agreed. "The clove trees, and further south, the nutmeg trees."

"I look forward to learning much more about you and your work, dear Laura, but it must be tomorrow. The sun has set and so must I." He discreetly bid Willem and Laura goodnight and moved inside.

Willem and Laura looked out to the panoramic view.

Laura broke the quiet by saying, "Willem, Ternate smells of cloves! I could smell cloves before we came ashore."

"Yes, but only when in season, when they're laid out to dry on mats on the roads, like now."

"Willem, are you Catholic? And by the way, how do you spell your name?"

"W-i-l-l-e-m."

"You pronounce it with a V?"

"Not quite, but closer to V than W."

"Okay, Villem to me, then."

"To your first question: I was born and raised north of the rivers, in Utrecht."

"What do you mean, north of the rivers?"

Willem drew a map of the Netherlands in the air. "Three rivers cross the country, horizontally on the map." He drew two lines. "At the mouth of the Rhine and the Maas rivers [it's the Meuse in English] is the city of Rotterdam. Busiest port in the world; did you know that?"

"Nope. Wow!"

He drew a third line. "The *Schelde* – Scheldt in English – flows further to the south with its mouth at Vlissingen. And why 'the three rivers?' Because the Spanish conquest and occupation from 1556 to 1714 mostly didn't get above the three rivers. To the south of the rivers, they converted the Dutch population to Catholicism. The Spanish were finally expelled, but even today, Dutch people to the south of the rivers are more Catholic, and to the north, they're more Protestant... But why did you ask whether I'm Catholic? Going off course here, aren't you?"

Laura smiled big, delighted with this exchange. "I'm still on the mesmerizing fragrance of cloves. I wondered if you could remember the first time you went into a Catholic service, and..."

Willem interjected. "I was 17 and still in school when I agreed to join my friend Jaap before we went on to the beach on a Sunday morning. But why, dear Laura?"

"Because, you said you were older than an infant, so you might remember your first experience of inhaling herbs in the service."

"Yes, incense! Very strange to me, a little scary."

"Yep."

"You too?"

"Yes. I was a teenager too when I first went to a Catholic service, together with a Catholic girlfriend. Strange to me. It was before incense became common at parties, co-occurring with the arrival of cannabis into our university department in the fall of 1967. The new graduate students, the others all from East Coast major universities, brought both the incense and the pot. And that was the end of our dancing at parties! The students just sat, smiled, listened to non-dancing music, and passed around a joint."

Willem asked, "So do you know what spices are in Catholic and other incense?"

"I looked them up. Haven't seen much use of our favorite spices, the ones from these islands. In both Catholic services and in incense sticks – which came from India, I think, – frankincense is a big item, a resin from a thorny desert bush in Somalia. And myrrh is similar, and both are still used. They're tree bark oils. But I have had a similar experience on entering a Catholic church to smelling cloves here in the open air: mysterious and mesmerizing."

Willem closed his eyes and tilted his head toward the darkening sky. "When I walked into a party where incense sticks were burning, the atmosphere was startlingly special, and I'm not sure I liked the smell."

"How about your first experiences with our special two spices, Willem?"

"Well, in the Netherlands we use nutmeg a lot in vegetables, like potatoes, cabbage, spinach, squash. I don't know of any other European cuisine using nutmeg in savory dishes."

"Only rarely in American savory dishes as well. We stick clove nails in onions for soup, and in meats like ham and in beef stew. And about cloves: my dad chewed on a clove 'nail' when he had a toothache and was waiting for his dentist appointment. So I've chewed on one as well now and then, but just for the taste. A little bit burning and numbing."

She added, "Americans are more likely to season savory food with onions and garlic, and salt and black pepper shakers are on most dining tables. Nutmeg and cloves are usually used only in sweet foods. Do you think that maybe you in the Netherlands use these spices for savory foods more than other Europeans because you were so involved in the Spice Trade?"

"Hmm, maybe so."

"Well, maybe the Netherlands is not unique if you look at the cuisines of countries more to the east. If you follow the Spice Trade from here, Ternate, through all the countries that the traders passed through on the way to Europe, that's where you'd find local cuisines that include these spices. I know that these and other eastern spices are used a lot in Indonesia, Malaysia, Thailand, and India. Continuing westward, use of them tapers as you sail toward the Near East and Africa, and then you find little use in Europe. I've read that the Netherlands uses the most of any European countries."

"I think so. And as you know, I, a Dutchman, am here to study these trees."

"How come?" Laura asked. "Are you in the Spice Trade?"

"I'm a botanist, actually a dendrologist, the study of woody plants. We Dutch could take some responsibility for these trees. They've been very important for our history, and actually, for the rest of the world as well."

"Didn't Alfred Russel Wallace also come here because of these two trees?"

"Yes. Oh, you know of him?"

"Yes, contemporary and competitor of fellow Englishman Charles Darwin, mid 19th Century. And hey, have you noticed that Russel is spelled unusually, with just one -l-, and it doesn't even match his last name with two -ll-s? What were his parents thinking?"

"*Ja*, ha ha, why not call him russet – potato?"

She laughed.

He continued. "I have to admit that I was lured here to the Spice Islands after reading about Alfred Russel Wallace. But he concentrated on animals. During his ten years here, he sent 125,000 specimens – dead, of course – back to London! Some were big mammals, including our local *orang utans*! I first came 20 years ago to learn more about the trees, their history and their botany, especially the beneficial fungi associated with them. Now I've come back for a follow-up."

"Beneficial fungi?"

"Yes. All trees growing in their natural setting – and these little islands are where these two trees evolved – have beneficial fungi associated with their roots in a symbiotic relationship. For all the service they give to the trees, the fungi can take up as much as one third of the tree's production of nutrients."

"Wow. So you're back for more?"

"There's plenty more to learn. Especially, what happened to the fungi and the mutual relationship when so many trees were cut down by the Dutch in the 17th century? Is any vestige of the original symbiosis left? Or, how have the trees and the fungi adjusted to all the disruption? Is their communication with other plants severed, reduced, distorted, destroyed? And do these two spice trees, two separate species, communicate with each other via their fungi?"

Laura's eyes opened wide. "What do you mean, communicate? You're not saying that these trees talk to each other!"

"Not just these trees. All trees."

"What? I've never heard this." Pressing her elbows onto one armrest of the chair, she leaned toward him to experience more.

"Yep. They communicate with their fellow trees, and I learned twenty years ago that nutmeg and clove trees communicate with each other, now that they're planted nearby one another. One way is via the vast fungal network connecting the tips of their roots, underground. Another way is by scent. A third way is by their behaviors. For instance, they send nutrients back and forth, nurturing both their own and other's seedlings.

"What!"

"Yes, they take more care of their own than others' seedlings. They help one another in storms and in other difficulties. If they are kind, and they usually are, they don't crowd other trees with their branches so that they don't shade them out."

"This is all news to me, Willem. I can hardly believe it. Surely they don't talk to animals…"

"Well, you already know that of course they do."

Laura interjected. "You know that song? Well, probably you wouldn't, from *Paint your Wagon*, a movie that came out in 1959. Clint Eastwood – he has a good voice! – sang the song himself, 'I talk to the trees, but they don't listen to me.'… But remind me how trees communicate with animals!"

Willem pressed forward. "Of course you know that many plants put out flowers to make cross-pollination attractive to bees and even birds. They make their male flowers brighter so that the bees visit them first, before carrying the pollen over with them to visit the female flowers."

"Well, birds and bees, then," she conceded.

"But other insects as well: bad taste to the beetles; no fruits in alternate years in order to deter attracting deer and boar..."

"Surely nothing audible, though; right?"

"You can hear if you listen carefully."

"How, then?"

"For instance, put your ear to the ground under a tree, and you might hear root action."

Laura frowned. "Or maybe I would hear just insects down there. How would I know?"

"Aah, you're skeptical, I see. A real scientist!" He smiled, pulled himself out of his chair, and offered his hand to Laura. "Come with me to that tree over there; you might hear something." He led her to a ficus tree at the edge of the garden.

"Put your ear against the trunk like this." Standing, he pressed his ear against the trunk.

Laura took her turn. She listened for a few seconds, and suddenly her eyes lighted up. She pulled back, looked to Willem, and said, "Yes. I did hear something, definitely inside the trunk. Sounded like ... like... water coming up a drinking straw. Or running through a garden hose. What is it?"

"Water and nutrients traveling from the soil up through the tree to its top."

"Wow!" She stepped back to look at the treetop. "By the way, how *does* water get all the way up to the top of the trees?

If I suck on a straw, the liquid overcomes gravity by my creation of a vacuum, right? But trees can't do that, can they?"

Willem answered, "Well, they can and do, by transpiration."

"Oh... yeah... uh, I kind of remember that from junior high school science. Leaves evaporate water and create a vacuum..."

"You're right, but that's not the only way that water defies gravity to travel to the top of trees."

"Oh?"

"Two other actions help. Capillary action helps a little. You know, how water molecules bond together but then attract to a solid, for instance a paper towel picking up water, or the surface tension of water in a glass causing the water to rise above its flat plane at the edge of the glass."

"I think I understand. And there's another action?"

"Yes, osmosis. Water will travel through its cell wall into a neighboring cell that has more sugar until they have the same concentration of water. This is the most important way that water rises, like taking steps of a ladder."

"Is this what I'm hearing inside this trunk?"

"Yes, especially during the warmth of the day, so let's listen again tomorrow morning."

Then she frowned again. "So trees make internal sounds. But surely, they have no way, or don't want, to talk to us humans, do they? The only sounds I've heard from trees are of leaves blowing in the breeze. Maybe with big winds, creaking branches now and then."

He smiled again. "Listen more closely. Let's go to some trees again tomorrow morning."

15. The Linguist

The next afternoon, as Laura walked back to Clifford's villa from another solo tour of Tolukko fort, she saw Willem talking with a young local man who appeared to be showing him a notebook. The two men talked, and then Willem reached into his pocket and counted some money out to give him. The young man looked for Clifford in the house, said "*selamat tinggal* (stay well; goodbye), and rode off downhill on his bicycle.

Laura greeted Willem as she passed him to put her bag inside the house. "Hello, Willem. Oh who's that man?"

"Oh, Ali, he's been working for me, collecting photos, specimens, and seeds. He looks for certain fungi in roots of clove and nutmeg trees.

"So he's had botanical training?"

"Yes, I've been training him."

Before long they sat with their host on the terrace having afternoon *camilan* (snack) of beer and tiny dried and salted anchovies. Once again, they admired their broad panorama of the little town of Ternate below them, and behind and above them the almost perfect cone-shaped Gamalama mountain, and to their right, across the Ternate Strait, Tidore's forested volcanic mountain to the south.

After a quiet period, Willem said, "I've been thinking about what you told us last night, Laura, about your field of linguistics and your fieldwork. And I was wondering, shouldn't linguistics be considered a humanities subject, not a science?"

Laura replied, "It's the most patterned of human behaviors. All human languages are much more similar than dissimilar. Human languages are narrowly structured, with many more universals than differences. For instance, of all the possibilities even within audio range, from the mouth, apart from hands clapping and so forth, all human languages use only a very finite set of sounds, and most of these are common to all languages. For one example, the speech of most languages is uttered on exhalation. One exception is Bantu languages, that have what we call "clicks," and those are uttered on inhalation. And, linguists use scientific methods to study languages. One universal analysis is that (almost) every six-year-old has learned to adhere to the myriad rules of her language, even though she's not consciously aware of those rules."

Clifford joined in. "I've always been wondering, Laura, aren't some languages better than others? More highly developed? Better able to express thoughts? And how did humans get languages in the first place?"

She looked at each of the two men. She figured that Willem, who spent most of his adulthood at a university, would likely know more about the scientific study of language, and he was baiting her, in a friendly tease, to talk about herself. Clifford, now living out here in the tropics as a gentleman farmer on his parents' plantation and dabbling in the nutmeg and clove business, perhaps had less university study. She decided to go "introductory" in her response to accommodate Clifford.

"Linguists are still looking for the evolution of human language. They've given up on finding a missing link, because scientific reports have come back from every language, or at least every language family, in the world. Their data and analysis have shown that there's no human 'primitive' language."

Clifford asked, "If so similar, did human languages get invented just one time? And in fully developed form? If so, why do we have so many?"

Laura answered, "Probably only one time, but we don't know. And about many: languages diverge when speakers diverge. English was brought by Englishmen to America, and our speech diverged from that of the folks back home. Language drifts with lack of contact. And every living language is constantly changing."

"Oh, how many are there?" asked Clifford.

"Maybe 7,000 languages."

"Seven thousand?!" the men exclaimed.

"But sadly, around three languages are dying off every month, languages now spoken only by older people."

"Being killed off by humans, like disappearing flora and fauna?" Willem asked.

"Not killed, just dying, mainly when old people die. Two American Christian missionary organizations can take the credit for finding, counting, recording, and translating the Bible into most languages. Yeah, starting in the 1930's and 1940's the Summer Institute of Linguistics, the Biola Bible Institute, and the Wycliffe Bible Translators took on the mission to bring Christianity to everyone in the world, partly by translating the Bible into every language."

"That'd be costly," Willem said.

"Umm." Laura continued. "And they had a special interest in dying languages. These organizations attracted many missionaries to study linguistics, and they gathered church donations to send these linguists off to fieldwork for years at a time. They were mostly young married men who took their wives and little children with them to the "field" for decades, many out to remote places with primitive technologies. "

"Please continue about missing link: none has been found yet? How can that be?" asked Willem.

"Yes, we think there's enough evidence by now to know that every natural human language is fully formed, and none is more primitive than any other."

"Oh, that cannot be." Clifford emphatically set down his beer, and he then signaled to Hammid, who was discreetly watching from the kitchen door, to bring more beer.

Laura said, "Surprising to everyone. We know that "traditional" people usually have little or no advanced technology. So we're surprised to learn that they have languages as complex as those in 'modern' cultures. They can say anything we can. There's no simple hierarchy of human languages in overall complexity or capability."

Willem protested. "But some languages are a lot harder to learn than others, right? So they must be more complex!"

She calmly answered. "Kind of surprisingly, perhaps, but not illogically, the languages that traditionally more adults learn as second languages, or as *linguae francae,* have become – apparently but not factually – somewhat simpler grammatically. For instance, English has dropped most of the declension markers of other Germanic languages, probably because English came to be learned by more adults as a *lingua franca.* By 'apparently' I mean that some of the grammatical meaning has been taken up by word order and intonation, which most adults find easier to learn than case endings."

Willem knew three Germanic languages well: his native Dutch, and German and English. "Yeah, I suppose it's got a simpler grammar, though English pronouns *do* have declensions."

Laura added. "And yes, they're almost the only vestiges. And to your question, is one language harder to learn than another? It all depends on what language(s) you're coming from. As *first* languages, all children everywhere learn around 90% of the surrounding language(s) spoken to them by the time they're six years old."

Clifford thought of an exception. "Even Chinese, with all those – 10 thousand, isn't it? - characters?"

She quietly sighed, while hoping that he didn't notice. "That's the writing. Writing systems are only feeble approximations of spoken languages. No writing system measures up to all the communication of the spoken language. Some writing systems are vastly more complicated than others, in particular, Chinese. But this is quite a separate topic from spoken language."

Clifford accepted his new beer; both Willem and Laura signaled polite declines to Hammid.

Willem sat back and spoke up again. "So back to how humans came to have language!"

She looked at each of the men, who both appeared to be actively waiting for her to continue, and who likely would flood her with more questions.

"Well, humans are not completely unique in our communication or cognition. Many studies report complex communication by other animals - primates, even bees, who can even communicate about experiences far away and in the past."

The two men looked at her. Willem said, "I've heard of Eibl-Eibesfeldt working on bee communication at the Max Planck Institute in München."

"Oh, you know, then. And even our vocal cords don't completely set us apart from other animals. For instance, adult male Gelada baboons in Ethiopia make sounds eerily like adult human men."

"I thought we humans were unique; made in God's image!" Clifford teased.

"Even centuries ago people wondered how human languages evolved. We now have a revival of interest from the 1950's up to the present: animal languages, babies learning their first languages, children and adults learning second languages, ASL (American Sign Language) and lately, studies have started of contact languages. And I wondered why all the contact languages we knew about were European-based. I've heard that one is now developing by workers brought together to build the Aswan Dam in Egypt, with the source language being Swahili."

"So tell us about your special Spanish dialect or language, Laura. What drew you to study it?

"At first I had hoped it might hold a clue to the evolution of human language. I was intrigued that I could understand a lot (though I missed a lot). And if I responded in Spanish, they (at least the adults) could understand me. Especially my short utterances, they could mostly understand."

Willem asked, "So are contact languages similar to each other?"

"They're amazingly similar. Of course, in the last 600 years, physical contact is recorded, of crews, for trading. For example, Portuguese sailed down the west coast of Africa, and they established ports and made long stops as they moved southward and then eastward. In those ports, Portuguese pidgins developed. And whatever the source language, the grammar is surprisingly similar to that of other contact languages."

Willem persisted. "So how did this grammar come about? And is it different from baby talk, or even animal communication?"

"Different, linguists have learned. How developed? Linguists are working on relatively new pidgins. Creoles have been around longer. But hey, guys, I'm talking too much."

Both men immediately protested. "Please continue!"

"Oh, okay. So the goals of my research are: one, to describe and analyze the phonology, morphology, syntax – that is, the sounds, words, and grammar - of Chabacano; two, to compare usage across age, gender, and knowledge of any second language; and three, to interview people in my community of Ternate for historical memory.

"Shall I go on?"

"Yes, please!" Clifford added, "I had no idea how people study a language, or even what can be studied about a language!"

"Okay then: four, to conduct exhaustive search in Philippine and Spanish archives for early documents on the language."

Clifford interjected again. "So how do you go about studying it? I mean, how do you learn a language if you're not taking a language class? Kind of like babies do?"

She smiled. "Well, without a class, we have two possibilities: either without, or with, a translator. Without is more effort, but we know of efficient sequences of learning."

"For example?"

"For example, I can start out by holding up a stone. A cooperative informant will say something, and I'll try to repeat that – maybe receive an apparent correction – repeat it again and write it down on my notepaper. Then I'd hold up two stones and repeat that process. Maybe ... maybe, I'll have glimpses of one or singular, and two or plural, and stone, and whether that word changes when plural."

Willem asked, "So in general, what are you looking for with a new language, that is, new to you?"

"Besides the basic of learning to understand and to speak, I'm looking for the structure and the vocabulary. I want to learn differences from other contact languages, and I have descriptions of other contact languages with me."

"So how do you go about it?"

"Well, I make recordings of speech; I transliterate and transcribe these, and I've started out with the work of a translator, usually a local person who is not skilled in language study. And then I form hypotheses, and I return to speakers to test my hypotheses."

"About vocabulary: I make a 3x5 card of each word including its variations, and I record it especially within a context – an utterance - which I also write down.

"Then, I research the etymology of each vocabulary item. – And I have etymological dictionaries of Tagalog, of Spanish, of Sanskrit, and of Arabic."

"Remind me what that means" asked Clifford.

"Etymology means, what's the origin of the word? When did it first appear in print in this language, and if already researched, was it borrowed or evolved from another language?" she responded.

"Go on, please," said Willem.

"Okay, so I look for varieties in the several sites in the Philippines: Ermita, the neighborhood in Manila, in Cavite, in Ternate, where I do most of my research, and 600 miles to the south, in Zamboanga.

"I compare my data with that of other known contact languages, such as Southeast Asian Portuguese pidgins and creoles, including Macao Patois and Malacca Portuguese Creole.

"And I will try to find a 300-year-old grammar and dictionary recorded by Don Diego de Esquivel, the Jesuit priest who in 1662 took the speakers from Ternate, Indonesia, to Ternate,

Philippines. I'll have to go to Sevilla, Spain to look for it, and if not successful there, then to Santiago, Chile. I'll go sometime next year to look for that document."

Willem asked, "Have you been surprised by any of your discoveries so far?"

"Well, as I expected, the grammar is like that of other creoles and definitely not like those of either Spanish or Tagalog. Not exactly surprising, but certainly exciting.

"The sounds, as I expected, are similar to those of Philippine languages, especially Tagalog, nearby. This is the same pattern as of other known contact languages, so no surprise."

She continued. "The vocabulary – and I have 12,000 unique items so far, are 80% Peninsular Spanish, not Mexican, even though the priests and even sailors stopped over in Mexico on their way here. So that's a little surprising. Most of the rest are Tagalog, even down in Zamboanga's Chabacano, where no one was speaking Tagalog as a first language. So that's also surprising, and hints at mobility during these 300 years after immigration to the Philippines. The few Sanskrit and Arabic vocabulary likely came earlier into Tagalog. Some words are Portuguese not Spanish. These words are found as well in local Philippine languages, words borrowed from Spanish. One word startled me: *pikininny* "young child", used by an old man, because I've found it only recently in Chabacano in the Philippines, and it is also found in other European-based contact languages globally, so in Africa and the Caribbean."

"Laura," Willem asked," you told us yesterday that finding a job in an American university is a difficult reach. Will your work on this language get you there?"

"Well, interest in contact languages is flourishing in the field of linguistics. But everywhere they're spoken, they tend to be disdained. And I have missionary zeal to improve the reputation of the language in the Philippines. Filipinos dismiss Chabacano, saying that it has no grammar. Even its speakers say that. I want to show them that it does indeed have a grammar, just different than that of Spanish. Actually, in the Philippines I've been – maybe jokingly – accused of having the mission to build Filipino self-esteem by showing them that Chabacano is not a "bastard" of Spanish. Separate from the reputation of the contact language, I also have a big concern that Filipinos act as if the U.S. were close to heaven, and they want to become 'refugees' there. Their adulation bothers me so much! They have more respect for us than we deserve, and they deserve more self-respect.

"Maybe if I show them that Chabacano is a vestige of their importance in the great Spice Trade, I can help them gain respect for their history and culture."

Clifford interrupted her. "You mean that Filipinos were involved in the Spice Trade? I didn't know that."

She was delighted by his question. "The Spice Trade was what brought Spaniards to Southeast Asia, and because they valued Manila's bay and because Dutch sailors chased them out of here – the Spice Islands - they headquartered in Manila. And with their discovery of the best ocean route eastward to the New World, which they were also colonizing, they developed tremendous trade with their enormous fleet of galleons. And by the way, the contact language was created because of the Spice Trade. It's still spoken in the Philippines, but is no longer found in Indonesia."

"Wow, you're showing us how important the consequences have been of the spices on these tiny islands!"

"I hope so! I've had a passion for the contact language. Now I'm developing a passion for the bigger picture," a saga that encompassed 5,000 years, a good share of the globe, and a big role in global history."

All three looked out over their incredible panorama.

After a while, Willem said, "So the Spice Trade brought you here, Laura. Me too, because of these unique trees."

Laura said, "I'm really just discovering that the trees brought me here, too."

16. One Afternoon

A few afternoons later, when Laura had gone for another visit to the ruins of the Portuguese fort, Benteng Tolukku, Clifford took his chance to talk by himself with Willem.

Clifford discovered himself excited by this potentially budding romance. But he had mixed feelings. He didn't quite approve of Willem's possible philandering. even though Willem's wife was geographically and emotionally distant. Maybe he was not quite disapproving, just sad to discover that he was providing "opportunity" for yet another of his international friends. And he was starting to care about Laura's welfare. He didn't want to see her get hurt.

"No more children?" he asked Willem.

"Oh, no, we wouldn't want another pair. And...and... it turns out that my wife still suffers from a bad encounter with a gang of teenage boys, some years before I met her. She's had a lot of counseling, but it looks like she might never overcome it."

Clifford decided that he had probed deeply enough.

17. I Climb Trees

Laura told Willem, "I came here to see the trees. I'm surprised they look so ... modest; they've been so important in history."

Willem responded, "As a botanist, I can point out that a lot of tropical forest trees look very similar to each other even though they're different species. They don't interbreed, but they look very similar."

"Surprising?"

"No, it's a regular feature found in a center of biological diversity: large numbers of species, many of them similar to each other. Clove trees, for example, are one of about 500 species in its family, the *Syzygium aromaticum*, and they all look similar to one another."

"What do they look like?"

"Well, they're evergreen, and tropical, of course. They don't grow over twelve meters tall. Their bark is smooth and gray, and they have long leaves, maybe twelve centimeters, that look like bay leaves. The little flower buds, the cloves, are two centimeters long and they gather in clusters at the branch tips. They're red like holly before they're harvested and dried."

Laura gazed out over the big sky landscape from Clifford's terrace. "Do people climb them? Like they climb palm trees for their fruits?"

"Forest trees like cloves? Yes, they do, but they're hard to climb because for most of them in the dense forest, the first branches are high up, way too high to reach."

"So people do climb nutmeg and clove trees?"

"Yes. Why?"

"I love to climb trees."

"You came here to climb trees?" He smiled.

"Well, mainly to learn more about these trees, and mainly to see these formerly famous Spice Islands."

"You're still a kid!" He laughed.

"Come on. Do you still enjoy living? I mean, I loved climbing trees when I was a kid. Neighbor boys teased me for being a tomboy, but I saw that as a compliment because they were impressed by my prowess. Back then, I could jump up to grab the lowest branch and then swing my leg up and over and then pull myself up to sit on it."

"Impressive."

"Hmm. My mom once came to call me home and found me in a tree. I clambered down and saw that she was kind of nervous, but she didn't say anything, I think because she had told me that *she* climbed trees a lot when *she* was a kid. And she loved the monkey bars at school. I guess the perspective looked different for her as an adult while watching her daughter."

"You never fell?"

"Not from a tree."

"So what did tree climbing mean to you? Escape?"

She quickly looked at Willem. "What, didn't you climb trees as a kid?"

"Not really. I was raised in the city."

"But you study trees now. Hmm, unattainable pleasure?"

"Ha-ha. Maybe!" He smiled, apparently delighted with her teasing.

"And climbing for you?"

"Hmm, about climbing." She paused. "I climbed buildings to the rooftops as well. And stairs up towers. But I lived in the country, and I was attracted to the trees."

"Why, then?

"Hey, don't rush me, I'm thinking." She paused. "I liked their fragrance, even if sometimes I got pitch on my hands, and occasionally, splinters. Higher up, I delighted in the perspective they offered near the top. They reached into the sky. Birds rested on them up high, but my rustling up the branches would of course scare them away. Up high, I had views like the birds, as if I could fly as well."

"So, mainly better view?"

"View, and fragrance, and you could count on each tree always standing in the same place. Dependable. Most trees have perfect posture. But their branches and leaves are constantly moving, usually gently. And the sunlight dances on their leaves. They bend with big wind and usually return to upright. I like that when the sky grays and darkens in the fall, they resist with bright colors of their leaves. Then they sink into the dark cold by losing their vulnerable leaves to get through the winter, but later they spring back with new tender yellow-green leaves. And they welcome me to climb, like a ladder, with their branches spaced out for my hands and feet."

"I think I missed an important part of childhood, Laura."

"Never too late, Willem." She looked out over their grand vista again. "So the clove and nutmeg trees: I wouldn't want to intrude on anyone's private trees in their gardens, but plenty of wild ones are standing in the forest here, isn't that right?"

"Sure, but..."

"Before coming here, I read that these two species grow only 40 or 50 feet tall, and, traditionally at least, harvesters used to climb them. So the branches must start out low enough and be spaced far enough apart for a human body to fit."

"Yes, I guess. I'll show you some nearby ones tomorrow. But I'm reluctant to help you go up!"

"I'll climb only if I can reach the lowest branches, and I won't need help."

18. Trees Talk

The following day, Willem showed Laura how to identify
clove and nutmeg trees near Clifford's house. Then he left for
downtown to examine the new samples his assistant had
brought in. Laura waited for the afternoon rain to finish, and
then she walked toward Mount Gamalama, looking up
toward the many nutmeg and clove trees. She carried a large
plastic bag, now folded, as a ground cover. Close to town and
houses, these trees were widely spaced and appeared to have
been planted for commercial harvesting.

She walked a little way up the alluvial plain of the volcanic
peak, into what appeared to be natural forest, with a variety
of trees growing closely together and taller. By the side of the
path, she found what she was looking for, a natural grove of
clove trees. Under one tree she smoothed down fallen leaves
with her foot, carefully spread out the plastic bag, and gently
sat down on it.

She looked around the ground and wondered what might be
under the springy pile of leaves. *Leeches under there?* She
looked up the trunk and into the branches of her tree, and
down again. Now and then she heard a *betjak* – a motor
scooter with sidecar - on the dirt road down the hill, about
a mile away. Here under her tree, she found warm, moist,
musty quiet. A cicada screeched its song somewhere not so
far away, and then another, farther away. *Responding to the
first one?* Laura wondered. The noise dissipated, and her
little grove returned to quiet.

She timidly put her ear down to her plastic bag and pressed
toward the earth, but she heard only the crackle of her bag.

Better to listen at the trunk, she thought, and stood up. The
trunk was bare of branches to about eight feet - *too high up to
start a climb* - so she easily pressed her ear, and listened.
Have to settle in, get oriented, and she waited. And just as the

night before, listening at the trunk of the ficus, within a few seconds she could hear the same soft sound of liquid moving up a hollow tube. She listened for several minutes, and the sound steadily continued.

She sat down on her bag again, and she looked up into the branches. Afternoon sunlight brightened the upper branches, but down closer to her, the tree was in shade.

Hmm, if this tree could talk to me, what would it say? I wonder if listening to a tree is something like listening to God? A lot of the world's population think that God is a man who talks to them, so they pray to Him. And they hear God. I wonder if I could do the same here? I learned how to pray, long ago:

> *Be grateful for what's going well today;*
> *Express concern for others in need;*
> *Sort out and define today's concerns;*
> *Sort out and reflect on decisions that need to be made; and*
> *Reflect.*

I can do that!

Dear clove tree, I'm so grateful that I met Willem. We both came to Ternate because of you, Clove, and the others, nutmeg and mace, only I didn't know it until yesterday. Willem came here to study you two species. But I hadn't yet quite realized how important you and the nutmeg tree became for people, even starting more than five thousand years ago, when they discovered not just your delicious tastes, but also your miraculous medicinal properties.

She patted down her plastic bag in order to smooth the leaves underneath and looked again up into the branches and leaves.

Oh my heavens! Dear Clove Tree, I'm thinking, that it had to have been because of you and nutmeg trees that my language, Chabacano, came to be created! You brought peoples of different languages and cultures together for the creation of a new language. And that's how "my" language came to be. Was it around 400 years ago? And now it's still spoken in the Philippines but is no longer spoken here!"

She watched a little bird land on a branch for just a moment before it flew off again. *We both came here, a linguist from the States and a botanist from the Netherlands, because of you two. I came to study a language that was created because of you.* She paused. *And we met because of you.*

Laura continued her silent secular prayer to the tree. *I worry about your welfare. You've been so exploited, so many of your ancestors were cut down, so many have been planted now commercially that your natural life has been almost destroyed. And Willem told me that not all fungi are beneficial. Have phytophthora water molds ever damaged you?*

*How can I help? Will Willem learn the best way for you trees to survive and thrive, and can his report have impact on the commercial industry? And can learning about you and your history help **my** study?*

19. Culture Shock

Willem and Laura sat on Clifford's Ternate sunset terrace looking southward across the one-mile Maluku Strait to the island of Tidore. Tidore, like the island of Ternate, rose in the center in a volcanic cone and wore a wide skirt of lush green, black beaches, and one town. Tropical trees, including cloves, nutmegs, and some coconut palms, covered both islands' eight-mile diameters.

Once again, the two people admired the setting sun, the very rapid descent into dark, and then the few lights from the houses below them. They each sat on *bangkirai* chaise lounges, protected by *katol* coils underneath, their little wisps of smoke curling up around the humans to ward off mosquitos.

An hour after sunset, Clifford again had discreetly gone inside to his bedroom, leaving the two.

"How come you waited twenty years to come back here?" asked Laura. "Did you have to get more financing?"

"That, and... frankly, when I came here twenty years ago, I couldn't adjust. I later learned I was experiencing culture shock. Laura, how did you manage when you first came across the Pacific from America?'

"Well, the first few months were hard. But some people have real trouble. What did you experience?"

"Well, you'd think, as a kid in summertime with my parents, vacationing in Italy and Spain where I didn't know either language, that I'd know about arriving in a new culture, but..."

"Yeah, they don't tell us about culture shock in graduate school before going off to our solo field work. How about in your university in Holland?"

"Nope. I discovered and confronted it on my own. Thought I was unique. Didn't know what was happening to me; wondered if I was going crazy… I really mean that. Couldn't get the dreams out of my head; they plagued me. And I felt so lonely that it was unbearable."

"What happened?"

"When I first came, I was exhilarated, in all my senses. Everything looked beautiful: people, clothing, plants, weather, mountains. I loved hearing the language and was excited to start working on it. The music was enchanting: gongs, bamboo flutes like birds in the trees. And I heard tropical birds. I was intrigued by strange smells: spices cooking, sweet tropical mildew, ripe fruits. Tasting new fruits I found enticing, hyper sweet but decadently mellow. I felt the humidity softening my skin. People were friendly and tried to help me when I asked, for instance, for directions. And on the flight eastward to these Spice Islands, I saw cloud formations completely new to me, tropical fluffy rain clouds, *cumulo-nimbi*. I looked down on small islands ringed by white sands and brilliant turquoise water. Arriving here in Ternate, Mount Gamalama looked even grander than in photos I'd seen: rising majestically out of the clear sea, and surrounded by similar volcanic-coned, lush green islands. I'd arrived in paradise."

"Yes, yes! But go on."

Willem poured refills into their glasses from the plastic jug that had been sitting in an ice bucket, and he then leaned back again. He looked up at the sky and saw the first star appearing. Laura looked up as well and wondered, *Couldn't be Venus, could it? We're viewing the sky from the southern hemisphere now.*

He continued. "Dreams flooded me, not just while sleeping, but during the daytime as well."

"Nightmares, day-mares?" She smiled, wondering if she'd invented a novel term.

"No, not bad dreams. But so many were about my life long ago, even in my childhood. I dreamt of my father carrying me onto the beach in Katwijk in the summer, with a pail of toys for my brother and me. We met up there with my mother, who was spreading a blanket on the sand."

"Enjoyable memories, then?'

"Not quite memories. I don't know... sometimes fantastic dreams, like mixing up yesterday's experience of sitting in a little boat passing a mangrove swamp, and then coming to the playground of my elementary school in the Netherlands, where we'd all run inside when the rain turned heavy. I'd pulled my jacket up over my head."

"So not just memories, then."

"No. But one day, I had been here – on Run Island in the Banda's, south of here – for a few weeks, progressing nicely on the language.

I'd found people to help me with day tours out to find some of Alfred Russel Wallace's flora and fauna, doing reasonably well. All of a sudden, I didn't like it here anymore. I wanted to go home.

"Ah... You weren't staying here in Clifford's villa?"

"Oh, no. I didn't know any European here, and I don't think there were any. Clifford came just five years ago, after he finished university and then worked for years in Amsterdam. I met him in Den Haag's annual Pasar Malam, an annual Asian night bazaar event. These Pasar Malams are important for the older Indo-Dutch and Indonesians, significant minorities in our country, who are valiantly trying to keep up awareness of Indonesian culture for their children. Clifford wanted to come back to his roots, even though he'd been in the Netherlands for years. All through Clifford's youth, his grandfather had reminisced about his home, Ternate. When Clifford retired – his grandfather long gone – he decided to come back here, and then he decided to live here at least half of each year."

"Is he Muslim?"

"No, but his grandfather was, and some older people remembered him, so he figured he'd be accepted. And so far, it's working out."

"God, your English is good!"

"Hey, thanks, but don't distract me! You already said that last week."

"It's still true."

"So, back to you, Laura: did you go home when you experienced culture shock?"

"My first stay, I felt committed to finishing my work here, that is, in the Philippines, and I did stay. But I felt so lonely! People were friendly with me, but I felt no one understood me. Sometimes when they laughed, I didn't know why, whether they were laughing with me or at me, or because I was making them nervous. You know how Indonesians laugh sometimes when they're nervous? Filipinos do as well. I didn't understand why I was so distraught. I couldn't explain it to anyone, or to myself, and besides, I was just starting out with the language. I even let the little girl in my guest house, maybe six or seven years old, look for *kutu*, head lice, you know, in my hair, just because it felt good. And I did wonder if I might get *kutu*, because the kapok pillow on my cot smelled rancid, of old coconut oil. Oh, do Indonesians out here in the *rimbu*, the countryside, also put coconut oil in their hair? I think I've seen that they do."

"I don't know; haven't noticed."

"Hmm. This is painful work, don't you think, Willem, focusing on these early experiences? But I hope to have a full catharsis, revealing it to you – and to myself, I guess." She chuckled.

"Ja...yeah, about language: we Dutch all learn the languages surrounding our tiny country, but of course they're all European languages. We can't expect anyone to learn ours. So by high school and certainly by university, most of our texts are in English. And half of all the programs on television come from England or America, with no dubbing, but usually with Dutch subtitles."

"So then what did you do?"

"Twenty years ago? Back then, I tried to reduce my loneliness by looking for Europeans in Ambon and here in Ternate, in cafes and at the port. Didn't see any. None on the Banda islands including the island of Run, where I was doing research on nutmeg trees. I was just counting the moments until time to leave. Felt I was barely escaping with my senses, and yet I still didn't understand why I fell down the deep black well of loneliness."

"Wow, you're describing classic culture shock, stages one and two, honeymoon and then disillusion."

"Sounds like you also didn't expect culture shock, is that right?"

"Well, after that first trip to the Philippines, I talked about it when I got home to California, and an anthropologist friend told me about a study on culture shock. Turns out there's a pretty regular progression of four stages. First is euphoria, then the dark, and then, after a few months, coming to terms with the new culture. And fourth, finding some real comfort in learning the language and peoples' behavior, and even the climate, of the new place."

"Yes, that's where I am now, Laura. I love these people, I love the language... but I also like the comfort of retreating up here to Clifford's luxurious villa at the end of the day."

"He surely enjoys your company as well."

"I think so; he's very hospitable. Oh, I do pay him for room and food, but he didn't ask for it.

"Now, Laura, back to what I love here: I love that you can expect rain to come every afternoon for two hours, so I take a nap or read, and then I can expect the sun to come out again, so that I can return to work. Ali comes to fetch me, and we go out to gather specimens."

"So you've completely left behind any shock?"

"I think so, Laura, but I'm not positive; I wonder if I might have a recurrence. It threatens. It's not 'island fever,' like some people talk about in Hawaii, I've heard. I wonder if I have a little PTSD [post-traumatic stress disorder]. Maybe I came back here partly to prove to myself that I've overcome it. I do wonder what's going on in the rest of the world. I try to think of this place as 'where it's at,' never mind Europe or the U.S. or Latin America or the Near East. I remind myself that four hundred years ago, Europeans were already here on these little islands, the Spice Islands. And of course much earlier, Chinese and then Arabs came here, all for the spices."

"As you know, that's what brought me here as well." She leaned back into her chair. "Both of us."

He smiled. "Surely not just Alfred Russel Wallace? Or that priest, Esquivel?"

She smiled as well. "No, I was enticed by the longer story of the Portuguese, the Spaniards, and of Europeans' interest in spices, cloves and nutmeg. They wanted medicines and food flavorings, not just covering up the smell of old meat!"

"Any other culture shock episode? Tell me more, and how did you – or did you? – overcome it?" Willem leaned back in his chaise lounge and looked up at the stars. The sky had by now turned a smooth black on this moonless night, but dotted with lights.

She added, "I'll give you a couple of examples from my first visit to the Philippines, at age 24. I had read so much, seen so many photos. I found everyone and the scenery so beautiful, the air so caressingly soft damp-warm, the smells so tropical moist.

"On first arriving, I was so excited to finally get to my destination, that little village on a small island in the south. Plans were working out so well: my letter from the president of the university led to good introductions. I was given an introduction and so met a young man who had graduated from a missionary high school and who knew English well. He agreed to work as my assistant. He introduced me to his uncle and his family, and they said they'd be happy to have me stay with them."

"Good start. You weren't yet feeling uncomfortable?"

"Not in the slightest at the start."

"But...?"

She smiled. "Sure, you know. Like, this one time, still in the city waiting to go out to the island, sitting in a jeepney with the driver outside, waiting to get enough passengers before he would take off. A young man came up to the open window from outside and from behind. 'Oh, excuse me, Ma'am, may I know the time?' I looked at my watch and told him the time. An older Filipina waiting with me then told me to guard myself, because the armholes of my sleeveless shirt were not tight enough. If I raised my arm to look at my watch, a man might be able to peek inside my blouse."

"Ha!" Willem lowered his head, closed his eyes, smiled and brushed his lips with his hand.

Laura said, "Another example: I quickly became accustomed to a small crowd of children following me around, not just when passing through a neighborhood of a small village, but even in Manila. Groups of kids formed everywhere and followed me. They sometimes ran forward to look at my face, continually jostling their companions and laughing raucously. So I kind of announced my entrance anywhere by the crowd of kids around me."

"Oh, sorry, Laura. Here too. You've experienced crowds of kids in my Ternate as well, right?"

"Yeah, probably this is all familiar to you. Another experience when I first came to the Philippines: I was new to the country and the language, so my local companion translated this one for me. A tiny boy, maybe three, asked his mother, 'How can she see out of those eyes?' Apparently to him, my blue eyes looked like they were blinded by cataracts."

She continued. "So, at first, I experienced euphoria here, but before long I also felt lonely, homesick. I had a strong longing to understand and to be understood, but simultaneously I craved privacy. The kids constantly following me didn't relieve the loneliness, but rather intensified it. I didn't have any refuge, no one to talk to, no one to ask if they'd had similar experiences. No one to easily speak with me in English. And, I was struggling to communicate and understand in a couple of new languages."

Willem said, "In the meantime, you've told me you'd learned that these are near universals for new foreigners, experiencing culture shock."

"Yes, and here's another one: now and then I noticed a pregnant woman would divert her direction of travel in order to pass behind me, and to brush her hand against my shoulder. A colleague told me, 'She's hoping your light colors will come to her baby.'"

"Funny!"

"Ha ha. In general, I felt like a Hollywood starlet on achieving sudden fame but who couldn't handle all the attention."

He said, "I don't like the excessive attention, and it sounds like you don't either, but some foreigners really like it."

"Definitely not I. In general, Filipinos, wherever I have traveled, or stayed, treated me with courtesy, and appeared interested in me. But somehow, they didn't notice my ever-deeper developing loneliness. They didn't understand me. They didn't recognize my mortal need for a long-term position, and they wouldn't be able to help me get one. And I didn't understand them, either their languages, their motives, or their way of life. How could they be happy living in such primitive conditions?

"What if I were to get stuck here, would have to spend the rest of my life here? I was once again experiencing classic culture shock; something was either really wrong with them, or with me."

Willem asked, "So why didn't they tell us in advance that this would be hard, like people learn before a space missile takeoff?"

"Yeah. We needed a course called 'Entering a New Culture 101.' I needed privacy, private thinking, because I had no one to talk to who would understand. I'll remind you that out on that little island in the south during my first year in the Philippines, I slept in a one-room house with at least six in that family. Anyone getting up at night, even turning over on his mattress, shook the whole little house high up on its stilts, like an earthquake. And oh, we also experienced real earthquakes there as frequently as once a month."

"So, it was hard for you to be alone, that is, as the only foreigner?"

"Well, I did find a couple of comforts to protect me from culture shock. I discovered two quiet times of the day. One was in the middle of the day, after lunch. I'd go out snorkeling by myself. Little kids didn't follow me. They took naps like everyone else. Occasionally I encountered deadly sea snakes, small, light blue and white ringed. I was told that they were so deadly that I wouldn't even be able to make it back to shore alive. But I was so needy for privacy that I took the risk. Snakes can stay down for maybe 1-2 minutes but have to come up for air, and mainly, they float on the surface. So, frequently I raised my goggled, snorkeled head above water to scrutinize the water surface around me.

"The second quiet period was at dusk, when people said that *multu* and *djinn* – evil spirits – came out, and people retreated into their houses. I took to walking away from the village at dusk, and after the evening meal. No one could see me, I thought. I even did some calisthenics in the cooler air: arms out, swinging them in big circles, narrowing the circles to little 12-inch rotations, first forward, then backward. Swinging one leg up as high as my head, then the other. Maybe someone might have observed me and reported back to others, but I never did hear anything. I so craved that privacy that I was willing to take the chance."

He looked at her inquiringly for a moment. "Laura, how long did your discomfort last?"

"Well, by the end of my first year in the southern Philippines, I managed to feel more comfortable. Much less needy or lonely."

"And when you came back last year, to a new field site?"

"Somehow I became more focused on them than myself. The people were proud of their history, that they had come from "the Spice Islands" in Eastern Indonesia 300 years earlier. Their ancestors had named their town, Ternate, after the main Spice Island in Indonesia. – Your Ternate, here!

"In their church they had a 'Santo Niño,' a figure that their ancestors had brought from Indonesia.

"Even nowadays, in their annual January Santo Niño' celebration, thousands of Filipinos travel to visit, because they have heard the figure has curative power. A water procession, many boats, some outfitted with floats, and the figure, floated to the church, and then the figure is placed back in the church. He has an angry face and is holding a sword, and people say that he protects the village."

"So they are Catholics, not Muslims?"

"Yes, they came partly because they had become Catholics here in your Ternate. Spaniards had converted them, and then in 1662, when the Dutch were taking over the whole Indonesian archipelago, the Spaniards rescued them when pulling back to the Philippines."

She continued, "So back to my Ternate: those people are proud of their heritage but not of their language. What loyalty they have to their language came from their strong interest in remembering their history. They were delighted to hear that I was there to study their language and that I insisted it did indeed have a grammar, just different from that of Spanish."

"So they welcomed you."

"Yes, they were very kind to me, ready to answer questions, but allowing me privacy when I needed it. And the village was pretty, green, clean, with a beach looking out to the mouth of the Manila Bay and the Island of Corregidor to one side.

"They had another, more recent, history they wanted to tell me about: they showed me bullet holes in buildings from WW II, and they've kept those buildings as honorable reminders of their difficulties on May 5th and 6th of 1942."

"Oh, yes, I heard of the Battle of Corregidor, but that's all I know."

"Well, that island became famous as a battle site early in World War II, as the American military worked to chase out the Japanese occupiers. Instead, the Japanese chased out U.S. troops, for three years.

"Back to culture shock. Within a couple of days of arriving at my new field site, I once again felt utterly lonely, imprisoned. 'What am I doing here? I'm stuck here for two *years*! How can I manage this?"

"So this time, how long did those feelings last?" His concern for Laura brought a frown to his face.

"I tried and tried to understand *why* I felt so bad, again! I mean, I could talk with these people. I could immediately understand maybe half of the words in their language – more than half were Spanish vocabulary – so I had a great head start. If I spoke in Spanish, adults could – somewhat at least – understand me. Some people knew some English, which helped me at first. So it was an easier introduction than being dropped into a place with no common language."

"What, then?"

"I once again became aware that my discomfort was that no one understood *me*.

"That is, learning this language, and learning about it, was my ticket, I thought, and my only ticket, to getting a university position back in the States. At first it appeared so easy, but I quickly learned that the simplicity was deceptive, and that I had a lot more to learn than I had thought at first. It was more than learning to communicate. I needed them to understand my high stakes but felt it would be futile to try to explain, and besides, I felt kind of ashamed at using them for my own gain." Laura looked up at the dark sky and then leaned back In her seat.

"And, you overcame all that?"

"I started learning about individuals: first, Corazon, the niece whose house I was living in. She had a lot of gumption, worked hard, had been trained as a pharmacist, and sold medicines in her little sari-sari store, along with gasoline for motorboats and candy to children. Her husband worked his oyster beds in the river. They had two little children and a young girl to help care for them. But finances were really on the edge and the adults were always tired."

Laura brought her gaze back to Willem. "And I came to know other individuals, among others, an elementary school teacher who invited me into her class, and I read stories in English to her children. Within a short time I noticed that I was becoming interested in their lives. I tried to imagine life from their perspective, living in this little village. And as I developed (maybe very slowly) some empathy for them, I felt less lonely. My need for them to understand *my* struggles felt less urgent."

"Wow. Maybe that's what I missed, 20 years ago."

"Maybe. So I started doing things for them, with my access to the city Manila, that they didn't know about."

"Like...?"

"Like, in Manila, I had met the Secretary of Agriculture, Arturo Tanco. When he heard that I was working in a little village, he offered tree seedlings. So after I had been in Ternate just a couple of weeks I went into the city and brought back out hundreds of tree seedlings: mango, tamarind, even kapok. And you know, within a couple of hours everyone in the village knew about the seedlings and came to the sari sari store. They lined up very calmly and picked out a few for the gardens around their houses or out in their fields."

"Wow!"

"Yes, and I did the same with reading glasses. I read somewhere that I could get donations of used reading glasses from the U.S., and my APO address facilitated speedy receipt. Once again, people calmly lined up, and each recipient tried on several before choosing a pair."

"So you felt better?"

"Yes. That was the key. I felt, I don't know, I guess, just less self-centered."

They looked down to the lights below and up to the stars above.

Laura said, "So we've both had serious challenges with culture shock, and maybe we've met the challenges."

He was quiet for a moment before responding. "Yes, I do hope so."

20. I'm So Impatient!

"Laura, please tell me another of your stories!"

She smiled, closed her eyes, and then said, "Here's another one. This happened about two months after I came back to the Philippines and had already been working in Ternate. One morning I was working with Antero, the man I hired. We were transcribing our latest recording of Chabacano speech. My main data was to interview people, and record them, for instance, about their means of livelihood. We sat on the deck in front of his house, maybe eight feet above the sand on stilts behind Ternate's beach.

"And then for a moment my thoughts wandered from our task. I knew that the cool air wouldn't last much longer, even in the shade under overhanging palms. I could see that not far ahead of us, the sun shone brightly on the sea. And then I noticed a small single hull boat with two fishermen, using oars.

"So I asked Antero, 'Unusual, isn't it for fishermen to be working this time of morning? Most fishing is done at nighttime, isn't it?' Antero glanced up for just a moment, mumbled "mm-hmm" and returned to his writing. We still spoke in English because it was still early in my research year. Antero knew English pretty well and was skilled in several languages important to me.

"I noticed that a mild sea breeze caressed my neck and my bare arms.

"Now, thinking back, I was startled out of my small reverie because of what happened next. One fisherman paddled the boat to shore, jumped out in thigh-high water, and ran along the shore, around a bend and out of sight.

"I said, 'Hey, look at that!' to Antero. 'What's happening?'

"The other man started to climb out of the boat but then fell back into it.

"So I jumped off of my little bamboo stool, I clambered down the ladder to the sand, and I ran across it toward the boat. At that moment I noticed women from three nearby houses moving toward the boat as well, but they were a lot slower. All four of us waded into the sea water, which was still cool and clear, and we pulled the boat up onto the sand, and then we helped the fisherman out.

"I saw, 'oh, Lord,' enormous, deep bolo cuts! So much white of his humerus bone exposed! But no blood! – Why no blood?? One of the women spread out a nipa palm mat in the shade of a coconut tree, the other two women and I helped the fisherman to sit down and lean against it. And here came yet another woman who brought from her house a cup of hot tea for him. I noticed profound quiet, just the soft lap-lap of tiny waves reaching the shoreline."

"So did he live? What happened next?" Willem asked.

"Well: Antero by now came down from his roost. I thought he had been kind of slow! He sat down next to the fisherman, asked him a question, and listened to the very quiet response. I couldn't understand; I was still learning Chabacano, and besides, the men talked very quietly. Antero asked another question, heard no response, stood up, and motioned to me to follow him back to his deck.

"I hurriedly whispered to Antero, 'But we – they – have got to get him into the city to the hospital! He can't survive otherwise!' I was very agitated, frustrated, and wondered *why they weren't **doing** something!* When I – reluctantly - climbed the ladder back to the deck, I looked back to the beach. The women were sitting near the man, one holding his tea. No one was fetching a boat to get him into the city.

"I had to work hard to resign myself that I couldn't take any action. I quietly asked Antero 'What did he say?'

"'They're from Mariveles over there,' and he pointed to an island some distance across the sea, beyond Corregidor. 'They had an argument, and his brother-in-law hacked him. He wants to rest here a while.'

"I said, 'He's not bleeding! Those enormous slashes!'"

"I've seen it before."

"And then I told him, 'I've never seen someone hacked, and I've never seen a big cut not bleed. Well, maybe the first few seconds, but then gushing.'"

Willem swallowed hard. "Wow, you must have felt helpless when someone really needed you!"

"Yes, but no one else acted like this was an urgent problem! And then, about three weeks later, and I was sitting on that deck with Antero again, working, I asked him if he had heard what had happened to that fisherman.

"Can you believe this, Willem? He said that he's doing fine, and that he had seen him over in Cavite City the other day. He wasn't wearing a bandage, and he showed Antero his wounds, that they were healing well."

"So-o, were you surprised?"

"Yes! I noticed how different my response had been from everyone else's! I'd have rushed him into a boat with an outboard motor, though maybe those boats were all out with the men, who had taken their night fishing catches into the city. No bleeding! I still wonder why. What do you think, Willem? Could it be his quiet, and their calm? Did he go into another state while I was in 'flight' state? He survived; he's getting well. Would my way have done better, or worse?"

21. A Daughter?

"It's much easier for me this time." Laura set her drink down on the arm of her Adirondack chair.

"Oh, why?" Willem asked. He re-crossed his legs to face her.

"One thing, I've come back to a – by now – familiar culture. Southeast Asians are not so strange for me now. Same as for you, you just said."

"*Ja.* Yeah."

"Another thing, I *know* this time that because I have a ticket in my pocket, I can go back home again. Comforting. At least I think I can. I need to go back for a job, but I don't know where that will be because I don't have one yet." She added, I'm counting on my work in the Philippines being important enough that it'll get me a good faculty position."

"I do hope so, for your sake. *Veel geluk daarmee*, lots of luck with that, we'd say in the Netherlands."

"Thank you. But back to culture shock vs. settling in: most of all, I have a daughter now."

Willem opened his eyes wide. "You have a daughter?"

"Yes, she's four."

"You're married, then?"

"No, I'm a single mom." Laura picked up her drink an inch and resettled it on her chair arm.

"How about you?"

"Yes, two children; they're in college now."

"And married?"

"Yes. But, uh, tell me about your daughter." He looked at his glass for a while, and then inquiringly into her eyes.

Laura looked up to the sky, now dark, and noticed that stars had emerged, ever more brilliantly. "Charlotte is a great companion. She embraces new experiences. She's quite ready to meet new children speaking a language that is new for her. She's not put off by squalor. She treats new communities like an intriguing picture puzzle, looking for the one piece that can start her entry to the new place, like if she saw a toddler staring at her, she'll find a ball and gently roll it toward him. And then the older children might show they'd like to play with her."

"Oh, how valuable for you." Willem reached for his glass, flicked condensation off the side so that it wouldn't drip on him, and took a long swallow.

Laura continued. "Yes, and arriving with her, people immediately see that I'm a mom, and that I interact with her in familiar, I suppose universal ways, like helping her take off her sandals so that she can run in the water at the shore. When Charlotte is with me, I don't seem so strange to Filipinos as before. And here in Indonesia these weeks, even without her, I feel more comfortable with these people because they seem culturally very similar to Filipinos."

Willem asked, "Back to your daughter. Where is she now? Is she with her father?"

"Not with her father; he's out of the picture. I left her with a friend in Manila for this short trip here. She's with a family with two sons who are close to Charlotte's age, and with maids to take care of them."

"And you didn't bring her here…"

"No, mainly because now she's in a nursery school, and I came for just two weeks."

"Just two weeks!? Oh yes, you said that the other day." He furrowed his brow but smiled.

"Yes, I came for initial exploration of the place where my Ternate people came from. If I found any vestiges here of their lives 300 years ago, then I might return."

"Well, my dear, have you found enough to return here in the future?" He rubbed his hands together and smiled.

She laughed. "The only human signs of their lives back then are the ruins here of forts, especially the Portuguese ones and the Dutch one. Of course no one here speaks a creole Spanish; I had already expected that. But the spices! I have been delighted to see clove and nutmeg trees growing here and still harvested for their spices. And of course it was the spices that brought the Europeans here in the first place."

"Yep, they brought me here too, as you know." His smile grew wider. "And we met."

"Yes, and we met." They smiled at one another.

She continued. "We followed a star, and we met. But the star is crossed: you're married, and I have a child. Now what?!" She raised her shoulders in a shrug.

"Let's toast to meeting, at least!" He raised his beer toward her, and she brought her glass to his with a clink. They each took a ritual drink.

Again, they looked at the stars above and then down to the few lights in the town below them.

She frowned. "But one discovery I made on my boat trip here is disturbing enough that I'm going to have to write to a journalist friend about it."

"Oh?"

"Yes, on the boat coming here from Davao, I talked with Filipino lumbermen; they were the only other passengers. They told me that they were hired to harvest timber just like they did on Mindanao in the Philippines, clearcutting. They've cut down so much of the forest in the southern Philippines that their firm has moved them here to Eastern Indonesia."

"Filipinos are here?"

"Yes, they're hired by an American firm, Weyerhaeuser, out of Seattle."

"And what would you do about that?"

"Expose the clearcutting. This journalist friend, if he likes the story, would distribute it internationally."

"God, you're asking for trouble, my dear!"

22. Homeless?

 "You were *homeless?*" Willem turned to look more seriously into Laura's eyes. They had just passed a beggar in the dirt on Ternate's main street, a middle-aged man sitting on a wooden board with wheels that looked like a primitive skateboard. His withered, misshapen legs were curled up mostly underneath his core except in the fold of one knee was nestled a small tin can which held a few coins.

A half block later, Laura quietly said, "I feel for him. Where's his family? Not enough social services here, or in the Philippines. I'm grateful that I never got that powerless."

"What do you mean?" asked Willem.

"Uh, I was sort of homeless for a year before I started graduate school."

"What??"

"Well, only minimally. I mean, I had my car, and I parked it in my sister's driveway every night and slept in it... for a year."

"You couldn't sleep inside your sister's house? And why didn't you have your own place?"

"Well, my sister and her family had a small house with no extra bedroom. She offered me to stay there, but they needed their privacy. Her husband told her that he felt judged by me. "

"How come?"

 "Oh, I don't know. Anyway, so she and I worked out this compromise. I ate some meals with them, and I babysat their two little boys now and then."

"Why didn't you have your own place? No money?

"My job paid so little, back then as an elementary school teacher, that housing was almost beyond my capacity. I decided to save the little that I could, by camping on my sister's driveway. I wanted to continue graduate school, to get a Ph.D. so that I could become a university professor, and I'd earn more. I knew that my field was very specialized – linguistics, but I saw all the professors at Cal appeared to be doing fine financially. I considered medicine; even had an interview with an admissions officer. He discouraged me, saying that at age 23 I was already too old to get into any medical school in the country. And besides, students with Ph.D.'s in linguistics were getting good faculty positions at major universities. So I got into this Ph.D. program. But after entering, I learned that all the students were expected to do one or two years of fieldwork on a language in a developing country."

"And so you came across the Pacific!"

"Yeah. I learned how to write a good grant application for the field work, and I got one, from the National Science Foundation (NSF). So I came to the Philippines, twice, first for the Ph.D. fieldwork, and then I came again, and here I am."

"Taxpayer money, then?"

"Yes, and I'm grateful. It's still hard to believe that taxpayers are paying for linguistic research!"

"But your taxpayers didn't pay enough for a decent teacher's salary, you said, not even enough for your housing."

"No..." She shifted in her chair. "Are teachers paid well in the Netherlands?"

"Dutch taxpayers don't let people go homeless, plus we pay for research like yours and mine. We pay well for teaching salaries too, for teachers in universal preschool through university."

"Well, Willem, I'm glad to have the research money, and I'll do my best to make the research worthwhile. But I suppose most taxpayers couldn't understand the value of studying low-profile languages, or why public universities would have faculty positions to teach about contact languages. Maybe if we would show a direct relationship to how people learn languages in general or how human languages emerged, or how this research could be used for developing machine translation."

"Wow. Laura, you're hoping for a faculty position in a public university?"

"Yes, public or private. Anywhere, but I hope California, because it's my home."

"In the Netherlands, we have only public universities, just thirteen of them in our little country of thirteen million people. Separate from those, we have institutes for teacher training. And for a lot of careers we have extensive apprenticeship programs in partnerships with private industries."

"Boy, your taxpayers pay for a lot! And, additionally and especially, they pay for that safety net against homelessness. What an impact it must have on the public, to not have to fear about going homeless!"

"I suppose. Our population is almost all middle class economically. Oh, we do have the royal family, but the rich are not mega-rich like in the U.S. In general, people don't worry that they'll fall into deep poverty, like becoming homeless."

They looked at one another, both absorbing their new information.

"But how did being homeless affect you, Laura?"

"A lot! For example, I empathize with that man back there. I had been so worried that I'd become a bag lady! Still am. I saw them on the streets of San Francisco, hunched over, missing teeth, hair uncombed and straggly, smelling of old urine, pushing loaded grocery carts of their stuff, alone. They didn't even travel in clusters for safety. I wondered if they could sleep at night, they'd be so vulnerable in a store doorway. Can you believe this, Willem? One of my graduate program classmates, two years ahead of me, couldn't find a job with her Ph.D. She got involved with drugs, and she became one of those street people in San Francisco! And you can read in the paper about other street people who have major college degrees, and not just in liberal arts or social sciences."

"God, this can happen in America? Are *you* going to get a job there, Laura? And if you don't get work, there isn't a social welfare system to take care of you?"

"I do still get notices of university positions. They're sent on to me in a newsletter from my university department. So there are still jobs, some even in California, but the forecast is for ever fewer open positions. I need to finish this research, write it up, get it published, and find a job to apply for and obtain before the jobs all dry up. I've got to find a job. No unemployment insurance would be available to me, because, being a student now for three years and even with this grant, I haven't been working."

"Nothing?"

"Nope, therefore we have street people, even some with Ph.D.'s and good work records."

"High stakes for your research on contact languages, hmm, Laura."

"Yeah, and a rush to finish."

23. Trees Talk to Me

Laura walked by herself late one afternoon toward Mount Gamalama, as soon as the rain had finished.

She now knew how to recognize clove and nutmeg trees.

Trees root in one *place. The only ways they travel are to cast off seeds or send out shoots.*

They're never completely quiet, but communication is mostly not auditory.

Even most human communication is not through our "languages" but by gestures and by other sounds we make.

She reflected on what she had been learning about information that humans can get from studying trees.

- *Suzanne Simard studied fungi in roots, which share nutrients, and trees protect their own seedlings.*
- *Trees communicate with fauna, including insects, birds, squirrels. Two ways are by fragrance and by color.*
- *We can listen to trees, as Willem showed me.*
- *Breezes blow trees' canopies, which make noises, communicating about wind.*
- *Trees are symbiotic with other organisms, including saprophytes, that is, with decaying matter.*
- *We can learn about the earth's past from trees, especially from rings of their trunks.*
- *We learn about trees' evolution from earlier plants through fossils, and from their present distribution. (Greatest variety is center of dispersal).*

She continued to wonder. *Do trees offer to their offspring information about the parents' past? Anything like crows teaching their offspring to avoid certain humans?*

Laura skipped a couple of steps, feeling light on her feet, as if, with these thoughts, she could walk all day.

Clifford's Hammid told me that the oldest living clove tree, named "Afi," is 350-400 years old and he'll show it to me. That'd make that tree's "birth" be around 1572!

Gosh! That tree must have been maybe 87 years old when that Jesuit priest Don Diego de Esquivel fled with his 200 Christian Moluccans back to the Philippines! How would that old tree have escaped the "extirpation" by the Dutch colonials when they overtook this island? I read that they cut down thousands of clove trees in order to control all harvesting!

She was delighted to continue to walk by herself, her thoughts flowing.

If the trees really could talk to humans, they might tell:

> - We, the clove and also the nutmeg trees, have had a difficult history with you humans. The first few thousand years were okay: you just ate a few of our fruit, like insects do.

> - But by 2700 BCE, other people came. They took so much of our fruit. (Humans know about it, because archaeologists found some cloves in Israeli *tels* from back then!) The first spice traders were Chinese and Indians.

> - Then, by 1100 CE, Arabs brought Islam, and took yet more of our fruits, and selling our fruits back home paid for their trips to us.

> - In 1492 Europeans came; they wanted to bypass the Chinese and Arab traders. The Portuguese and Spaniards even fought back in the Mediterranean Sea over us!

> - Europeans overcame the Arabs, who had for a few centuries been more advanced in science.

- The Italian Christopher Columbus got the idea of going westward to get to us. He convinced the Spanish Queen Isabella to spring for funds, but instead of reaching us, he discovered the New World.

- Then by the late 16th century, other Europeans vied for us: English, Danish, French, and especially the Dutch. They took us over, for 300 years. By 1650 they wreaked genocide against our local people and killed thousands of us to control us. The Indians, the Chinese, the Arabs, they didn't have the concept of monopoly. Their way was to meet traders at every port who took the harvest to the next port, so the spices traveled like on stepping stones. But the European each wanted a monopoly on our harvests. They waged wars with each other. Even their Crusades, 1200-1500, were funded by selling our fruits. The Europeans wanted, and got, all the profit.

- But by 1800, interest in our fruits dwindled, mainly because people turned away from our medical properties. Bacteria were discovered, and medicine became more scientific.

Laura wondered if she also heard this:

- Please tell our story! – We are beneficial. We can still help humans and other fauna with our preventative and curative powers.

A memory startled her of her talks two weeks earlier with the Filipino lumbermen who were her fellow passengers on the boat returning to Indonesia from their "furlough" in the Philippines.

Oh Lord, they're killing precious trees! And Americans are hiring them, big lumber companies. If I get the word out to fellow Americans, maybe they can stop the lumber companies. They're clearcutting, and they might even be cutting down clove and nutmeg trees!

As she walked along the earth path back to Clifford's villa, she thought, *maybe I'll write about the clearcutting of Indonesian forests and send it to my journalist friend... And maybe even, how about doing a documentary about the Spice Islands?*

In the near distance she heard someone playing gamelan music. Is *the sound coming from a house beyond these trees? Is it live, or is it a radio?* She knew that a gamelan orchestra could well have twenty gong players. *They sound like leaves in the trees.* To the chorus of gongs, now a bamboo flute soloist entered. *A bird flies onto the tree!*

Oh, what a beautiful place, here where the clove trees evolved! Beautiful sight, beautiful sounds. She noticed a woman walking ahead of her along the path. *She appears confident ...not quite cocky, but rather, energetic. Wearing those classic black coral bracelets bound by embossed silver tubes. She's got several of them gently clicking together with every step.*

Laura thought of the New York poet John Ashbery's poem, that she had memorized in her English 201 class at Cal:

Some Trees

These are amazing: each
Joining a neighbor, as though speech
Were a still performance.
Arranging by chance

To meet as far this morning
From the world as agreeing
With it, you and I
And suddenly what the trees try

To tell us we are:
That their merely being there
Means something: that soon

We may touch, love, explain.

And glad not to have invented
Such comeliness, we are surrounded:
A silence already filled with noises,
A canvas on which emerges

A chorus of smiles, a winter morning.
Placed in a puzzling light, and moving,
Our days put on such reticence
These accents seem their own defense.

24. Exposé

She wrote a 500-word article to her Associated Press friend
in Manila, J. Jackson, who broadcast it to U.S. newspapers.
Several papers published it.

The gist:

"American lumber companies, with impunity, are
clearcutting primeval forests in Indonesia. (They have
already decimated massive forests in the Philippines. Where
do you think they get their lumber for all the plywood
we use?) Sukarno started it up, allowing Weyerhaeuser and
Georgia-Pacific from the U.S. to take from their forests,
the second largest in the world...

"Even four species of little arboreal marsupials live in these
forests!"

25. Hide!

Three nights later, Laura was awakened by men talking. She peeked out her window and thought she could recognize Clifford's young servant Hammid out on the terrace, talking quietly but using emphatic gestures, with Willem. After a few minutes, the two walked away together. She continued looking out for a few minutes, wondering what she had observed, but then she went back to her bed and slept.

Sometime later – *an hour?* – she was again awakened, this time by several knocks on her bedroom door. She opened it to see Willem with Hammid beside him and Clifford coming down the hall in boxer shorts and carrying a candle on a saucer, rubbing his eyes, in an apparent effort to wake up and grasp the urgency.

"Laura, sorry to disturb you, but we must leave immediately. Hammid has just helped me book passage on a small commercial diesel boat leaving in an hour for the Philippines. You must be on it."

"Uh… okay… What's this about?"

"It's about your exposé article. We've learned tonight that the POLRI are looking for you with a warrant for your arrest because of your exposure of lumber extraction in this country." [POLRI = Kepolisian Negara Republik Indonesia, started in 1964 by Sukarno. Part of the national military until 1999.]

"So my article did get published, then! – I wonder where?"

"Wherever, the Indonesian government didn't like it."

"They've had a very fast response!"

"The captain told me that he wouldn't let a woman onboard traveling by herself, to be the only woman on the boat. I'm going with you."

"You can't leave your work here!"

"I'll be back here in four days, on the same boat."

"Oh... oh. I didn't mean to be so disruptive. I've just wanted to save the trees!"

"Well, now we're going to save your freedom. Bring only your passport and your money, your *olos* (a big tube-skirt/scarf – Laura had used the Filipino term), and a jacket.

"And we must be fast. Hammid said that the POLRI are downtown looking in the *rumah tidurs* for you. Ready to leave? Goodbye for now, Clifford! I'll try to contact you with an update. And Hammid knows how to get us onto the boat quietly, but he'll stay here. Let's go!"

Laura immediately thought of Charlotte. "Clifford, any way we can contact the people taking care of my daughter?"

Clifford responded, "I think not. The word would get out."

"Oh... so difficult for me." And she thought further, *I can't tell Belen and Steve, either.*

By eleven p.m., their copra cargo boat departed from Ternate for Davao on the island of Mindanao in the southern Philippines, 400 miles to the north across the Sulu Sea. The other passengers were about 30 Filipino workers on their one-week family leave.

PHILIPPINES, 1972

26. My Brother Will Help You

Though somewhat rickety and grimy with diesel exhaust, the boat rode the waves well, and the two foreigners were able to sleep a few hours each of their two nights onboard in a little alcove on deck.

Under way, they planned their arrival in the Philippines. "In Davao, I'll get you to the airport for a plane for Manila, and then I'll return to Indonesia on this same ship."

"Oh, thank you, my dear, but I can manage that part myself. You'll need to stay on the boat to ensure your return."

"Well, the captain was uncertain about the length of stay in port, so maybe you're right. But I want you to be safe. At least I'll walk you to your bus."

They smiled at one another; their gaze lingered; they sustained their hold of hands.

After some 28 hours at sea and two mornings after their late evening departure, at around three a.m., the boat docked at Davao's port.

All passengers crowded on the port side for debarking, with the two tall foreigners among them, both taller than the others, but dressed similarly as the others, with *olos* scarves used as minimal blankets around their shoulders. Most looked drowsy, but a few waved their arms up high as they recognized a family member waiting on the dock for them. All the men on board were carrying bags of fruits for their families.

But then she saw something alarming. Beyond the dock she saw two uniformed PC (Philippine Constabulary) arrive on motorcycles. They parked and then stood to one side, scrutinizing the bulk of the passengers as they shuffled past them to the dock and proceeded to the bus stand nearby.

"We must cover up and go to the buses," she quietly told Willem. She pulled her *olos* up to make a hood over her head, and she discreetly pointed. *Urgent change of plans!*

He looked, and responded "Oh, *ja,* yeah!"

While Willem and Laura were still on the dock and amidst the throng, a man pushed his way to them. "I," and he touched his chest, "Balayam. Binyak my elder brother."

"Oh, *asalem walaykum*, may God be with you, Balayam!" said Laura, and she pressed her palms together in prayer position, and then, following Muslim custom, brushed them down her cheeks and on down her chest to her waist. Balayam returned the same gesture.

"You must follow," he said as they continued shuffling toward the parked buses. They saw some people climbing into one bus, others into another.

She leaned toward Willem and gestured with her head. "When I came to Indonesia two weeks ago, on the boat I talked with a man named Binyak. He gave me the name and village name of his brother, Balayam, in South Cotabato, in case I ever got into a fix in the south. And here he is. I don't know why but I wonder if these PC are looking for me, and Balayam knows."

Within another half hour, at 4:13 a.m. their intra-island bus lined with rows of wooden benches filled with passengers rolled out of Davao.

"God, now what?" asked Willem.

"I don't know but now we're completely dependent on this man Balayam."

Under way, Balayam explained. "Elder Brother said take care of you, Ma'am," and nodding toward Willem, "and your companion."

"Binyak call me from Indonesia to our village center. They fetch me, I say hello. Binyak tell me meet two people in Davao. Waiting for the boat, I learn the PC looking for two 'wantid' foreigners."

Willem looked solemnly at Laura. "With this difficulty, I must stay with you." She swallowed hard and nodded her head and her eyelids.

After 5-1/2 hours they arrived in General Santos City, 120 miles along the coast to the south. The bus stopped, and Balayam signaled that they should get down. "We take our breakfast here."

On scooting along their wooden bench and climbing down from the bus, they were surprised that another man joined them.

"This my brother Kodon."

The brothers led them to a food stand. "Last hot food for a while." They bought rice and *menudo* and sat to eat on bamboo stools in the shade of the corrugated tin roof. They ate quickly. Several children gathered to watch, smile, even laugh at the two foreigners, and then they poked each other for more laughing.

Balayam pointed to a flat-bed truck; the waiting driver started up the engine. "He is going to Tboli Village to collect copra, and he will take us."

"How far?" asked Laura.

"Maybe 60 kilometers. Come on."

Willem whispered to Laura, "Even if this tiny village has a telephone, I can't call Clifford now to tell him I'm delayed."

Laura thought, *I'm so tempted to try to send word to Marilu! But of course it'd endanger everything.*

The driver locked his door for his safety and then leaned against it in order to accommodate the four passengers on the long bench seat beside him. They stuffed their small bags and the brothers' large *bolo* knives behind the seat. Willem eased the crowding by offering Laura his lap.

After two hours of bumpy, sometimes muddy, sometimes dusty travel, and perhaps ten miles before Tboli, Balayam lifted his hand, signaling the driver to stop. "We walk now," he said. He led them to a trail.

How long? How far? Where are they taking us? Well, at least away from the PC.

In the now broad midday daylight, they hiked. They saw no other humans. They passed by wet rice fields, then climbed past dry rice fields. Hill, valley, hill, valley. They filled their water bottles in streams. They worried about the safety of the water. They worried they might be followed. They frequently looked behind them. Their trail followed a river, then dipped into the rain forest. They hiked for hours.

Under way, Laura worried. *Oh oh, I can't even contact Marilu to inform her of my delay. What will Charlotte think? Will she be okay?*

I've got to stay alive, and out of prison, for her, for myself. So I've got to hide for now. How long? I'll miss her so! And she'll miss me.

Shortly before the usual sudden end of daylight in the tropics, Balayam and Kodon stopped near the river. They cut a dozen palm fronds with their *bolos*. They laid several fronds on the ground next to a forest tree, and then they leaned others against the tree and tied with a "string" from a palm branch. Finally, they laid several longer fronds diagonally against the tree. Balayam said, "we sleep in here tonight." Willem and Laura sank onto the ground, put their little bags of belongings (hers holding her jacket and her wallet) under their heads, and slept, too tired to ask, to stir, or to worry.

.....

At the faintest light of dawn, Balayam gave Willem and Laura's feet a little shake. Both sat up, startled and groggy.

Balayam quietly said, "We stay in the forest two months. Then, the PC forget you 'wantid.' We cannot make fire. Must eat food natural. I have two bolos. Maybe we must keep moving. Gather food, build lean-to's for night. Cannot see the sky, only trees above. Must stay inside forest, not by river, open sky. Hide palm leaves, leave no... tracks."

Laura exclaimed, "The only way?" She turned to Willem. "Willem, what'd I get you into? Oh God, do you agree? And are you up to this?"

"Well, I'll do my best to measure up. We had hoped that you would be safe once we got you out of Indonesia. But after seeing those Philippine Constabulary at the Davao harbor... We did worry that they might be looking for you in this country also. Who knows what they would do to you, perhaps with your American CIA behind them urging their search? So now this must be your best chance to stay out of jail."

"Yeah. I didn't realize that just writing that one short report would put me, and now you, into such a dangerous position, in Indonesia and in the Philippines as well!"

They all stood up, stretched, reached for their water bottles, and drank.

27. How Can We Eat in Here?

She turned to the brothers. "Balayam, how can we manage? I mean, how can we eat? And do you think we can be safe here?

Willem added, "We don't know how to survive in the forest. Can you teach us, Balayam and Kodon?"

"*Oh ho*, of course, Miss Laura and Mr. Willem. For food we eat like our Manobo fathers here in the forest."

"You can do that?" she asked.

"Yes, Ma'am. Plenty of fruits, and nuts. Some leaves tasty, and ginger roots and fruits. Many crabs and small fish in the rivers, some frogs and snails. Sometimes we catch a bird. I teach you how to catch a fish with your hands."

"You eat them raw as well?"

"Oh yes, Ma'am. If cook, PC smell smoke. If airplane pass by, can see smoke above trees. Little animals, not hard to eat. If lucky, grubs in caryota palms. If we find Caryota palm, maybe we stop to make starch. Make us feel strong."

Laura quietly said, "Oh my God," and looked up into the thick tree canopy high above.

Balayam added, "This first forest - original forest - so many kinds of plants and animals."

"What do you mean, Balayam?"

"If burned already or trees cut down, not so many different plants or animals."

Willem added: "Original or primeval forests are much more diverse, with trees of different ages, heights, diameters, and different species, and so they support more diverse fauna.

In contrast, succession forests are what we call forests that have grown up after destruction such as fire or flood or human tampering such as logging. They tend to have more uniform sized trees and fewer species. As a consequence, they support far fewer species of fauna."

"Oh, then are succession forests less healthy, say, for the trees?"

"Yes in primeval forests, the fungi are more beneficial. In such forests, fungi fix the nitrogen to be most beneficial for the trees, and they decompose the decaying organic matter, providing nutrients for the trees. Succession forests are impoverished for some time without beneficial fungi."

"We're in your field now, aren't we, Willem. May this be a good place for food for us!"

"I hope!"

And here's what they ate in the forest:

- ripe fruits, including of *ubud, natok,* rattan, climbing *calamus*
- ginger roots
- wild yams
- rattan
- (The two Filipino men decided against caryota palm starch, because evidence would be left behind.)
- nuts
- betel chew ingredients, include Areca palm nuts
- seeded banana
- small animals caught by trapping: mammals, birds
- fish, snails, crabs, tadpoles, frogs caught in or at the river
- edible leaves
- edible flowers

They could hardly store or carry much, so they continually foraged and snacked as they moved along through the forest but not far from the river.

Balayam instructed them. "We sometimes spread out to find food. Sometimes Kodon go ahead, set trap for small animal. We find him later, maybe he have food for us."

At first Willem and Laura managed to eat only the raw plants, but little by little they managed the raw river creatures as well.

28. Dragon's Blood

Balayam and Kodon had awakened several times in the night to listen and look around them. They had heard only the usual insects, their buzzes and hisses echoing through the tree trunks.

At the first sign of light, they all stretched and crawled out of their lean-to. Balayam and Kodon scattered the fronds and lightly covered them with brown leaves from the forest floor.

All four walked out to the river, and they cautiously looked around before stepping out to its bank.

Had they left tracks in the sand along the river? Did their two guides - and protectors - hack any branches with those bolos to ease their passage? No, Balayam had been keeping close attention to "leave no track."

"Beautiful, beautiful," Willem said. "So peaceful!"

"Listen to the birds," Laura said. "They're happy it's morning."

All four hunkered down, filled their water bottles, took long drinks, and refilled their bottles. They each dipped their cupped hands into the water to wash their faces. Kodon and Balayam stood to remove their shoes, waded into the water, and reached down to rub their feet. Willem and Laura watched and then followed their example.

Kodon walked a few paces to a palm vine with little brown fruit, and he picked four. He brought them back to the group and gave one to each. Laura and Willem watched him peel and open the fruit, and then put the flesh into his mouth. The flesh was smooth and shiny, peachy in color, but the dripping juice was red. After Balayam opened and ate his fruit, then Willem and Laura followed.

Laura took a little bite and immediately winced. "Sour!" But she took a second bite. She and Willem both made "sour" faces as they ate, but they also smiled. Kodon returned to the palm to fetch more, and Balayam said, "Maybe this will be our breakfast. Rattan fruit."

"Dragon's Blood," Willem said, looking at the resin. The botanical name, in Latin, is *'Daemonorops draco.'* 'Dragon's Blood Palm.'"

They considered whether to stay or to move. Balayam and Kodon recommended that they continue northward, further into the expanse of rainforest, an area least traveled by hunters.

If they moved, then how? They saw no trail anymore, not even a trail trampled by animals. Balayam agreed. "No trail; we manage by ourselves." Should they follow the river upstream? Out there by the river they would experience sunlight. They saw that despite the undergrowth that grew only at the riverbank, they could walk along the bank for a while, but they would surely eventually encounter bushes and steep banks. And besides, might they be seen? If they traveled in the forest, they could walk more easily because of the lack of undergrowth in the deep shade. But almost no fruit or nuts were to be found down at their level. Leaves as well were too high above to reach. They needed to find food.

Their feet dry by now, they stood up, put on their shoes, and picked up their little bags. They resumed their positions of the day before: Balayam led Laura, then Willem, and Kodon kept the last place in their single file, except on the occasions when he went ahead to scout their route or to set his crudely-made trap.

"Listen!" Balayam turned back to Willem and Laura. In the distance, to the south from where they'd come, they heard a helicopter.

"We go inside the forest," and Balayam led them through the riverbank bushes back into the dark, moist, cool, quiet. Their eyes took a few minutes to adjust.

"I need to pee," Laura announced, and for privacy she walked beyond the tall buttresses of a few gigantic trees.

A few moments later she returned to report her scary experience. "First time I've eliminated inside the forest, and I didn't know!

"Know what?" asked Willem.

"Well, I hunkered down as usual. Just dead leaves under me. But as soon as pee fell onto the leaves, an *army* of leeches advanced toward me! I was immediately surrounded. They marched slowly, but like gymnasts!"

"How do you mean?" asked Willem. Balayam leaned over to Kodon, spoke quietly, then the two smiled broadly and turned to hear more.

"Have you seen them before, Willem? No? Well, they travel end over end! Like back bends, and they flip, one end, then the other. Slow, but ...look, eek! I've got one on my ankle."

The brothers were laughing by now. "I help you, Miss Laura," said Balayam. "I show you." He pressed one finger near the leech's head and slowly, gently, but firmly, pressed his fingernail underneath, releasing the leech. With the other hand, he quickly flicked the leech away. Laura's ankle bled profusely at the wound.

"I read that their bites don't hurt, but with all that blood, I'm surprised," she said.

Willem watched, and then said "Ugh."

"Yeah, I read that they first inject an anesthetic and then an anticoagulant, so it'll bleed for some minutes. But chances of infection are low, even in this humidity. Can't sit or I'll get more leeches, and we really should go only very rarely out to the river to wash." She took a mouthful of water from her bottle, and while standing, lifted her ankle onto the knee of her other leg, and spat the water, washing off some of the blood.

Willem was startled. "But listen, the helicopter is coming our way!"

They all looked up. The occasional insect and bird calls had quieted; they heard only the helicopter.

"Would they have a way of seeing us, like an infrared sensor?" Laura asked.

"I don't know," Willem said.

Balayam pointed to a recess in a large tree buttress. Maybe we wait inside there?"

"Or," Willem suggested, "how about if we spread out and wait individually? If they do have an infrared sensor, then four single bodies would be less noticeable than a cluster of four. What do you think?"

The helicopter was quite close by now.

Laura and Balayam nodded, Balayam quietly spoke to Kodon, and each quickly moved to a separate tree to stand inside a buttress recess.

The helicopter hovered, almost overhead.

Willem looked at his watch, and in the forest dimness could just read the time, 9:14 a.m.

They listened, and waited.

After some minutes – Willem looked at his watch and saw 9:19 – the helicopter continued northward. Its sound diminished and finally could no longer be heard.

"Phew! Think they'll come back?" Laura asked.

"Guess we'll have to stay alert and inside the forest," Willem said.

"No one came out of it, did they? This low, they'd have to climb down a rope."

"Don't think so. We'd have heard different sounds, I think."

They remained at their posts for a few minutes longer. Balayam then said, "We eat more rattan fruit. And then maybe move away. Maybe they mark this place on their map."

After a while they ventured out to the river, picked a few rattan fruits, and ate, wincing with each bite. They picked more and put them into their bags for later. Kodon came back from a little foray with *kenari* nuts, carrying them in the fold he had made with the front of his tee shirt. He and Balayam retrieved stones from the river, and they showed Willem and Laura how to crack the nuts open without smashing the flesh inside.

Balayam plucked bunches of grass from the river and brought two handfuls back. The four sat down on damp sand at the riverbank. "We eat these leaves too. Not bitter." He stuffed a few into his mouth, including the roots. Willem and Laura looked at one another and grimaced slightly. The three followed Balayam's example and finished up the grass.

"But we can't stay out here in the open," Willem said.

They stood up, brushed sand off of their pant bottoms, smoothed away their tracks, and retreated into the forest. Once again, the quiet astounded them. The occasional insect buzz echoing through the trunks only emphasized the stillness.

They wouldn't, would they, capture my Charlotte to force me out? Oh, God. Surely, they wouldn't go that far. More likely, they'd interrogate Marilu, maybe even stake out her house while waiting for me!

They walked, and occasionally Balayam, in front, or Kodon, at the rear, found fruit, nuts, or leaves for them to eat. They came to streams, refilled water bottles, and quickly returned to the forest. They hiked uphill and down to another stream. Willem and Laura marveled at Balayam's sense of direction.

Finally, she asked him. "Balayam, where are we going? And how do you know how to find your way? We're not going in circles, are we?"

"Oh, Ma'am, I know this forest. Hunting many years here for viand. I know these rivers and hills. We stay far away from the villages. And I know about the sun."

"But we can't see the sun!"

Balayam pointed upward. "See up there? Some leaves, you can see shadows. This side, not that side. Maybe two more hours, then the sun go down. We stop soon."

29. Luya

"Laura, let's stop and look at your leg."

"What?" she asked, looking down at her ankle where the leech had attached itself. "I hadn't noticed it. No pain, but it's swelling, isn't it?" she said, looking down.

"Let's go over there into that ray of sunlight near the river." Willem called to Balayam ahead of them, "Let's stop for a moment."

Laura stretched her leg out into the small patch of light. Willem bent down to look carefully; Laura did as well.

"Several red lines coming up your leg. It's gotten infected, and very quickly."

Balayam and Kodon looked closely at the wound as well, and then talked quietly in their language, Manobo. Kodon walked away in the direction of the river.

"We didn't bring any medicine," Laura said.

"No," Willem said. "And this infection is developing fast." He looked up to Balayam, who had stood up and looked in the direction of his brother. "This is the biggest danger of the rain forest, isn't it, Balayam?"

"*Oh ho*," (yes) said Balayam. "My younger brother is looking for medicine." He pointed with his lips in the direction that Kodon had gone.

Willem said, mainly to Laura, "I wonder what Kodon will bring back." He then turned to Balayam and said, "I'd think that you young men have become accustomed to modern medicine, is that right? Maybe you don't use traditional medicinal plants anymore?" Balayam didn't respond.

"Now I can feel it swelling," Laura said. "And it's hot."
She cupped her hand around the wound, and then released
her hand. "Doesn't hurt a lot, maybe because of the leech's
injection of anesthetic."

"And it's red," Willem said.

Kodon returned with his bolo and a large folded leaf.

Balayam turned to Laura. "We start with rattan sap, from the
palm. Kodon cut the palm trunk, catch this sap for you."

He looked to Laura and then Willem, who both nodded. "Put
sap on leg now." He broke off a piece of the leaf and used it to
press the sap in and around the wound. "Kodon go out, get
more."

Willem said, "I know just a little about traditional medicine in
this part of the world. "Dragon's Blood" from the rattan palm
is one of the most widely used medicinal plants, for lots of
ailments, including skin wounds. And it's the same plant's
fruit we've been eating! It's antiseptic and helps the blood
form a scab. But it's not very antibacterial, and besides, the
bleeding from the leech has already stopped. So blood can't
wash out the toxin."

They waited. Their sun ray slowly shifted, and so the group
of three moved. Laura again positioned her leg in the sun's
"spotlight", and they continued to look at the wound.

Kodon returned, again with a leaf in one hand and two stones
from the river. He cradled his bolo knife between his other
upper arm and his body. Around his neck he wore a large
glossy dark green leaf from the river tied with some thin
plant strands. He handed the stones to his brother, with a
few words.

Balayam set one stone on the forest floor, took the contents
of the leaf from Kodon, and told Willem and Laura, "Kodon
bring back *luya*, ginger root. He peel the skin off at the river

and wash the root and stones. Now I smash the root, and we get paste."

Kodon cut several thin slices of the root and handed them to Balayam, who hunkered down to grind the slices with the second stone. He used a torn piece of the leaf to scoop up most of the smashed ginger root, by now a loose paste, from the bottom stone. He motioned to Laura to position her leg horizontally, and then he gently applied the paste to the offended area. Willem and Laura watched, fascinated.

Laura said, "Gently, please. Starting to hurt."

"We must tie *luya* to stay on." Kodon used the leaf and plant fibers to tie the leaf, first at its bottom, then the top, around Laura's leg, to hold the ginger paste in place.

"Maybe you stand up," he asked, and he motioned to Laura, who carefully complied.

"Now, you must eat *luya*. I smash more." He took several more slices that Kodon had made him, and with the stones as mortar and pestle, made more paste. "Cannot make tea; not enough sun to heat water; cannot make fire. Must eat *luya* every day now."

"Oh, why?" Laura asked.

"Make body strong. Fight wound," Balayam said.

Willem added, "Ginger root is one of the most widely used and most effective of all the herbal remedies, and it readily grows by streams at the edge of the forest. It heals many ailments, reduces pain, and it builds the immune system. " He looked up the sun's ray to the small opening in the tree canopy far above them. "*Zingiber officinale*," he said. "This one-two treatment just might work." He brought his gaze down to Laura and smiled. He nodded to Balayam and Kodon, smiled, and said, "Thank you very much." Balayam and Kodon each gave a single nod and looked down.

Willem then asked, "How long before we know. I mean, how long does it take to heal?"

Balayam answered, "Maybe Miss Laura can sleep tonight. Tomorrow morning maybe no more red lines."

30. Walked All Day

In the morning, Balayam looked at Laura's wound: it appeared the same as last night: not bigger, not smaller, same color, lines a little shorter. He applied more rattan resin and then more ginger poultice. "We wait and see."

They walked all day, staying under the forest cover but near the river. Occasionally they ventured out into its sunlight to gather fruits, nuts, and grasses. They rested while they ate; they again took off shoes to wash their feet in the river. One of the brothers always kept watch with eyes and ears and feeling for vibrations, upriver, down river, and at the sky above.

Didn't know I'd get in this much trouble writing that story about the logging. And probably even from my own government! But I had to take responsibility, Fellow Americans devastating primeval forest in another country. Oh, I've been an innocent abroad. And maybe even at the expense of my daughter's welfare. I sure hope not! I've got to get back to her in order to take care of her! And I've got to work, have to have an income.

I miss her so much! I'll try my best to imagine that she's doing fine, that I'm the only one of us doing the missing.

Surely Marilu and her staff and her sons are calm. Charlotte will just go to nursery school every day. Each day will be normal. And what does a four-year-old know about the number of days?

Or is she suffering? Maybe not trusting what I told her, about when I'd be back? I even marked on a calendar for her, hung it on the wall! Asked Marilu to show her how to mark off each day. But I've left her before on short trips, and she knows that I've always come back.

I have a taste now of what so many nurses in this country go through. The Philippines supplies the nurses of the whole world! So many of them are moms – and dads – and they leave their children for years in order to send money back home. They leave their children with grandparents or aunties. I've always wondered how the moms or dads can handle being away from their children for so long.

Back under the forest canopy, they easily stepped over the thin carpet of brown leaves between tall, straight tree trunks spaced far enough apart that they occasionally walked abreast. The four people had a visual radius of easily a hundred feet. Occasionally they stepped over a rotting tree trunk. Now and then a bright flower surprised them, white, pink, red, fallen from the canopy above. Occasionally they diverted their course around ferns, some dwarf palms, or small thickets of aroids – dark glossy-leafed low plants.

The sounds of their steps were muffled in the thin layer of leaves. The air was cool, usually still, and they looked up into the dim light coming down from the canopy high above.

"Awesome," whispered Laura to Willem. "If I were alone, I'd be scared. It's so grand, so vast, I feel insignificant. I'm reassured to be here with you, and with the brothers."

"We're utterly dependent on them," Willem said. "Like passengers in a plane. We share this grand, solemn, mysterious place with only our two protectors."

"Well, yes, and all the plants, occasional insects, and that little primate that Kodon showed us high in a tree back there. A tarsier, wasn't it?"

"Yes, you're right. This enormous world exists fine without humans. Out there in civilization we have the illusion that we care for each other. This vast forest doesn't care at all about us, and so we're dependent on our two protectors. But that also means that we never have privacy."

"I long for private moments with you," said Laura. She reached her hand back toward him; he squeezed then released it. They continued their quiet, careful now single-file stepping behind Balayam, with Kodon taking his usual last place in their procession.

Toward dusk, Balayam signaled their stop for the night. Kodon brought back new palm fronds from near the river. Balayam assured Willem and Laura that Kodon would make his cuts for the palm fronds without leaving a trace for others to notice. Balayam and Kodon secured their by-now familiar lean-to shelter against a tree trunk.

The four prepared to sleep together in the same arrangement as the previous nights: in two pairs, the brothers, the couple. Their four heads together, they stretched their feet outward in two directions by the side of the tree. All four slept lightly, hyper-vigilant, like young cats, ready to spring into action if necessary.

No little Charlotte next to me. I'm so accustomed to feeling comforted with her beside me, knowing that she's safe.

In earlier discussions of forest dangers, Balayam and Kodon had told them to not worry about creatures. Against leeches, they could hope that their frond mat would protect them. About mosquitoes, their lean-to was far enough away from the river that mosquitoes wouldn't venture.

"No worry about reptiles, rodents, mammals: we find very few," Balayam said. "About other humans: we try to leave no trace."

"If we hear or see anyone, what then?" Willem asked.

 Balayam answered, "If night and lying down, we stay quiet. We signal others: we touch other heads. That means we must stay quiet. If found or caught by other person, we give up quietly. But each night when we lie down, we hope for good sleep. We wake up at dawn, not earlier."

Feeling their way into the lean-to, they settled down. In the forest dark, they knew that the moon shone above the high canopy, for they could just make out glimpses of their own moving forms. Side by side now, with Laura next to the tree's buttress, they laid on their backs in order to listen and look outward. Behind them, their heads less than a foot away, Balayam and Kodon stretched out in the opposite direction.

Willem reached for Laura's hand next to his. With her other hand, Laura reached for and caressed Willem's hair. He gently squeezed the hand he had been holding.

She turned her lips to his ear and very, very quietly whispered, "I wish we could touch more." He gripped her hand again.

He whispered into her ear, "I want to kiss you." Laura turned her head toward the brothers, saw no movement, heard no sound, and then she turned back to Willem. With her free hand she felt his face, found his lips, and then brought her lips to his.

Their lips stayed long together, very quietly. But their bodies became anything but quiet! They inhaled sweet, exciting smells of their togetherness. They felt rushing, racing movements of - electricity, of blood? – from their lips, down through their bodies to their cores. The energy raced up again, up and down, into their limbs. So hard to remain still, quiet!

They both pulled back from the kiss; they listened, they looked. Danger of intruders? Danger that the brothers would notice them? All was quiet.

One set of hands still together, they returned to their kiss. They once again became absorbed in their sweet smells, the racing sensations in their bodies, the sounds of their breathing. Their breathing tempo was accelerating. But oh! – the danger out there! A fleeting thought flashed though

Laura's head. *Oh, he's married! He's married ... way out there, somewhere, over the horizon.*

But the kiss was overwhelming. Each noticed their own, and their partner's, breathing accelerate, both in tempo and in sound. Noise! Both tried to return to complete quiet, to hold still, except to squeeze their two hands together.

Lips together, Laura felt, "it's happening. Now I can control the quiet, remain still. I can let it happen." Her breathing built to a crescendo, and then, calm. Willem? He shared the experience. His rapid breathing also suddenly subsided. He restrained himself to remain quiet. He moved away, rustled about, looked for something. Laura heard his quiet noises. *Leaves?* He returned his hand to hers, his lips to hers. They kissed sweetly, calmly, shortly, pulled their heads back, each smiling, and slept.

31. The Wallace Line

Day after day they woke at the first sign of dawn and followed a routine. They hid all traces of bedding, found and ate food, hid their tracks, and walked. Balayam had told them that the forest was big enough to walk toward the west, in the direction of Cotabato, but to still stay far away from villages. And they needed to move to reduce the risk of detection.

Before each evening they selected a place to sleep and then prepared the place. Gradually they became accustomed to their routines, and slowly their anxiety dissipated. Even their two guardians relaxed somewhat, the main evidence being that, instead of one walking last, both walked ahead of Laura and Willem, and they quietly talked together. Walking between the enormous buttressed tree trunks in the shade with canopies high overhead and decomposing leaves underfoot, sounds were muffled. Balayam and Kodon seemed alert even to ground vibrations, sensitivity to even faint vibrations which could warn of large fauna, or, unlikely but possible, humans nearby.

During relaxed hiking, the two foreigners walked and quietly talked, sometimes about other places and other times.

"Tell me more about your man Wallace, Willem. You've come here to follow up on his research of a hundred years ago, didn't you say?"

"Yes. Hmm, where to start: I told you about The Wallace Line, yes?" Willem asked.

"Yes, and that over the following 50 years, five other researchers modified Wallace's original line. They moved it, in their theories."

"Well, no one has really examined those lines, not even after the major theoretical shift by geologists."

"Hmm? Remind me."

"Yes. It was just five years ago, that the world's geologists agreed that the theory of plate tectonics best explains large-scale movements of the Earth's crust."

"Many plates?"

"Seven or eight large ones and at least seven minor ones."

He continued. "Hard to believe, but Wallace, a hundred years ago, advanced a theory about the locations of flora and fauna that implied plate tectonics. He developed incredibly good hypotheses about why the flora and fauna, even those under water, are completely different between the Spice Islands and the rest of Indonesia. Such a phenomenon, such a discrete separation, is found nowhere else on Earth."

"Does it have anything to do with our spice trees?"

"I'll come to that. But mainly he's best known for his theory of evolution, which he developed at the same time as Charles Darwin, but independently of him."

"So why does Charles Darwin get all the credit?"

"I'll come to that, too. By the way, they were both Englishmen, contemporaries, and similar in age and dates of research. They even exchanged several letters. But they were of different economic and cultural classes. Darwin had a much more privileged background.

"Wallace developed his theory of evolution while conducting ten years of research in our area, the Malay Archipelago, and mainly in our Spice Islands. He gathered and sent to London125,000 specimens of flora but mainly fauna, of evidence for his theory of evolution. And his analyses were even grander than Darwin's. He had a second major analysis, and that was of the discrete distribution of flora and fauna, not crossing over what came to be called 'the Wallace Line.' It could be as long as 2,000 miles, south to north."

"Wow. How does one even go about gathering data over such a vast geographical area before there were airplanes, not to mention analyzing such a vast quantity of data without a computer, and eventually developing theories?"

"*Ja* – yes, he was a marvel. Can you believe that the London Museum of Natural History has one whole enormous wing on him? But the general public doesn't know about him."

Laura pondered. "Did you go there?"

"Yes, I spent a few days there in London. A small army of volunteers are still working on his data. They're kind of like volunteer astronomers searching the heavens and contributing to scientists' discoveries. They call it 'The Wallace Project.' They contribute documents and information as they are found, and they post their work on their public website. I've been following them for years. In fact, their work stimulated me to apply for the WOTRO research grant to come to Ternate."

"So, have you been collecting specimens in Ternate?"

"Well, Wallace killed. He pinned butterflies and beetles to boards. Killed mammals, even around 27 orangutans that were captured in Borneo."

"God."

"But, mercifully, we don't do that anymore."

"Thank God. We both know that by now, orangutans are almost extinct!"

"Yes, They're in just two reserves now, one in eastern Borneo, the other in Sumatra."

"Yep."

Willem then described his visit to London a few years earlier, just a 45-minute flight from Amsterdam, to see what he could

learn from Wallace's notes, after having read his major
publication, *The Malay Archipelago*, about his ten years of
work and his theories. They had been published in London in
1869.

"Did you know, Laura, that the British Library is the largest
library in the world? – that is, by number of items
catalogued?"

"No, wow."

"At the main building of the British Museum they sent me
over to the Museum of Natural History, which had throngs of
tourists waiting for opening time. But I had an appointment
and was privileged to skip the line. And better yet, inside,
I was able to hold in my hands Wallace's original journals!
And they let me photograph the entire volumes. Took me two
days."

"What a valuable experience!"

*"Ik voel me zeer geëerd deze honderdvijftig jaar oude
documenten aan te mogen raken.* – Oh, excuse me, Laura,
I was back in my thoughts back then. I thought, 'I'm so
honored to be allowed to touch these 150-year-old
documents.' I read each page slowly and reverently, and then
I photographed it before carefully turning the page. They had
me handle them with an elaborate set-up of cloth-covered
foam wedges, and a beebee-weighted rope to hold down the
page."

"Wow."

"It was like church; you could feel the reverence. I whispered
to the librarian when I finished the journals. My last step was
to look through a 100-page, A4-sized, photocopied index of
'The Wallace Project' holdings in various locations in the U.K.,
including in Dorset, 122 miles west of London and at
Wallace's burial site."

"Do you think Wallace learned the Indonesian language on Ternate, Willem?"

"He must have. He had local helpers to find and kill all those specimens. No mention of anyone helping him who was from Jakarta, or Singapore, or farther away."

The four travelers in the forest stopped to gather some rattan fruit by the river. They ate, and then three of them took a short nap in the sun. Kodon stayed awake to keep watch.

A half hour later they returned to the shady refuge of forest and resumed walking.

Willem and Laura continued their talks, learning about each other. Willem started. "Laura, I'm still astounded that our quite different academic fields have brought us together in a very special place in the world."

"Mm-hmm, even though the events that attracted us occurred centuries apart in time. Started even millennia apart."

Willem stopped to hold her hands and look into her eyes. "Must be manifest destiny."

Laura said, "Well… we *do* wonder. Haven't heard or read of any other botanists or linguists around here nowadays."

"Nope. We're kind of pioneers."

She smiled. "And few international traders either. Imagine, Arabs came all the way here, more than 5,000 miles, for spices, and they took them back to Europe, starting around, you told me, at least 1300 years ago! And the Spice Trade led the Portuguese and then Spaniards to start exploring. The Crusaders brought spices back to Europe. Competition over spices led to exploration, opening up to Asia, and then 'discovery' of the New World, all because the spices were seen as so important to human health – and taste."

"And we do both hope that our research will advance knowledge of languages, of botany, and of world history."

They both delighted in their shared topic. Laura said, "And *your* research follows on an English zoologist's consequential work here a little over a hundred years ago. But his work hinted at the early formation of our continents and islands, and that your island of Ternate offers crucial information."

"Yes, continents moved several times, starting around 500 million years ago."

She asked, "Hmm. The Earth is four-? five-? billion years old?"

"They say around four and half billion."

"That single continent of all landmasses, Pangaea, that was the start of land; do I have it right?"

"Well, geologists write that Pangaea was formed around 250 million years ago. Rocks from Australia and all the way up in China, Burma, Thailand, even Tibet, and as far west as Sumatra, were determined to have formed together, in a much earlier and vast supercontinent called Gondwana, around 500 million years ago. Twice as old as Pangaea. And animals swarmed it and the surrounding waters."

As usual, the terrain for the four travelers was easy to navigate, with no brush under the high trunks that reached up into a complete canopy that always shaded the floor. The forest floor was mostly flat with a thin cover of fallen leaves. They followed Balayam and Kodon, who carefully moved between the buttresses reaching out from the trunks.

Laura asked, "So back to Wallace: He wasn't doing geological work, was he?"

Willem said, "In the 19th century, those naturalists were generalists. Before coming to Eastern Indonesia, earthquakes and volcanoes were real mysteries and this was an especially active area. We're still studying the why, how, or the when of their activity."

He continued. "So Wallace discovered a discrete line – that he drew in the seas on a map! – that marked this division of living things. The entire population of animals and plants to the west, where there were big mammals such as elephants and tigers, and even their insects – were separate from all fauna to the east of his line. He drew the line at its southern end between the islands of Lombok and Bali, just 35 miles apart. His presentation of his discovery astounded scientists back in England. To the east, the biggest animals were only marsupials, with kangaroos the largest. This discrete separation caused him to wonder why. He came right to the line and lived here for ten years. He pondered a geographical explanation, especially continental drift."

"So now, Willem, what can *you* add to Wallace's 1860's report? Degradation by humans? Another refinement to the Wallace Line?

 "Well, it wouldn't be completely unheard of, to discover such a fundamentally new phenomenon. It wasn't until 1967, a hundred years later, that geologists discovered plate tectonics, a major reconsideration of theories about the formation of our earth."

"But plate tectonics were already known back in Wallace's time, right?"

"No. Continental drift was theorized by a geologist colleague and even by Wallace. But even up through the 1960's, the theorists of plate tectonics were dismissed by mainstream geologists as kooky, until 1967, in a seminal report. Mainly, up until then, geologists were saying that the causes of earthquakes and volcanoes were still a mystery. Mainstreamers theorized it preposterous that large land masses could drift.... And by the way, Wallace himself was considered kooky in general by others, for other reasons, later on in his life.

"So what convinced geologists?"

"I believe it was the discovery and then confirmation that the layer *under* the land masses was much more fluid than the surface land. Magnetic "stripes" were discovered on the oceanic floor, using equipment that had been developed during World War Two to detect enemy submarine activity."

"No kidding! So does that mean that the Wallace Line shows that the distribution of flora and fauna - that their distribution took place *after* a single large landmass separated into continents and islands, divided by water, and therefore have remained separated after water divided the landmasses?"

He responded, "Flora and fauna evolved, west and east, indeed after the separation into landmasses and islands, west and east of this enormous tectonic plate. Wallace showed the remarkable separation of all species of animals, from beetles and butterflies to large mammals, even birds."

"And you said others contradicted him and his line?

"Yes, five modifications to his line have been published, the most recent one by Weber in 1902."

"No complete contradiction of his line even after plate tectonics were discovered?"

"No. That's why I'm here."

So, Willem, we're sitting on a plate tectonic border? That is, walking on it?"

"Yep. It's not just under water."

"Your Mount Gamalama on Ternate is quiet now, but didn't you say it last erupted in 1962, just ten years ago, and for a whole year?!"

"Yes. We live dangerously, don't we?!" He reached for her hand to hold it.

She gave a quick smile but pressed on. "Do volcanoes occur just at the borders?"

"Well, sort of. Convergent boundaries are a main place to find active volcanoes. That is, plate boundaries can be destructive, and that's what we have here."

"So what difference will your research make? What do you hope to contribute?"

Willem answered, "I want to look at how closely animal and plant distribution follows the relatively new knowledge of plate tectonic borders. And my geologist colleagues in Utrecht will compare my findings with what is known now about continental drift in this part of the world. Together, we'll confirm current geology theory, and I'll be able to report on how close The Wallace Line is to what we know now of plate convergence. It might even bring us a little closer to predicting future earth movements: earthquakes and volcanoes. More specifically, I'm studying what has happened to the roots and above-ground communication between clove trees after a few hundred years of human manipulation."

They walked silently for a while.

"Willem, it's astounding that these very special spices, clove, and nutmeg and its companion, mace, evolved only here, on Ternate and the Banda Islands nearby."

"Yes, I agree. To think that they developed only on those islands, at this convergence of tectonic plates, in this beautiful tropical setting..."

Laura stopped to look at him. "Yes, we each entered this vast domain through a tiny window, yours of updating Wallace's work in this place, and mine to study a certain contact language."

"Yes, and hey, let's continue now about *your* work as well!"

"Oh, okay!" She quietly took several steps before answering.

"As you know, Portuguese were the first Europeans to start exploring over here."

"Sailed down the west coast of Africa, right?"

"Yep. They were motivated to bypass the expensive eastern trade routes, figuring, correctly, that transporting spices by ship all the way to Europe would be cheaper and they could subvert the hegemony of the Arabs' land routes and traders at ports. The Spice Trade route overlapped somewhat with the Silk Road.

"The Crusaders, you know this, right? funded their travels by bringing back spices. They started in, um, 1092 C.E. in France, and the last crusade took place starting 1291. As you know, the goal of the crusades was to boot the Muslims out of Jerusalem.

"Portuguese made big progress in the late 1400's, when they first succeeded in rounding South Africa."

"So the first contact languages were started, or stimulated, by Portuguese?"

"Well, at least European-based ones. The concept is relatively new and therefore we've a lot more searching to do. The Portuguese set up forts on the west coast of Africa, and in these forts, for instance, in Ghana, Portuguese pidgins and then creoles developed. Crew members were left at various ports along the way, including Goa, Penang, Malacca, Macau, Ternate. Spaniards followed and competed with the Portuguese, and some of the pidgins and creoles were relexified into Spanish words: Malacca, Macau, and then on to

Ternate. The two languages Spanish and Portuguese, as you know, are very closely related.

"And let's remember that Christopher Columbus, of course an Italian, got Spanish funding and started his effort to go westward around 1475, and finally sailed across the Atlantic in 1492. This was the same year that Portuguese navigated around the south of Africa into the Indian Ocean! Columbus's main motive, after scholars generally accepted that the Earth is round, was to find a westward route to the Spice Islands. Portuguese had been fighting Spanish sailors on the Mediterranean Sea over getting to the Spice Islands!"

"Busy year for global explorations!"

"Yes! Willem, have you ever heard of the Tordesillas Treaty?"

"*Ja*, Yeah, but tell me."

"Well, did you ever wonder why Portuguese is spoken in Brazil but not in other South American countries?"

"Uh, tell me."

"Well this treaty was signed between Portugal and Spain in 1494, dividing the very newly discovered lands outside Europe: Spaniards would have those to the west, Portuguese to the east. You'll note that Brazil sticks out to the east of South America, into the "Portuguese" side, and that's why it is the only Portuguese-speaking country on that continent."

"Yes, it does stick out…"

Laura continued. "The biggest goal of all for the Portuguese, and then other Europeans who competed with them, was the spices. Nutmegs and cloves were tasty in foods. But they were also considered a necessity, especially by those who had money, for medicines, preservatives, and ultimately prestige. And now we know that even ancient Egyptians, who started mummification around 2700 BCE, had used nutmeg to embalm their dead. The spices were so expensive in Egypt and in Europe that a small pouch of nutmeg could be sold for so much that an explorer making one voyage could live comfortably for the rest of his life."

"You had already told me that the Philippine contact language that you came to study was taken there by people from our Spice Islands. So your language has a rich Spice Islands history as well!"

"I agree."

"See? Destiny!" He reached out to press her hand.

32. Almost Evicted?

At midday, they sat in the shadows near the river after eating.

"Laura, you said you were almost evicted from your first field site? How?"

"I had to prove myself on first arriving in the Philippines," she said.

"What happened?" Willem looked up from his task. He was scraping wet mud off his shoes with a short stick.

"Well, I came loaded with help, sufficient, I thought. I arrived carrying a letter from the president of my university, which I showed at the U.S. Consulate in Manila and at the Philippine Office of the Ministry of Interior Affairs there as well. That minister wrote a nice letter in English and in Tagalog for me to show in the south; great letterhead."

"A lot more than I did in preparation for my work in Indonesia. But for me, getting the visa to enter the country took three years! Is that how it's done in the Philippines?"

"Wasn't so hard to get a research visa. But yes, anthropologists everywhere, and surely in other fields as well, such as yours, always want good local support before entering a new field site."

Rain had been falling quietly, steadily for three days now, and the four walked slowly and carefully, each holding a fantail palm frond overhead for protection.

"I was told to meet a man, Sam, who had an uncle out on the island where I wanted to work. Sam took me there. We traveled by bus and then double outrigger canoe, to ask permission of the local leaders. I was awestruck by the natural tropical beauty.

"After rounding a swamp of mangrove trees, a point sticking out into the azure Sulu Sea, I could easily see white coral sand below. Sam pointed out coral table heads beneath us, dark against the white sandy bottom. The helmsman, his brother, carefully steered around to avoid each table head. We entered a tiny bay, shallow enough that we had to walk some distance through knee-high warm water through sea grass, the water gently lapping in tiny waves. The white, steaming hot beach ahead of us formed a wide arc, and several little boys, maybe ten of them and all nude, had noticed us coming. They jumped into their tiny canoes, double-rigged like the boats adults used, and paddled out to us, boisterously laughing at us. Their smooth brown-skinned bodies glistened from seawater and salt crystals.

"Just behind the white sand beach, a wall of coral rocks formed a barricade, but we saw gaps here and there for access to the houses just behind and where the first row of coconut palms grew. Sam asked for his uncle's house, and the boys pointed to one of the houses close to the beach.

"Uncle Omar seated us on his balcony cantilevered out in front of his house and around ten feet above the sand. He looked at my letter and then up to Sam, who explained it to him in Samal. 'That's why she wants to stay here, to study our Samal language,' Sam said. The uncle considered, talked with the two equally old and dignified-looking men who sat with him, and then looked back to us. "We will help her," he said, and Sam translated for me. Back then, it was a completely new language for me.

"I was offered to stay in the house (one-room – they were all one-room) of the local policeman, a young man, Samad, along with his wife, two children, and his mother. The policeman, who knew some English, would answer my questions to help me start learning the language. All was well for a week or so."

"Go on!"

"Well, the village had some two hundred people and the island had three other villages. You could walk the perimeter in two hours, and I did, many times. They were subsistence farmers and fishermen, and they also grew palm trees for copra, which they sold in the city. They got to the city, Zamboanga, by boat and bus, a full day's round trip. A few men also earned cash by smuggling cigarettes and clothing fabrics from Malaysian Borneo to the south. The Malaysian items were fetched by outboard motor boats, much faster but much more costly for the fuel of gas and oil.

"The main smuggler in our village was suspicious of me, and he called my host, young Policeman Samad, into his house. Policeman Samad told me that the smuggler, Sabirin, said he had learned that real Americans have little spots all over their faces. He suspected I might be an 'East German.'"

"Wow! Did you find that absurd? *Zonnesproeten* in Dutch; what do you call them?" asked Willem.

"Freckles. And, by the way, Doris Day was in American movies back then, and had freckles."

"Fun!"

"Mm, funny... Yeah, I tried my best not to scoff, just a small smile and said just, 'huh?' Well, it turns out that young men in that village, if they had any cash at all, and the young men working for the smuggler certainly did, would take the day-long trip into the city of Zamboanga, and there they would see American movies. And just the previous month, my assistant, Ahmad, told me, the movie in the city cinema had been *Pillow Talk* with Doris Day and Rock Hudson. So she, with her freckles, was the 'real American.' I think the 'East German' suspicion also came from another movie in the city."

"And so?"

"The policeman took me to see Sabirin. The smuggler was angry. Until then I hadn't seen much anger by Filipinos, so he surprised me. He talked to me in a little English – I couldn't do much with Samal yet – and he insisted that I show my passport to the Mayor of Zamboanga and get a letter of endorsement from him, and not return to this island without it!"

"So did you pack up?"

"I had to. I didn't have much, just two small suitcases, one with language books and papers.

"So, back to the 'eviction' story. That day, I hired a young man to take me in his small boat to the larger island, Mindanao, and a larger village, Taluk Sangay, where I'd catch a bus into the city, Zamboanga."

"And then?"

"Next day I collected my passport, my letter from my university and my letter from the Philippine Ministry of Interior Affairs. I had put them in a safe deposit box in the small hotel where I had stayed in the city, and I headed to City Hall to make an appointment.

I was immediately ushered into the mayor's office. It was old-fashioned, like you see in movies of banana republics. The mayor sat at the end of a large assembly hall, windows all along two long sides. Next to him, at a smaller desk, was a man with papers talking to a young woman who sat at a typewriter. The perimeter of the hall, and below the windows, was lined with fold-up chairs, all filled by men, many with papers in their hands.

Whatever business was being conducted stopped when I entered. A receptionist had entered with me and she walked to the mayor, spoke quietly but audibly for all of us, and explained my business. Quietly, but everyone in the room could hear. The mayor was super polite to me, and he appeared honored by my visit. He looked at all three documents, and he smiled at me, saying that these looked legitimate."

"So the challenge had become easy, then?"

"Well, wait! Then the mayor had his male assistant carry them to... to whom? I was surprised to see Mr. Smuggler Sabirin sitting among the men along the side of the room! So then the smuggler and a man on each side of him looked and looked again at my passport and my letter from the president of my university. Smuggler Sabirin held up my letter to the light coming in the window and showed it to the man next to him. That man took the letter back to the mayor, who held it up, looked at it. Then he laughed and said something apparently dismissive, and had the letter and passport brought to me. And what was that? In the middle of the letter was a watermark showing 'University of California, Berkeley.' The smuggler looked chagrined.

On returning to the little island, of course I was worried I'd get retribution for having publicly humiliated the leading smuggler. After that I was always on the alert, but I never had further trouble with him. But also very little contact. For my research I didn't try to interview him about smuggling!

The four forest travelers, now silently, continued their long day's walk under the enormous forest trees.

33. Gotta Keep Moving

"We must keep moving; leave nothing behind," Balayam told Willem and Laura the next morning. "Maybe the PC hire persons who know this forest to search for us."

Willem turned to Laura. "They've been so quiet, I thought they were calm. I hadn't realized how worried they are."

"The Filipino way," Laura said. "Not blustery, like us Americans. How about Dutch?"

"We'd have shown more anxiety as well."

"Balayam already told us that he's compromising our hiding by following the river upstream."

"But of course we have to have water. And otherwise, how would they know directions in this forest? – With no compass, and it's really hard to tell where the sun is above this tree canopy."

"Yeah, we've got to follow the river."

Again on this morning, the four walked quietly, almost reverently in the stillness of their vast cathedral. As usual, even the soft sounds of their steps were muffled by the shallow dead leaf carpet on the forest floor. Their voices as well were absorbed by tree trunks and woody *lianas* climbing up them, sometimes looping down from the canopy high above. Slightly cool humid air felt calming to human skin, and the pervasive mold smelled mellow and sweet.

In the dim brown and green light, Willem said that he thought that the brothers walked a bit farther away this morning from him and Laura: Balayam farther in front, Kodon farther behind.

He picked up his pace to move closer to Laura ahead of him and quietly asked, "Do you think they noticed us last night?"

"Hmm, I wonder. Let's see if they sleep a little farther away tonight. But, for safety we'll still all need to sleep together."

"Yeah. Protection from danger is more important than privacy, isn't it?"

She responded, "And probably for them, our privacy isn't crucial."

"What do you mean?"

"Well, I've slept in several one-room houses by now in the Philippines. In the countryside, most people still live in one-room houses, up high enough on stilts that you can walk and work underneath, and up high, it's cooler, with breeze coming up through the smooth bamboo-slat floor. Very attractive houses. Everyone sleeps in the one room, and I've learned that sex certainly takes place in those houses at night."

"No privacy, then?"

"Well, a little. One, the couple waits very quietly until others are (maybe) asleep. Two, I think that anyone still awake pretends not to notice."

Willem considered. "So, if the brothers' heads are a little farther away from ours tonight, then we'll know, right?"

"Ha ha! Already we have a hint, that they're walking farther away from us."

They walked silently for a while, alert as always since they had entered this world, in awe of the beauty, but vigilant for danger.

"Laura, I'm overwhelmed by our experience last night."

"Me too. Everything is more vivid now! Smells, vision, rainbow aura around any leaf or flower that floats down from above. "

"Yes, for me as well!"

"I wonder, Willem: do you think that we're falling into each other's arms because we're excited to be together in this incredible forest and because we're in danger?"

They continued walking. Willem said, "Well, the danger is important, isn't it? Our senses are already in high arousal."

"Arousal! Ha! She looked back at him and gripped his hand. "I bet you were surprised you could... mm... come to completion without you know what."

"Oh yeah! It was like being a 15-year-old kid again. Special experience! But I do wonder if our companions noticed!"

"For me too. And all the excitement around us, maybe the PC looking for us, and now Balayam says maybe local people, people who know the forest, could be hired to look for us."

"And I'm still on the lookout for tigers and pythons, even though they tell us they're not here."

"No tigers here in the Philippines, but tiny creatures, mosquitos and bacteria. They're probably the biggest danger. Sure hope this sore on my leg goes away."

"Laura, I made the right decision to come with you, I've come to care about you so much. But we're such babes in the woods. And it's hard to have to depend on these men we hardly know to protect us."

"I sure think about them as well. Can we trust them completely? We can't afford not to."

"And the farther we go in this forest, the more dependent we are on them."

"Yeah, we're getting in ever deeper. We could never get out on our own."

Laura's thoughts drifted. *Not handling my responsibility for her! – Abandoned her! Oh, God, what if What's-His-Name learns that I've left her for a long time? He'd use the information to intensify the custody case!*

What can I tell Willem about this? Would he understand? Hmm. His own children have left home for college. I wonder if he can remember how intensely parents care for little ones before they gradually grow ever more independent. My friend Diana told me "The Lord loans us our children for 18 years." Lord, I can't imagine Charlotte really moving out and away. Way too early for that!

But about Willem: I wonder how involved he was taking care of his children when they were little. Or did he just leave all care to their mother? surely they had the traditional division of labor in the Netherlands back then. That's the way it was here; my dad was pretty distant... Everyone's dad was. No, Willem likely wouldn't understand.... I could ask him... Or not.

Little Charlotte: an impediment to romance? Yeah, men don't want to forsake their own children in order to take care of some other man's child! Even if his own are out of the house now. And Charlotte: could she accept a stepfather? If this would become a relationship, it is structurally flawed. Anyway, I didn't start this romance thinking of the long term. It just kind of came upon me, and it's probably temporary. I may even have wanted it to be temporary, taking up with a married man. I'm certainly not going to choose a man over my daughter. If I had to choose, of course I'd choose for her... wouldn't I?

She came back to their topic. "Maybe we've learned enough that we could now forage for food for ourselves."

"But how about listening for danger?"

"And how about leaving no trace? – Cutting branches, and we have no *bolo*, then hiding the branches in the morning?"

34. Searching for Long-Gone Men

Willem and Laura sat next to the riverbank in the morning sun, making their preparations for the day. The brothers had gone to scout for food.

"Hey, Laura, we're both amateur historians, aren't we? We're both looking for documents written by long-dead men." Willem looked up at Laura, who was tying a rattan strip around her dilapidated shoe.

"Yes, one man's language work, Esquivel, whom I told you about, got me to your Ternate in Indonesia."

"And Wallace's book *The Malay Archipelago* got me to Ternate as well, where you then came, and you met me!" he responded.

They smiled at one another. "So these men, in the mid 1600's, and the late 1800's, brought us together."

She had been weaving several short strips of river grass together underneath her right shoe for a mat to hold the dilapidated sole. Now she wove the ends of the strips on top, in order to secure the mat to the shoe.

Willem asked, "Do you think we went into our respective fields because of our fascination with these men?"

"Not me," she answered. "I first became fascinated with creole languages. *Then* I discovered Esquivel in the process of my research about varieties of Creole Spanish. And I've found him surprising, but my search for him is tangential. I don't expect this research on him will enhance my chances for a good university position. How about you?"

"Oh, Wallace definitely got me to Ternate. Studying biology when I was a *prekandidaats* student - what you call an undergraduate – in Leiden, learning about Charles Darwin and his *On the Origin of Species*, I thought back then that his contemporary and competitor, Wallace, never got the recognition he deserved – and still deserves. With my search about him and his work here in Ternate, I hope to finally give him the credit." Willem looked more closely at Laura's work on her shoe and smiled. "But I don't expect any job enhancement; my position in the university is already secure."

Laura patted her shoe and then put her foot into it. "So both of us want to learn about people long gone. Do you think I might learn any more in your Ternate about Esquivel? Maybe I could go there again, this time with my daughter. Might be good for me to leave the Philippines for a little while, after being 'wantid'. And I'll take those trips to Spain and Chile soon for the same reason."

"…If we can get out of here! But of course, I'd love you to come there again. And I want to meet your daughter."

She reflected. *If this romance lasts any length of time, he'd have to fully accept my daughter.*

They saw the quiet approach of the brothers and stood up to receive them.

Balayam, eyes wide, raised his index finger to his pursed lips. Then with his thumb he motioned that they must follow him and his brother *now!*

35. Long Wait

Balayam quickly but quietly led them into the forest from their small low-growth clearing next to the river. Willem and Laura exchanged puzzled, worried glances before they stepped into the dark shade. They passed many enormous tree trunks in the dim light before Balayam and his brother turned around to look back. Willem and Laura looked back as well and saw that they could still make out their little clearing in the sunlight next to the gently gurgling river, maybe 60 feet away.

The brothers moved behind the buttress of a tree and motioned to Willem and Laura to join them, and to remain standing. Balayam leaned to Willem's ear and then to Laura's, whispering "We hear people coming. We wait here." All cautiously looked around them in the near darkness and out toward the river. Laura felt her heart racing with adrenaline. She looked to Willem. *He's as scared as I am.* Balayam gestured that Willem and Laura should watch below him, in squatting positions, from his side of the tree, while his brother should look from the other side.

They waited. Laura's heart pounded so hard she wondered if others could hear it. But in the forest, she heard nothing unusual, only an occasional quiet bird song from high overhead. After a while Laura sat down, crunched one knee to her chest and then the other, and then repeated. Her legs felt heavy with the long standing. She noticed that the angle of the sun's rays had slowly moved toward vertical.

I hadn't even noticed earlier if the brothers had gone up-river or down-river, so I don't know which way to look and listen. She occasionally looked at her companions, and though alert, they also showed no sign of new input. Willem reached for her hand, squeezed it, and then continued holding it. The thick warm air surrounding them remained still. She moved her legs again, which were starting to ache.

Balayam motioned to us to stand, maybe to be ready to run?
To minimize insect invasion? Hard not to sit. They waited.
Laura became ever more aware of an urgency to pee. *Oh,*
I didn't have the chance for my morning ablution. Gotta pee!
But I can't, now!

What's that?! She looked in the direction of the slight sound
and then all around and up at the others. The three men were
all looking out toward the clearing, still on high alert. Willem
held her hand tighter.

She gradually recognized new sounds, of steps against bare
earth, of *soft crunching against loose sand, so out by the river,*
not here under the trees where we have leaves. Human
footsteps? She couldn't tell yet. The rhythm, the sounds, came
closer. *Human steps. But one person? More than one?*

She saw movement out toward the river, a flicker as a shrub
moved. Then another flash of reflected light. *"Shiny, sweaty*
skin. Bare chested, walking upstream. Two of them. Local men?
She looked up to Balayam, caught his eye. Willem looked to
him as well. She raised her eyebrows to Balayam. He
responded with shrugged shoulders. *Hard to breathe! I'm too*
scared to behave well.

She looked back to the two strangers. *Filipinos, surely; local?*
Wearing western shorts and flip-flop sandals, and carrying
bolos and small cloth bags. Each had a bolo sheath which was
tied around his waist. *Maybe in their thirties. Only two, or*
were there more after these? Hunters? - Of animals? Or maybe
looking for us? She caught Willem's eyes, and raised her
eyebrows and shoulders. He responded with the same
gestures but added lips pressed together, indicating "I can't
decide about them." He raised his eyes and brows toward the
brothers, indicating "Let's learn what *they* think."

The two newcomers stopped and looked carefully around. *Oh*
heavens, did we leave any trace that they might notice?! Laura
worried. *Grass matted down? Footprint in the sandy earth?*
Bolo cuts on the nipa palm tree? Fruit pits? Then the men set

down their bolos and bags, hunkered down onto their heels, and leaned into the river to lift handfuls of water into their mouths and then over their leaning heads. Next, they sat down on the riverbank, took off their flip-flops, and dangled their feet into the river.

They both reached for their bags and took out something. *It's wrapped in banana leaves – oh, they are rice cakes, probably fried in coconut oil, so travel food.* As they slowly munched, they looked up-river and then down, up at the sky, by now bright blue with late morning sun, and then all round them. *Oh, heavens, they can't see us, can they?!* Laura and her three companions all remained completely still in their very dim light. *Gotta stay completely silent!"*

The two strangers pushed their now empty banana leaves under nearby bushes. They lifted their feet out of the river, rubbed them thoroughly, put them back into the river, apparently to rinse, and then brought them onto the bank.

One man took out a small silver box from his bag. He opened it, prepared two betel nut – areca leaf – tobacco-chews, and handed one to his companion. They both chewed, they gazed out at the river and up to the sky, and they spat their orange-red juice into the bushes at their sides.

Laura leaned upward toward Balayam, who brought his head down to her lips. "Do you know them? Can you understand them?" He whispered into her ear. "People from east of us. Don't know them. Tboli speakers. Cannot understand them well. Maybe they are paid to find us; maybe they are hunting animals. We must stay quiet."

The two men stretched out on the ground, turned on their sides toward the forest – toward the four in hiding - and away from the river, and put their hands across their eyes, apparently to block out the sun. Before long, they appeared asleep.

"Not worried about *us,* are they! So maybe they're not looking for us?" Laura whispered into Willem's ear. Balayam looked down on Laura and Willem and motioned downward with his hand, apparently meaning "be quiet." Willem and Laura's hands remained clasped together.

After considerable time- surely several hours - Laura noticed that the sun's rays once again slanted down, now from their side of the river, the west side.

The men sat up, rubbed their eyes, leaned into the river for more water; and then sat back again onto the bank. They ate more rice cakes.

One man stood and walked to a small nipa palm tree, cut four fronds – *Oh! – we didn't get our fronds there last night, did we? Or did we?!* With his fronds, he walked back to the other man and sat.

The four people in hiding looked at one another, raised their eyes and eyebrows, looked upward, and slightly raised their shoulders. They looked back at the two strangers, who had moved to a forest tree buttress near the river – and closer to the four people in watchful hiding. The strangers arranged their palm fronds under and over them. In the near dusk, Willem and Laura and the two brothers could see that the two strangers laid themselves down and before long were completely still.

They waited. Willem shifted to one leg and then the other and whispered to Laura, "Can't wait; gotta go." Laura pointed to her chest and nodded, mouthing "me too." Willem looked up to Balayam, pointed toward his lower core and then behind them. Balayam opened his mouth in alarm, took in a deep breath, and then motioned with his two hands to walk very slowly, very quietly. He pointed downward, indicating that they should stay very near, and to stay out of sight behind their tree trunk. Laura gestured to show that she would do the same. Balayam closed his eyes and exhaled, indicating his resignation at their plan, but then pointed to his chest and to his brother, showing that they would soon relieve themselves as well. They all looked out at the by now apparently sleeping strangers before Willem and Laura moved.

They moved very carefully, just six feet into the forest, and then turned back to back, and both hunkered down. Their liquids sank silently into the thin layer of damp leaves and shallow soil. Laura noticed the urine smell blending with the musty, faintly aromatic fragrance of the fallen leaves. *Oh no!* she thought, as she noticed, even in the near dark, movement on top of the leaves, on all sides. *I should know by now; out here in the forest for many days already!* Leeches marched toward her newly released urine. *Not finished yet! Gotta finish! ...Takes so long!"* She finished, gave her body a shake, and stood up. Leeches had climbed onto her shoes. She reached down to flick them off before they could latch onto her skin.

She heard a twig snap behind her, and looked around at Willem, who had also just stood, and then had stepped on a twig under the leaves. Both quickly looked at Balayam and Kodon, who were watching the strangers. Willem and Laura, out of the strangers' view behind the tree, couldn't see them. Balayam touched his brother's arm. Indicating high alert. Willem and Laura didn't move. As Balayam again touched his brother's arm, both reached for their sheathes and pulled out their bolo knives. They watched; all four waited. Balayam signaled with his hand behind his back to Willem and Laura, indicating "stay where you are."

Willem and Laura heard movement out by the river and looked at one another with eyes wide open and eyebrows raised. *Stay strong, stay quiet, Laura!*

They heard sounds coming their way, even though muffled in the "carpeted chamber" in the forest. They heard first the crunch of steps on sand, and then the even softer sounds of steps on slightly damp fallen leaves. Very slow steps, pause between each. *Maybe getting adjusted to the dark in here. And listening. God, the suspense!* She felt so vulnerable, standing in the open even though very dim light; *Surely Willem is, too. Small comfort: adrenaline rush, and oh, my heart is so noisy!*

Balayam and Kodon each used only one eye for their vigilance, the rest of each face hiding behind the tree.

The two strangers, walking with hands on their downward pointed *bolos*, passed the hiding tree to discover Laura and Willem standing in the open and with scared expressions.

"Oh, hello!" said the first man (in English!) and gripped his *bolo* tighter. "*Milikanos ka'a?*" (You're Americans?) The second man looked around, discovered Balayam and Kodon behind them next to the tree, and likewise gripped his *bolo.* The men looked at one another.

"Oh, Tuan!" (Oh, honored sir!) said the stranger, still with his *bolo* pointed down. Laura was startled. *Why! That's a term of respect!"* Balayam responded in a few words. *T'boli? He just told us a while ago that he didn't understand T'boli.* The stranger switched to Tagalog; Balayam responded in Tagalog, and then the other two Filipinos moved over to join in, leaving Willem and Laura behind. Laura whispered to Willem, "So they've all been to school; to have learned the national language."

After a short time, Balayam turned to Willem and Laura. "They're out here hunting for toucan birds so they can sell to Japanese. They want to sleep here tonight. I think we'd better all stay here, so we'll be able to watch them to see if they're telling the truth."

Laura thought, Relief! *Calm down, body!* She felt the adrenaline gradually dissipate. Balayam turned around to continue his discussion with his brother and the two strangers, and Laura turned to Willem. Mildly alarmed, she noticed a leech on Willem's ankle. He mildly jumped at the sight but watched her with fascination. She gently pinched it with two fingernails, tugged on it until it finally released its hold, and pulled it out, relieved to see the head still attached to its body. Tossing the leech aside, she then wiped Willem's ankle with the back of her hand, brought her hand up to her lips, and licked it clean, with a small smile. She then whispered, "How much can we trust those men? And by the way, can we really, really, trust Balayam and Kodon?"

36. Trustworthy?

The six walked out to the river and sat, apparently amiably. The four Filipino men did their best to chat with their limited understanding of each other's language. Laura tried to understand but could catch only an occasional word. Balayam once in a while turned to Willem and Laura with a short translation.

"They say at first we frightened them; I said the same from us."

"They say they go home tomorrow; no catch of any toucans this trip."

"They ask if the foreigners are afraid of creatures in the forest."

Laura said, "Well, maybe you can tell them that we've had swellings from mosquito bites and from leeches, but the swellings have been healing. Tell them thanks to you guys for putting poultice on them. And you kept us from more bites by giving us insect repellent.

"Like what creatures are they talking about?" asked Willem. "What have we been missing?"

"They asked if you saw snakes here."

"Snakes? You didn't tell us about snakes," he said, startled.

The two Tboli men turned to him, smiling with mischief.

"I think we're being hazed," Laura said, turning to Willem.

The two men, Sabtu and Igtu, talked to Willem and Laura, one adding to the other, while Balayam translated, saying:

"Many, many kinds of snakes here, but only a few are poisonous. Back there in the dark forest, leaves are not down low, and fewer snakes. But out here by the river, you must always look when you pass under a tree branch or reach for a vine, especially in the bushes and vines near the river, where the foliage is at our level.

"Here in the forest, we don't see so many of the bird eating spiders."

Willem asked, "Huh? So big?"

"*Oh ho*! Their legs are longer than this!" Igtu showed his fingers stretched out, thumb tip to pinky tip. Laura said to Willem, "Bigger than our tarantulas in California."

Willem responded, "And I don't even like spiders."

"What else are they saying?" asked Laura.

Balayam listened, and then translated. "Big centipede, longer than this, showing fingertip to tip span again. Very painful; takes one month to overcome a bite. Crawl at nighttime."

"Oh, you didn't tell us about them, Balayam!"

"No, we just hope we do not see them. No way to guard against them in the night. Same with scorpions, but not so many here in the forest. Closer to the river. Same with crocodiles."

Willem opened his eyes wider. "You have crocodiles here?!" He looked at Laura with alarm.

"Yes." Balayam was kind of enjoying this topic by now. "Sometimes we see the little ones, only a meter long. But we also have large ones in the river. We didn't see any here yet. We looked and we would tell you, but we didn't see any."

Sabtu and Igtu talked; Balayam translated. "Worst is mosquito because sometimes you can get very sick, some people die from mosquito bite. But we just hope we can manage. Anyway, we sleep in the forest, fewer mosquitos than by the river."

"Balayam and Kodon, please tell them how you have been protecting us from bites and helping us heal when we get bitten by mosquitos and leeches".

"Oh, they know this. But I tell them for you." He turned to the two Tboli men and tried to translate Laura's words. She said, "For repellant they bring leaves, they smell a little citrusy, they crush them, and we rub them on our skin. They say, "all over.""

"Oh, *sambong* leaves, ma'am."

Willem added, "Yes, *Blumea balsamifera*. These bushes out here by the river," and he pointed. "One to four meters high. Strong fragrance of camphor and limonene."

Laura continued. "And then, when we do get bitten, they make a poultice of *sambong* and *luya*. Plenty of ginger plants everywhere along the river." She pointed to some nearby.

Balayam responded, "*Ugat ng luya*, root of ginger. I showed them that we make paste mixing these two plants together, root of *luya* and leaf of *sambong*. You men know, usually we make a tea of *sambong* and sometimes of *luya*, but not strong without hot water; paste is stronger than tea; paste made with water heated by the sun only." After his crude translation, the two Tboli men nodded, apparently in agreement, and stopped their teasing.

They talked, they napped, they ate fruits and nuts, they chatted.

Laura and Willem motioned to Balayam that they wanted to talk with him privately, and so he motioned to his brother to go help the two men to rearrange their sago palm fronds for their bedding. Nearby, Kodon uncovered their own bedding leaves from the previous night. Laura watched. *I wonder if he's putting them near us so that he and Balayam can keep a watch on them during the night.*

Balayam turned to Willem and Laura: "We must talk very short. When those two leave the forest, they will tell."

Laura asked, "Maybe they're even paid to tell?"

Balayam: "Maybe, I don't know. They said tomorrow they go home. We must also go, but another way so they cannot point to us. We go to the west, to Manobo village." Balayam went back to the others.

Willem and Laura talked alone quietly. Willem asked, "Then what about us? – I mean short term, long term?"

"Yeah. We've been together, let's see, almost ten weeks, and now we're in a predicament. We've got to get out safely. But we have the bigger concern: will we meet again?"

"I don't want to leave you, Laura. The whole universe has finally brought us together."

"Yes, but... is this just a summer romance? – Probably it can't survive because we live and work on different continents, right? And one of us is married."

"But I'm not being fair to you. You deserve to be with someone unencumbered by prior commitment."

"Oh, God." She put her face into her hands, and then raised up, resolved.

She walked over to Balayam. "How far are we from Cotabato, Balayam?"

"Only two days' walk, Miss Laura."

She returned to Willem, and quietly said, "Fastest way back to your Ternate is a big roundabout loop: fly to Manila, then Jakarta, then Ternate. Fast but long and pricey."

Willem responded, "My time is already up; I must teach two classes at my university in the fall semester. I can telephone my friend Clifford and my assistant Ali to store all my stuff. I'll go directly from Manila, and I'll return to Ternate in December, at the end of the term."

"Such a long time."

"Yes, where can we meet? We *must* be together again."

"Yes."

"So hard not to embrace!" Willem said, and Laura nodded. He walked over to Balayam and Kodon. "Please learn if it is safe for us to travel to Cotabato."

Now quite dark, they settled in for the night's sleep, this time all six in one large tree buttress. Arranging themselves for sleeping, Laura noticed that Balayam and Kodon turned now facing the two Tboli men. *Keeping a watch on them,* she thought.

Next morning, the four men appeared convivial, going off to find fruits and nuts. The Tboli men brought back leaves and ginger roots, and with a flintstone and the tip of a bolo blade, started a fire to heat water in a large metal cup that Sabtu had pulled out of his bag.

"Oh-oh, the smoke," Laura whispered to Willem. "Getting ever riskier." He nodded.

After eating, the four men talked. Balayam turned to Willem and Laura: "They offer to show us a waterfall. They say it is beautiful and is upriver only about one hour. Maybe we cannot say no."

"Are you worried they're setting a trap?" asked Laura.

"Maybe we must stay near them to watch them," Balayam answered.

So, for the first time in two months, they left their bedding leaves without hiding them, and they followed the two Tboli men up-river. And rather than stepping quietly in the dark of the forest without talking, they walked along the river bank, sometimes leaving footprints in the sand, sometimes jumping from stone to stone at the water's edge, sometimes exchanging words.

Laura noticed that walking out by the river was actually slower going because of frequent dense bushes by the river. But she relished the sunlight. She smiled to Willem behind her. "I've been craving more sunlight!" she whispered.

"*Ay yee!*"

Willem and Laura heard the shout, and immediately saw a flurry of motion ahead of them. Kodon pulled out his bolo knife and … "What's happening?" asked Willem.

Laura, who was ahead of him, said "I don't know! … Oh! Oh! Look!"

"What?!"

"He's… he's hacking a snake! Fell down on … on Sabtu!"

They watched as Kodon attacked, one thrust after another. They saw blood spurting.

"That's just the snake's blood, right?" asked Willem, and both he and Laura stumbled over the stones to see better. They saw the telltale two marks on Sabtu's arm that he'd been bitten.

"Yes, look. Oh, God." The snake's head was almost severed, but the yellow-green menace, maybe three feet long and a two inches thick, writhed.

Then they noticed Balayam, who had taken off his shirt. He used his bolo to cut into a side seam and then tore off the bottom six inches and made three long three-inch strips out of the piece. They moved Sabtu to a sandy spot on the river bank and laid him down. Balayam first tied one cloth strip above the wound on Sabtu's arm. "Oh, above the bite marks!" said Willem.

Igtu brought a large stick, as long as Sabtu's arm. Balayam placed it against the offended arm and quickly tied it with the cloth, making a crude splint. He checked snugness, adjusted, then checked again.

Sabtu appeared to be in shock. He looked dazed. The other three Filipinos talked in urgent tones, and then Kodon and Igtu hurriedly disappeared.

Balayam turned to Willem and Laura. "They look for poles and vines to make stretching."

Laura said, "Oh, stretcher. We'll carry him?"

"*Oho'* [Yes]."

Willem turned to the still writhing snake. "It's a Wagler's pit viper," he said. "Tree snake. Very venomous. We have them in Ternate as well. I wonder if Sabtu's going to make it. Depends on the amount of venom injected."

Balayam responded. "We get him to hospital and antivenom. Maybe he will live."

All three sat down around Sabtu and lightly held his limbs to comfort him. They waited. The two men returned before long with materials that they then quickly fashioned into a stretcher. Balayam showed Laura that she must hold Sabtu's arm "no moving!" and the three men carefully placed him into the stretcher. All quickly picked up their few belongings, and then Willem and Laura listened to the three men urgently discuss something.

"What are they saying?" asked Willem.

"I understand only a few words: hospital, Tboli, Manobo," she responded.

After their short discussion, Balayam turned to Willem and Laura. "We all go to Manobo village, not far. They take motor scooter to Tboli village, farther away, medical clinic, antivenom. Also, in Manobo village you will be safer." He looked carefully at both Willem and Laura. "We try to save this man, but now we very noticeable."

Balayam added, "Now Igtu walk beside him, keep him calm." The remaining four picked up Sabtu in the stretcher, one person at each pole end. Balayam and Kodon led the way, and Willem and Laura held the rear ends of the poles.

They all quickly fatigued from the carrying, and so they agreed to set the stretcher down every few minutes for short rests.

"I really want to get out of this forest," Willem puffed.

"Oh yes," agreed Laura.

37. Escape

Igtu took Kodon's place at the front of the stretcher, so that Kodon could scout ahead. Kodon returned late that afternoon from his foray into the regional town. He found the five very slowly moving along the trail toward him. He reported to Balayam who conveyed his news to Willem and Laura.

"No PC in Tacurong City, so your chances are good. Cannot take you to my *bahay kubo* (my nipa hut) in my little *kampong* (village) near Cotabato because my family and the neighbors will talk."

Laura looked to Willem and then back to Balayam. "No talking in the town?"

"*Milikanos* – westerners – pass through Tacurong now and then. But you must go by yourselves. You go to hotel – they have a hotel – and you sleep there. In the night, we come get you, take you to fishing boat. Boat will take you to Cotabato. Then airport."

She clapped her hands together, looked up to Willem and then to Balayam and Kodon, and said, "Well, then! More than two whole months!" She reached into her small bag. "How can we ever thank you enough? You've kept us out of trouble, and you've shown us how to live in the forest. You kept us alive, and you stayed with us all this time!" She reached for his hand without looking at it, in the Philippine way as did he in response, both of them pretending that she hadn't pushed a wad of peso bills into his hands. "And, Balayam, what can Willem take to your brother in Indonesia?"

By eight o'clock, two hours after sundown, the two westerners walked along the unpaved main street of Tacurong City, around small mud puddles in ruts from yesterday's rain, looking for the only hotel in town, the

Beldent Star. On each side of the street, dark brown, unpainted wooden buildings stood behind a raised wooden, covered walkway. Far ahead they saw two people stumbling away from them, apparently drunk men.

"Stage setting for a western movie!" Willem said. "Looks like one of your old cowboy movies, and I didn't know such a place really existed!"

"Like a dream, hmm. Basilan City, south of Zamboanga, is just like this," Laura said. "And hey, there's the hotel," and she pointed to the right, ahead of them.

She whispered. "Out here in the open, I'm more scared than in the forest!"

"Me too."

"No trees on the street, so we're exposed. No trees to protect us!"

Awakened by the opening of the hotel's door, the clerk quickly sat up and rubbed his eyes. Inside, the hotel was built of dark, unpainted, dark *lauan* plywood and framing: floor, walls, stairs, and ceiling. Other than the hiss of the kerosene lantern on the clerk's counter, the hotel was so quiet that Laura wondered if they were the only customers. The corridor was warm and humid with the sweet smell of mildew.

The clerk took their pesos, and then he handed Willem a long "skeleton-type" key attached to a large wooden block inscribed with the number 205. He gave Laura a candle, which he lighted, in a wine bottle, and a little box of matches. Laura noticed that the clerk put his head back down on the counter before she and Willem started to climb the stairs.

The room had the same dark wood, the same sweet smell of mildew, and it had, in a separate room, its own toilet and shower! The bed looked firm, a plywood platform on six-inch diameter solid legs. It held a three-inch kapok mattress covered by two mint-green cotton sheets and two kapok pillows covered by multi-striped cases. She set the lighted candle on the tiny table by the door, and Willem set the key next to the candle.

They both sat on the edge of the bed, sighed, and smiled at each other. "Can you believe that we get to share a real bed?" Willem said.

"New adventure!" responded Laura.

Laura took a shower under the unheated thin stream of water coming down from above, using the tiny bar of soap that sat on the shelf next to the plumbing. "Oh, heavenly! called Laura. Willem politely waited, then took his own.

The pillows smelled of slightly rancid coconut oil; hair dressing of their predecessors.

A very pleasant hour passed by.

They slept.

They were startled awake by a loud commotion of apparently drunk men coming down the corridor in the direction of their room. They both reached around in the dark, grabbed and hastily put on their meager clothing. The men outside laughed, they stumbled, they stopped in front of their door! Bang, bang, bang. A fist was hitting their door!

Laura heard Willem jump out of the bed, and...*What was that?!* A loud crash of breaking glass ... *What is he doing?*

Willem held the door closed and in his other hand, a jagged, broken neck of the wine bottle/candlestick, prepared for a confrontation.

But then from outside the door they heard both of their names: "Mister Willem, Miss Laura!" Relieved, they opened the door to familiar voices. There were Balayam, and Kodon, and two other men, laughing and reaching to hug them both.

"Why so noisy?" Laura whispered to Balayam when he hugged her.

"As if we are tipsy," he replied. "The only good reason for coming in so late. We have a boat for you, down at the river." In the complete dark, they touched the corridor walls to find their way to the stairs. Laura looked for the clerk at the front desk but couldn't see him; his kerosene lamp was out. They quietly stepped out to the dark street.

38. Genocide in the South?

In the regional city of Cotabato, Willem and Laura sat in the little airport to plan their flights. Willem would fly to Manila and then take the first flight to Amsterdam. Laura would accompany him to Manila.

"What's the buzz?" Laura whispered to Willem. Staff and customers formed small clusters and appeared to be urgently discussing something. Laura approached a uniformed staff member to inquire, who told her that President Marcos had declared "martial law" a week ago.

"Oh! What's happening, then?"

"Well, we don't know everything, Ma'am, because ordinary news is stopped. But today we hear that American navy ships are bombing rebel holdouts near Zamboanga City, on Basilan Island!"

American naval ships! Came over from Vietnam? Lord, what else is known? Is this public information?

She found a pay telephone and changed paper pesos to a lot of coins, to call Marilu, who asked, "Dios! Where have you been??" She then told her that Charlotte was fine and at nursery school just now, and that the whole country is alarmed about martial law. Laura asked about Basilan Island. Marilu said that her U.S. Embassy friend hadn't mentioned anything about that. Laura finished by telling that she'd be back in Manila in two days. She called her AP Bureau Chief friend, who told her that the rebels' goal was secession of the southern islands from the Philippines. She asked if Americans back home knew about this U.S. military action. *If people back home don't know, I might be the only one with the opportunity to tell them.* John Jackson encouraged her to find out more.

Americans don't know that we're secretly waging war in a friendly country? I must inform my countrymen. Laura decided to delay her trip northward by two days, which would even delay her reunion with her daughter. She decided to tell Willem only of her plan to visit Sam and his wife, not of her investigation. He would disapprove. *And I could get into more trouble with authorities. My kind of American patriotism, again! Got in trouble last time, but I'll find a way to avoid trouble this time!*

She took the one-hour flight to Zamboanga, where Sam and his wife, Rita, lived. They welcomed her and quickly updated her. "American ships are bombing every night. We heard that they want to get rid of the separatists because Americans have discovered oil in the sea to our west, and they don't want danger from these Muslim separatists. But our rice fields over there are getting ruined and our people are very afraid." For several months now, he told her, some thirty young separatist rebels had camped at his home village, forcing his relatives and neighbors to provide housing and food for them. These rebels were holding out against attacks by government military – and American bombs.

So the rumor I heard in Cotabato is true! American naval ships had come over from the Vietnam war, a thousand miles to the west, to aid the Philippine government in their effort to quell the insurrection.

Sam took her on the one-hour ferry over to Basilan Island, and then by bus, copra truck, and hike, to his home village. He and Laura interviewed the rebels and Sam's neighbors, and the rebels were proud to allow her to take photos of them "fighting for the cause."

She decided to write the story; it needed to be told, and she felt the responsibility as an American. John Jackson would publish it with international distribution.

But how can I avoid trouble? She pondered. *Hey, I can ask for the release of the publication to wait until I leave the Philippines. Now would be a good time to go collect the archival data in Spain and in Chile. By leaving before the story is published, I can protect Charlotte and myself. Hmm, but would we ever be allowed to return?*

That night, in discussion with Sam, she wrote it.

"It's Still Genocide Even if They Die by Starvation"

by Laura Rhodes, Ph.D.

Research Associate in Linguistics, University of California, Berkeley, California, September 1972. Reprinted from *Pahayang*.

The usually lush tropical countryside is now dead brown, dusty, and still. The houses are abandoned, the animals gone from their grazing under the coconut trees. Shriveled immature fruits are lying under the mango and jackfruit trees. The Samalan country of Basilan Island, Southern Philippines, is a wartime wasteland.

To the drought in the Southern Philippines has been added another disaster for the Muslim Samalans: they have had to evacuate their homes to flee from the fighting between the Philippine military in league with Christian guerrillas against the Muslim guerrillas. Most Samalans are caught between two poor choices. Either they must comply with the military pressure and evacuate their homes, leaving some relatives staying behind more vulnerable to attack by the military and themselves open to the disapproval of the Muslim guerrillas, called the Black Shirts; and leaving their sources of food, their crops and animals for another place of questionable safety; or, they remain at home or evacuate to a hill close by, risking the daily skirmishes between the Black Shirts and the Ilagas (the Christian guerrillas), and risking harassment by the Philippine military who would consider them sympathetic to the insurgents because they did not evacuate, and therefore, subject them to harassment whenever they passed through one of the numerous checkpoints. Some of the Samalans have already decided to join the Black Shirts. Estimates by the evacuees are that about one half of the adult men have joined up or are sympathetic. Councilor Purigay of Lamitan says, "They'd rather stay up in the hills and fight the army than die of hunger down here."

Most of the Samalans want to stay neutral. They have felt political, religious and economic discrimination like their Muslim relatives and neighbors, but they are not willing to join a war that looks hopeless and is led by long-time outlaws. Until now, the Samalans' anger over discrimination had not been directed toward their Christian neighbors, neighbors who are now picking up arms to join the Philippine military. On the other hand, the Samalans do not condone the actions of the government military who have shelled their houses, killed and harassed their relatives and friends, armed the Christian terrorists, and encouraged their raids into the Samalan hills.

This isn't a holy war – yet. Christian-Muslim conflicts started long ago, as soon as the Spaniards arrived in the Philippines during the 16th century. Basilan Island – and all the Southern Philippines for that matter – have been one of the most successful places in the world for the co-existence of Christians and Muslims. But more Ilagas are joining up largely because they are afraid of the secessionist threats of the Muslims, and Ilagas are rumored to wear amulets signifying they are fighting for God.

The next day, Laura landed at Manila Domestic Airport and stepped down from the plane.

39. Back to Manila

Even though very anxious to be back with her little Charlotte, Laura first wanted to pick up her mail. *Chance for a job offer in the mail?* She took a taxi to the APO Office on Roxas – formerly Dewey - Boulevard, opposite the U.S. Embassy on the Manila Bay. One perk of her research grant was to get U.S.-delivered mail, and within a week. Philippine post could take as long as a year!

Picking up her little stack, she noticed a letter from Attorney Bautista whom she had hired three months earlier to investigate Migo's attorney's request to provide a sample of Charlotte's blood for that so-called paternity analysis. Migo wanted to determine paternity, or, with blood type, at least narrow down the possibility. Atty. Bautista would investigate whether she had to comply, and whether Migo really wanted to open a case for custody. She didn't open it.

Out again on Roxas Boulevard, Laura hailed a brightly painted jeepney, with its routes scrolled on the outside and a string of colored lights flapping in the breeze. Marilu would call it garish. But the jeepneys were more frequent than buses, and Laura loved riding in them. Pressed together, with kids sitting on laps, everyone was polite, even with 15 people. And if too crowded, then men let the women and children sit inside while they hung onto the outsides, standing on the running boards, or they even sat on top with the chickens and other luggage.

This jeepney had plastic flowers, plastic flags, plastic tassels, and plastic flaps folded up on the sides that could be rolled down for rain. But it wasn't raining now, and the jeepney wasn't full. And the streets...why *so* quiet? Where were all the vehicles with their blaring horns, and the pedestrians jamming the streets? *Eerie,* she thought as she looked around at the few other passengers. But they simply smiled politely. *Because of martial law?*

Nearing her stop, Laura noticed a sign painted on the side of a passing jeepney:

> Ang katok, sa pinta,
> Ang sutsot, sa aso,
> Ang "para", sa tao.

She was happy to be able to understand it.

> Knocking is for doors,
> Whistling is for dogs,
> "Para" is for humans.

She thought back to her conversation with her dear friend and now landlady, Marilu, three months earlier:

"Oh Laura, you didn't ride in a jeepney, did you? I looked out the window from upstairs. I saw you walking here like usual; no taxi, so you must have taken a jeepney. You can't do that anymore!"

"Why not? I always do, you know that."

"They're too dangerous now, Laura."

"Oh, I know they usually belch smoke, and they break down, and the springs are so old that they don't take ruts or corners well."

"Laura, Nowadays, many bombings of jeepneys. And shootings."

"But don't you also love jeepney's outrageous designs?"

"God, way too garish."

"Precisely, garish: those intense multi colors, lots of chrome, sometimes "dancing" lights like blinking Christmas strings, bouncing with the ruts in the streets!

"Kind of embarrassing to me, our kitsch national culture on display."

"And, I know that you don't ride them, Marilu; they're for the common people, as you say; but I love them. Easy open entrance at the rear, easy exit. You can see their routes painted on the sides, in fancy cursive scroll! But better and more frequent than buses, jeepney drivers are much more flexible. As you know, if you have a heavy load, they might even divert to your destination for you."

"Yeah, that's true. Even I have ridden them when I had a big load."

"I knew it!" She hugged Marilu, who rolled her eyes, and they laughed.

This time, when the jeepney was nearing her stop, Laura smiled, and instead of signaling by knocking with her knuckles on the ceiling or with a coin on the handrail, she called "para" to the driver. He braked, and Laura jumped out at the gates of the exclusive neighborhood.

Charlotte will be at nursery school, not back for another two hours.

She walked to Marilu's, rang the bell, and was welcomed by a maid. Marilu ran in to the foyer to hug and greet her, and to exclaim, "Oh, you came safely! I've been so worried you'd get caught in martial law!"

Laura responded, It started September 22nd, (1972), two weeks ago, right? I didn't have any outside communication until day before yesterday. But coming from the airport, everything is much quieter than usual."

Marilu said, "Yes. Would you like to rest first? And then we will catch up on everything." Laura accepted her offer and went to her guest room, where she sat down and opened her attorney's letter, dated almost a month earlier. He reported on his letter from Migo's attorney. She read.

...The mother has been missing for almost two months...

...Custody!

She carefully folded the letter into its envelop and closed her eyes. *How'd Migo learn about this? Maids? Nursery school? Surely not from Marilu!*

Laura saw red. Shocked, she looked for Marilu, who was working at the kitchen sink arranging a bouquet of flowers.

"Marilu, I'm so angry that I saw red. Has that ever happened to you?"

"What are you talking about, my dear?" Marilu glanced back at Laura, saw her wide-open eyes and open mouth, and set her flowers down.

"First, look at this letter." Laura pushed it down on the counter to Marilu.

"*O, Dios mio*, Laura. But what do you mean, 'you saw red'?"

"I mean it literally, Marilu! When I read this letter, my anger practically exploded my eyes! For a moment, I saw only red, blood red. Have you ever heard of that?"

"I've heard the expression, but I thought it was only a figure of speech."

"Me too. I guess vessels in the eyes dilate, but for just a moment. "

"So now what're you gonna do?"

"I guess I'll call Attorney Bautista to learn whether I'll have to appear in court, or whether the attorney can appear without me. I have work out of town, this time with Charlotte, and I'm not going to let her out of my sight!"

She called Atty. Bautista immediately; he reassured her that he would contact Migo's attorney and surely, they would agree to meet without Laura.

Marilu wanted to hear everything, so Laura reported on her almost three months of experiences including why she had had to hide for more than two months, and she heard from Marilu about Charlotte's experiences, all good. They talked until the children came home from school. They heard them coming, and so they rushed to the front door to meet them. On seeing her mother, Charlotte shouted with delight. Mother and daughter hugged, laughed, she picked her daughter up, and then Laura sobbed almost uncontrollably. But she managed to pull herself together after a short time to share her daughter's big smile.

After dinner, in their bedroom, Laura and Charlotte talked and talked. Each wanted to tell how much they missed the other, each wanted to know all about the other, and each wanted to tell so much that happened during these almost three months. Finally, as Charlotte started to fade, Laura read her a story until Charlotte nodded off. Then she went downstairs to find Marilu sitting on the terrace.

"Lord, I'm happy to sit with you in your protected, luxurious garden." Laura sighed. A maid poured a glass of San Miguel beer for her. Marilu smiled. "And I'm so happy you've come back, dear Laura. What an adventure you had down there!" They each took another swallow.

"Look, we can see stars!" Laura pointed. "The forest was so dense that for those two-and-a-half months we couldn't ever see the night sky." She leaned back in her cushioned rattan chair, sighed again, and closed her eyes.

Marilu looked up. She said, "Your attorney is very good; he's helped our family for years, and he'll be able to take care of you as well."

They sat silently for a while. Then Marilu said, "Oh, more about martial law!" She told Laura what she knew.

Laura already knew of unrest during the last couple of years. Many people considered President Marcos' 1970 re-election the most corrupt election ever, and many protests had been held, nation-wide.

Random bombings had taken place even before the grenades exploded on August 21, 1971, at the Plaza Miranda rally of the opposition Liberal Party. Nine people were killed and a hundred wounded.

The many free newspapers still carried the news of growing unrest. The government expressed ever more concern about the rise of violence in Manila and other cities, declaring that communist insurgents were trying to take over. Critics said that the government was responsible for the bombings, to incite the people to agree to President Marcos taking ever more authority.

And now martial law had been declared, just two weeks ago, on September 22nd, with many immediate serious consequences. For the first 24 hours, all radio and television were silenced. After a day, a formal announcement was made of martial law. The free presses were immediately suppressed.

Last week, the venerable historian William Henry Scott, called "Scotty," whom Laura knew, was arrested and jailed in Fort Bonifacio in Manila for subversive support of the communists. Laura had once visited him at his house because she had learned that he was the "kiosk" of social science research in the country. He was an American but a 25-year resident and researcher in the Philippines.

Who else might be in danger of arrest? *They wouldn't come after me, would they?* She had already gotten in trouble for exposing the lumber extractions in Indonesia and the southern Philippines. Not yet published was her criticism of the American bombing to protect oil extractions in the Philippines...Would she be seen as a troublemaker?

"Uh, Laura, I have something I must tell you. It's not just Scotty."

Laura looked intently at Marilu.

"We've heard that other university professors are being arrested."

"Oh? Who?"

"So far, the pattern seems to be social scientists, researchers who have been working out there directly with people, who might have learned about any discontent with the government."

"Foreigners only, like Scotty?"

"No, Filipinos as well. Maybe fifty so far, mainly professors and researchers around Manila, but also up in Baguio and down in Cebu."

"How have you been hearing about this, Marilu? That is, with the suppression of the free press?"

"Only the *radjo kawayan* , the 'bamboo radio.' People can still travel, and they talk."

"Marilu, have you already heard about the bombings down in Zamboanga?"

"No, what do you know?"

"Well, when I came out of the forest to Cotabato City, people were talking about U.S. navy ships bombing people on Basilan Island and also on Mindanao. So on my way back here I passed by Basilan Island. I was concerned that my old research assistant and friend Sam might be in trouble, so I went to see him. I learned something awful and now I want to report it."

"Oh, about rebels? Plenty of rebels down there in Mindanao!"

"Yes, including in his home village, Bohe' Besse." To go behind military and their barricades, I had to get a ride with a copra harvesting truck. I interviewed a rebel. He is young, like us. He was happy to see me, happy that I would spread the word of their cause to the world."

"What is their cause, then?" Marilu frowned and set her glass down.

"Well, you probably already know that several American naval ships have gone down there to Mindanao Island, sent over from the war in Vietnam?"

"Yes, I heard about that. They've come to rescue us from the Muslim separatists. Go on."

"So I've felt during all my years here that Philippine politics were not my business to publicize. But in Basilan, after hearing that U.S. military were lobbing bombs onto rebel strongholds in Basilan, I feel some responsibility, as an American. So now I want to report about American military action down there."

"Laura, you'd be sent right to prison."

"God, I suppose so, from what you're telling me."

Both women sat quietly.

Laura spoke next. "Marilu, I don't want to go to prison, and of course I don't want to endanger my little Charlotte, but I feel the responsibility, as an American, to report secret American involvement in the unrest building up in this country."

"And *I* want you to be safe."

Laura continued. "Remember The AP bureau chief, John Jackson?"

"Yes, of course."

"I told you earlier about my report to AP about American lumber concerns decimating eastern Indonesia forest. Well, Mr. Jackson must have published it fast, because the search for me started very fast."

"Yes. So what about John Jackson?"

"Well, I know that Mr. Jackson would love to have this new story."

Marilu called her maid to bring two more beers.

"*Dios*, Laura, you're looking for trouble, aren't you? Why can't you just let it be?"

"I don't think I look for trouble. I just learned about the trouble the American military is making in this country, and apparently secretly. Because other Americans appear not to know about it, I feel the responsibility to report, as a good citizen, that is, an American citizen."

"*O, Dios.*" Marilu sighed and closed her eyes.

"Marilu, I know you care for me and are concerned for me. And I can never thank you enough for taking care of my daughter."

"Of course, dear Laura, and I know you'd have done it for me, too. I and the whole staff were successful in helping her to not worry about you."

"Oh, Lord, I'm so grateful to you, Marilu. Maybe I can offer you some reassurance about what I need to do next. I need to do archival research in Spain and probably Chile on the history of the Philippine Creole Spanish speakers – the Chabacanos - when they first came to this country in 1662.

Maybe I'll go do that work now, and of course I'll take Charlotte with me. I'll ask Mr. Jackson and the AP to not send out my report until after I leave the Philippines."

"But likely you would have no re-entry to our country, Laura!"

"Big risk. But, could you find out and let me know? I'll give you a telephone number and an address in Sevilla, and you can try to contact me, tell me if my name is on a black list. Would you do that for me, Marilu?"

"*Sempre*, of course, my dear."

The next day, Laura left her report with AP's John Jackson with the firm promise that he wouldn't release it until next week, the day after Laura and Charlotte would fly out of Manila International Airport. The report, along with a photo Laura had taken of the young rebel in Basilan, was picked up by several international presses, including *The Far Eastern Economic Review* in Hong Kong. It also became the headline story two days in a row in Jakarta, in Indonesia's biggest newspaper. Two weeks later it appeared in *Stern,* Germany's weekly news magazine.

40. Married?

During that long talk on Marilu's terrace, Laura had shared another topic with Marilu. "Marilu, when I was down there, I told you that I met a man. I didn't tell you until now that he's married."

"Not a married man!" Marilu sat back in her chair and looked intently for Laura's response.

"Yeah, I know, but I didn't plan to..." Laura closed her eyes and exhaled deeply.

Marilu interrupted. "I thought you were looking – at least hoping – for a lifetime partner."

"Yeah. But in all other respects, I feel this is the romance of the century! He's so..."Laura closed her eyes, smiled, and tilted her head upward.

Marilu interrupted again. "Other respects? How can there be other respects? That obstacle is so big!" Marilu carefully set her San Miguel beer glass on the table and leaned back again.

"But he's so wonderful. Like, we have so much in common. And I told you that we just went through that long life-threatening experience together. He's so good to me. And I'm not even gonna tell you about the passion!" Laura examined Marilu's eyes, hoping for a sign of understanding.

Marilu stretched her arm along the back of the empty chair next to her, looked away for a moment and then back to her dear friend. "I wonder ... there must be something in it for you, a married man. Have you ever wondered why? I mean, you once told me that you wouldn't date a man who smokes, that you can't stand the smell. So why isn't 'married' a complete turnoff?"

Laura scratched her head, leaned toward the table and rested her forearm. "Hmm, I've never wondered if there might be something positive in it for me. That is, about a man being married... I mean for a potential romance. Hmm." She rested her other arm on the table and looked to Marilu.

Marilu looked away. "I heard the main reason celebrities see prostitutes is that the pay is hush money. The women are paid for sex *and* silence.

"Yeah? So?"

"So, maybe a married man can be counted on to be discreet. Probably he wants silence, and maybe you do too."

"Oh, I'd tell anybody about this romance, even my mother! I'm not worried about getting found out, about being judged. So in that regard, I'm risky, right?"

"Well, *he's* likely worried about his wife finding out. But I'm leading to more than that. I'm wondering if the restriction on how far this relationship can go is somehow attractive to *you*."

"I don't think so! I mean, I might have found my soul mate."

"Let me continue. Have you ever noticed that a philandering married person often gets together with another married person?"

"Uh, maybe so. And sometimes they talk about two divorces and then marrying. But I recall reading that they usually don't get married. And even if they do marry, it tends not to work out. Like the man needs to prove to his wife that it wasn't just about the other woman, that he had other reasons for divorce. He wants her to know that she as well, not just he, caused it. So then he turns away from the other woman. Usually ends up with a third woman."

Marilu said, "Let me continue that thought. So if I'm married and you're married, you're not going to expose my infidelity to anyone, right? Especially not to my spouse. We enter a pact to keep it a secret, especially from our spouses.

She continued. "Well, not everyone is so secret. It involves a lot of lying, and people get caught lying. Some people just tell their spouses. But then, marriages do tend to break up over infidelities."

"True."

Marilu extended her idea. "So if I were a little worried about getting into another intimate relationship…"

Laura interrupted. "But I fell for him before I knew he was still married! I thought he was divorced; turns out just separated. And mainly just geographically separated. When he goes back to his university in the Netherlands, his home is with her."

"So," Marilu paused and looked into Laura's eyes. "Did he lead you astray? And what could you have been thinking about the wife? – Didn't you feel guilty?"

"Well, hmm, no… Marilu, you know about these men, I mean these American and European men out here in Southeast Asia, the ones who are here for a long time, a year or more. Some of them leave families back home. Some of them come out here for long periods in order to make some transition, maybe they don't even know what. This becomes a legitimate reason for separation without declaring their unhappiness with their lives back home. As for Willem, I'm not sure what he wants."

Laura poured the remainder of her beer into her glass, and she drank. "But I don't want to be a home wrecker… And yes, I've indeed been wondering what I've gotten myself into."

41. Letter from Migo

Two days before take-off, Marilu interrupted Laura's packing with a letter that had just arrived. Laura looked at the return address, and then with big, startled eyes, asked Marilu to stay. Laura read it first silently.

> 211 Hercules Street
> Bel Air, Makati
> September 24, 1972

Dear Laura,

We haven't communicated for more than four years, because I understood you when you said back then that the Pacific Ocean would be too wide for us to bridge, and that each of us needed to continue building careers in our home countries.

Now, I hear that you've come back to the Philippines, and that you have your *mestiza* daughter with you. Please don't be offended by the Filipino *radjo kawayan;* no one has privacy in this country! Of course I wonder if I might be your co-parent. I even worried about the future of that little girl when you were gone and for months out of contact with your friends. Please don't be concerned that I started a legal proceeding to learn if I might be the father. I might have needed a route to custody if you had met with mortal tragedy.

I'd sure like to see you again, and I'd like to meet your daughter, especially if I am her father. I wouldn't expect romance again, but I would hope that we could be friends. Perhaps you would be more comfortable if just we adults were to meet at first. Would the best place be your friend's house in Manila? Please give a date and time soon.

Very sincerely, Migo

She handed the letter to Marilu, who quickly read it and handed it back, looking inquiringly at Laura.

Laura finally said, "Now what?"

Marilu pondered. "You could squeeze in a meeting before you go."

"But why?"

"Maybe this whole legal thing could be dropped. Maybe he's not so dangerous as you're fearing."

"Could he stop me from taking Charlotte out of the country?"

"Hmm... That's a risk, but seems unlikely, because he'd know he'd blow his chances of cooperation with you."

"I suppose he could have already tried to prevent her departure, even if he doesn't know I have plane tickets."

"He probably learned about your tickets shortly after you booked. No secrets here, as you know!"

They sat for a short time.

Marilu spoke. "Looks to me like he's hoping for cooperation. We Filipinos don't rely on litigation for these matters."

"Hmm. I've been thinking about a question my classmate Grace asked me back in California: why did I shut him out of decision-making, from the moment I learned about my pregnancy? I guess now's the moment to revisit that decision."

"Do you want to talk about it?"

"Yeah, I'll try."

She propped the pillow against the bed's headboard and then pushed back into it to sit upright. "Back then, I thought that it'd be very hard for him to do as well in his career in the U.S. He was already building a strong reputation as a good journalist in your best newspaper, as you know, here in Manila. And I really wanted to work in the U.S."

"Was that it, then? Nothing about your feelings for each other? Love? On the other hand, perhaps you feared what he might do?"

"Hmm. I didn't think the romance was strong enough; didn't think it could survive the switch to the culture where *I'd* be the native. And yeah, fear… In high school and college, I heard from other girls that boys – men – were deathly afraid of getting stuck with a pregnancy charge… So, yeah, maybe I was afraid that he'd react negatively to my announcement. Maybe even accuse me of 'sleeping around.' I didn't, by the way."

"No fear that he'd try for custody?"

"No, not at all, but as you know, you and I talked about that just before I left for Indonesia."

"Why'd you risk coming back to this country last year, then? Surely you knew that you couldn't return without him hearing?"

"Well, I sure was naïve. I thought that because I'd be working out in that small town and going down to the south of this country and even to Indonesia, that people in Manila wouldn't notice me passing through."

"Might you, subconsciously, have wanted to have the confrontation with him about your decision to exclude him from your daughter's life?"

"No! … But I'm thinking, Marilu. I do believe in general that a child can do much better having experience with both parents. And I do believe that the father's involvement can be very important."

"So important that he should hear about what he's done? So that he can take responsibility?"

"Yeah... Marilu, I guess at the very least I could assure him that he's the father – that I didn't, say, adopt a child in California – and I could offer him visitation rights. But I still want to go back to the States. That's where I'd like to raise her. And I don't want to restart romance."

"So let's see if he can come here this evening after Charlotte's bedtime or tomorrow when she's having her last day for now in nursery school. Do you want me in or out of the meeting?"

"Oh, God, Marilu, you're such a valuable friend This is going so fast! Uh, how about the three of us at the start, and then you leave us on your terrace for a while?

.....

Marilu left, and then came back to Laura. "He'll come tomorrow at ten, in time for *merienda*."

.....

He came. They shared friendly but awkward greetings, tea, a little talk about the current feature story he was working on, about martial law and growing distrust of President Marcos. He inquired about Laura's work, expressed delight that Laura was working on the Chabacano language "that would help Filipinos respect the language and their heritage."
He inquired about Marilu's work on the ethnic minorities cultural museum at the new international airport. He asked about Marilu's children and about her husband and her parents. Her husband was at work, Marilu said, and that her two little ones were in nursery school today as usual. Laura added that her Charlotte was also in that nursery school.

Marilu signaled her maid for more tea, and then announced that she had some calls to make.

Now the two sat by themselves in the air-conditioned, shaded terrace.

"Laura." He held out his hands to her; she reached for them, and they looked intently into each other's eyes.

"I so appreciate that you're willing to see me. I want to reassure you that I won't try to rekindle romance. And I won't try to take away your daughter."

"Thank you for this, Migo."

They looked at each other again for a few moments.

"Can you tell me?"

"Yes, of course, you're the one."

"Oh, oh, oh! ..."He put his hands to his face, then down again. "But why...?"

She looked away, and then back to him. "It's so hard to justify. I was afraid you'd be angry, blame me, worry that I'd ask for support money or that you'd even demand abortion. Or demand marriage, and then on which side of the Pacific Ocean?"

"But I'd have welcomed..."

"I didn't discover the pregnancy until after returning to California. So I was already over there, and we'd already said goodbye. Goodbye, goodbye..."

"Now that you're here, and now that I know, what now, Laura? I don't want to hurt you, or her, in any way. I don't want to make you uncomfortable. Is there a way that we can cooperate? I mean, don't you agree that it's better for a child to have her father as well as her mother? We don't need any legal involvement."

"I'm thinking." She looked away for a while, into the trees outside. She looked back at Migo. "If there's no legal involvement, then my fears are dissolving. I'm willing for you to meet Charlotte. But it'd have to be this afternoon, because she and I will be leaving the country tomorrow for three months."

Taking the risk that he'd not keep it confidential, she told him about her two reports on U.S. involvement in Philippine matters and therefore her associated need to leave the country.

He responded that he had had communication with John Jackson and therefore knew that she had a report for him, but not the contents. "Because we're fellow journalists, and friends, you know."

"I really want to trust you, Migo. I fervently hope that you've earned it and will continue to earn it."

'They stood. He grasped her hands, and they both firmly squeezed.

God, does he already know about Willem? Maybe not, Cotabato is 500 miles away and now Willem is back in the Netherlands. Would Migo be so cooperative if he knew?

SPAIN, 1972

42. Sevilla: Find that 300-Year-Old Book!

Laura wanted to find Esquivel's 1662 document on the Spanish creole language then in the Spice Islands. She had learned about the document in California, in Cal's Bancroft Library. There she was excited to read in Murillo Velarde's 1749 book about an even earlier book, "*Gramatica y Diccionario de los Mardikas*" of Ternate, Indonesia, written in 1662 by Don Diego de Esquivel. Sevilla, she had learned, had the most extensive Jesuit archives. So she and Charlotte set out for Sevilla, Spain, to the best Jesuit archives in the world.

She and Charlotte found a little pension near the Archivo de las Indias in Sevilla, and settled in. The three-story building surrounded an open-air courtyard. The owner, Maria Hernandez, had canaries in several cages in the courtyard, and oh, did those canaries sing! Their melodies echoed throughout the 30 vertical feet of sunny, open space. They sang solos, they sang call-and-response duets. Furthermore, the six-year-old daughter of Maria and Julio, Elena, loved playing with four-year-old Charlotte. Before long, the family offered to watch (and play with) Charlotte while Laura went to the archives for their daily four open hours.

One large reading room in the archives held a small "club" of around 15 researchers who had converged mostly from around the Spanish speaking world. As a newcomer, she had a lot to learn, and others helped her, as they did each newcomer to the archives. Jesuit scribes through the previous five centuries had written carefully but with stylized handwriting, and they used many abbreviations. And the current researchers had to copy all by hand as well; cameras were not allowed.

She searched in vain for the 1662 document. She found other original documents from early European voyages, but no

Esquivel document. She continued to wonder about this priest who had written during his years in the Spice Islands about the Spanish contact language.

Each researcher was to sign in upon entering, and to specify certain documents, which the library staff would then retrieve in the closed stacks. This old-fashioned system of signing in served almost as a guest book. One day she discovered, by looking through this "guest book," that someone else several years earlier had been searching for the same document of 1662, Don Diego de Esquivel's *Gramatica y diccionario de los Mardikas*. He noted that he too had seen the 1749 citation by Murillo Velarde.

That researcher's name was Father Huberto Jacobs, s.j., of Antwerp, Belgium. Laura talked with the librarian who kept the guest book. He knew Father Jacobs, and reported the following to Laura. Father Jacobs had been searching for this document for a few years without success, and that his next and last place to search would be Santiago, Chile.
The librarian told Laura, "During the 18th Century, some of our precious Jesuit documents were used to polish shoes."

Our last chance as well, she thought, *We must go to Chile.*

CHILE, 1972

43. Chile: Last Chance

To prepare for the trip to Chile, Laura found in Sevilla the bibliographies of the Jesuit archive in Santiago. She sent letters to these Santiago contacts. One yielded especially good results, from an archivist and researcher in the National Archives at la Universidad Hurtado, Brother Rene Cortinez Castro.

On arriving in Santiago, she enrolled Charlotte in a nursery school nearby. Charlotte appeared to enjoy each of their few days in Santiago, even as she continued to learn Spanish.

Brother Rene Cortinez graciously met Laura. He managed his university's Antiquariat Library of Jesuits, and he graciously made an appointment with her for the next day. She met him in his office where he did a search in their card catalog, and then he took her into the stacks. With keys and ladder, he pulled out all the relevant volumes for her, and he seated her at a desk. He assured her that taking photos was okay. Using several rolls of film, she photographed all of the relevant documents, around 220 pages. Just one day in the archive sufficed, because, rather than handwriting as she had had to do in the Sevilla archives, here she could photograph.

What a quick way to capture this treasure trove!

Here's what she learned, of both new and known information for her:

First, Father Huberto Jacobs, the Belgian Jesuit priest, whom Brother Cortinez knew because Jacobs had come last year for research as well, and after his visit to Chile had just completed an enormous encyclopedia, in English as the *lingua franca*, of all the thousands of extant documents written by Jesuit scribes in the 16th and 17th centuries.

About Esquivel's grammar and dictionary, Jacobs had written "they've undoubtedly been lost forever." *Major disappointment!* thought Laura.

Second, Laura was fascinated to learn a little more about this man Esquivel from other documents delivered to her by Brother Cortinez.

- It was the clamor over spices that started European explorations in the late 15th century.

- In the 80 years after the Spaniards had conquered and expelled the Portuguese colonists from Ternate, and then settled there themselves, a creole form of Spanish had developed, perhaps getting relexified from a Portuguese creole, and that had taken on local language characteristics.

- By the 20th century, Spanish pidgins and creoles were still found in many of the places Portguese and Spaniards colonized as they had moved eastward to Asia and Southeast Asia, and westward to the Caribbean and Central and South America. But in the largest and longest-held colonies, local people learned Portuguese and Spanish, not a pidgin or creole.

In the 16th and 17th centuries, inter-European competition for these Spice Islands grew ever fiercer between Portuguese, English, French, and Dutch forces. During the 17th century, overwhelming Dutch power had been relentlessly moving eastward through Indonesia.

- Esquivel was born in Manila in 1620 to Spanish parents, and he probably never went to Spain.

- He became a priest around age 30, considered an unusually late age.

- Around 1650 he was sent out, probably by church headquarters in Madrid, on a mission to the small island of

Siao in Eastern Indonesia, at a time when Spain still had some – tenuous - control of the world-famous Spice Islands.

- The local "king," as he was called, of this small island then died. His widow begged Father Esquivel to take over the rule of the island. Esquivel complied but said he'd do it only temporarily while a successor could be found. Engaging in local politics was strictly forbidden by the Jesuit order.

- Word of this transgression got back to headquarters in Madrid, and the edict came back that Esquivel had violated the Jesuit charter. Therefore, Esquivel was ordered to move to his new station in Ternate, one of the (slightly) larger and more important of the Spice Islands, and where other Spanish Jesuit priests were stationed. Some 200 local people there had been converted (from a Muslim population) and now served as servants and guards for the missionaries.

- In 1662, the Dutch forced the Spaniards to pull back their SEA missions. They retreated to Manila, their biggest Southeast Asian holding. From Ternate, they decided to take the 200 Christians as well, who were in danger of losing their lives to the surrounding Muslims or to the inevitably conquering Dutch. Probably Esquivel had a big part in the decision to take these 200 to Zamboanga in the southern Philippines and to Manila, 600 miles farther to the north.

- Local Manila Filipinos didn't accept the newcomers, so, probably arranged by Esquivel, they were settled in an uninhabited area at the mouth of the Maragondong river which was at the mouth of the Manila Bay. They named their settlement Ternate after their homeland. There, they could serve the important function of giving notice to Manila if the Chinese warlord Koxinga dared enter the Manila Bay. Koxinga had sent a letter announcing that he'd be coming soon to conquer the Philippines. To give notice, the new settlers would set a bonfire at the peak of their mountain, and the fire and smoke would be seen by lookouts in Manila,

80 miles to the west. Not long after 1662, Koxinga died, so the threat was off. But the settlers stayed.

- In 1664, Father Esquivel died, at the age of 44.

Laura wondered why he had taken on the priesthood so late, at age 30. Back then, few people lived to age 40.

Laura also wondered about his language-learning skills. She loved the topic of language learning, both as a first and as a second – or more – language. She was fascinated with her daughter's language learning facility. Four-year-old Charlotte was now learning Spanish, and Laura had previously observed how Charlotte had learned some Tagalog and Chabacano in the Philippines. Of course Charlotte was learning these languages on her own, without a class, and without translation help. Laura reflected that she was curious about other people who probably learned local languages on their own, perhaps including Esquivel in the 17th century, and maybe Wallace, in the 19th century. Wallace had undoubtedly learned the Moluccan form of Malay (or Bahasa Indonesia) during his ten years in Ternate – but with some of that time spent in Singapore, where Malay was and is spoken. But for most of his ten years in "the Malay Archipelago" he lived in Ternate, a thousand miles to the east, studying the evolution of Spice Islands flora and fauna.

Laura also became more aware that her passion to learn about Esquivel, the Jesuit missionary of 300 years earlier, dated back to her first reading about him. She had for so long wanted to track down his volume, and more about him as well. *Didn't find it, or him. Gone forever!*

Now she found herself wondering about her current man. *Do I have as much passion about this new man, Willem? I'm discovering that my passion for him is dissipating. He's married. He was somewhat wimpy in the forest. He's very settled in another country.*

44. Letters Lumbered Along

Letters were carried over land, they sailed through doldrums on the tropical seas, they flew through storms, they were illegally razored open in back rooms of post offices. For the first couple of weeks Willem and Laura tried to exchange letters between Manila and Utrecht, a six and a half thousand mile journey. Each person wrote knowing that the recipient might never receive the letter, or it would likely reach its destination long after the recipient would have sent a missive. Their letters would cross in the mail. Willem wrote from his university office in the Netherlands, and Laura then reported on her investigations in Spain and her planned trip to Chile and stopover to visit her mother in California. And then, after three months, Laura and Charlotte would return to Manila and Ternate, Philippines, if allowed.

Each of their letters included questions about how the other's work was progressing and included reports on their own work. They always ended with tentative plans and definite hopes for meeting again, but where? – "Your country, mine, or one of the two Ternates?"

He wrote, "Why the hell did I come back here to the Netherlands? Your Ternate sounds great, and I'll dream of you in my Ternate.

"It's just got to be work, work, work for now. I must set aside so many recent memories and feelings... To set aside? Well, the work will not stop the welling images of you in the Cotabato forest and at the river.

"I received two of your letters at once, but apparently you'd received neither of mine. And maybe this one will cross with your next.

"All these words, to say what else, but Love, Willem"

Laura wrote: "Marilu has been advising me about my career. I told her a job is my biggest worry, so I'm sending letters off to 15 people this week. And I'm trying my darndest to rekindle enthusiasm for my work here in Ternate, the enthusiasm I felt before our experiences in Indonesia, the two plus months in the forest, and then coming back to live under martial law. Martial law here in Manila has left me with a strong impulse to run out of the country. Not martial law itself, because I'm very interested in what's going on, but because I'm worried what its impact might have on my Charlotte.

"Bob Fox, remember him? – American archaeologist, here ever since World War II – He and his wife invited me to dinner. After, he went outside with me to wait for a taxi, and he brought up the subject of Chabacano. He said, 'Don't get mixed up with Chabacano, whatever you do. If you do, you'll have all the Philippine linguists down your throats. They feel that that is a job for Filipinos.' I think it's about David [a Filipino anthropologist] and no one else. In fact, sometime during those few minutes I asked him who wanted to research the language, if it was David, and he mumbled something mildly affirmative. I really hadn't heard this before. I've been naïve, I think. And I did hear it from another linguist as well, But I'll continue my work!"

"For continuing to write up, I definitely cannot go back to Cal. In fact, I'll write to James, the department chair, to tell him I won't be able to teach a course in the Fall. Everything seems to depend on a job, that is, a real job, not a $2,000 per term Teaching Assistant job."

"Willem, when martial law started here, I almost called you to tell you not to worry about our safety. I had a friend call my mother on ham radio through the U.S. navy base at Subic Bay to a local person near her in California."

Two weeks later, Laura wrote from Sevilla. "We stopped in Cochin, India, on our way here to Spain. I found the spice market, and they are still selling cloves and nutmegs, but it's just a tiny vestige of Cochin's importance in the Spice Trade before 1662. And after we leave Spain, and then Chile, we'll stop in California to visit our family, especially my mother. We'll leave there after the December holidays to return to Manila – that is, if I can still get in. "Time to put Charlotte to bed. She's adjusting here in Sevilla very well. She has friends already, and she chases around with them a good share of the day when she's not in nursery school."

"It's only that I'm lonely. The slightest distraction seems to upset my work and my setup here. But loneliness is almost a constant. Why? Another touch of culture shock, I guess. What I'm missing here is a sign of real understanding about my situation. And I'm not even sure I understand myself! Marilu back in the Philippines comes close to understanding, but not quite..."

He wrote, "I think about you a lot, and daily, but by now I don't have that panicky, frustrated feeling of not being able to survive without you. This time, *verdomme*, (dammit), I'll be realistic about the impossibility of any commitment with you, and I'll simply accept what is possible. Oh, Lord, the prospect of seeing you say, for only a few days every two years, is grim. I can't even get out of here – the weekly teaching – to meet you in Sevilla!"

In another letter, he wrote, "Darling, I must be going into second youth. I go to the mail shelf with startling frequency. The secretary asks me, 'You expecting something important?' I prop your picture up on my desk, I look through my window at the sky and the linden tree and wonder where you are, if you're okay, what you're doing and, aw heck. Write when you can – like now! Love, Willem."

Laura wrote, "I worry about your wife finding out, and I don't want to hurt her. But it's your risk. ...But is it worth the sacrifices, to spend even a little time with me? I've worked very hard not to build any dependencies on you, or any foolish fantasies with you. And I'll go about my business of looking for a job.   I want to let you know that our relationship is safe, meaning that I won't be putting any pressure on you. Willem, don't worry about me thinking the relationship is too great a burden on me; it's you I'm worried about. But about gossip: I wonder if you might want to beat all the gossips and mention this romance to your wife."

Laura: "You said it: life's very short, and let's experience what we can and minimize the frustrations." ... Having Charlotte puts a big crimp in my possibilities with men, but I most certainly don't begrudge having her; I accept her as my biggest responsibility. Let's just do what we can and be discreet. Confining ourselves to communicating only with letters might be a heck of a lot better than having a crisis, a big mess, and possibly severing relations. This is to let you know that I certainly do not want to end things, but I don't want to cause a mess."

Willem: "I just have to see you, so your contact info is very important, be it via cable or telephone."

Willem: "You'll say I'm inconsistent. True, but what else can one be in this kind of situation? To have you. To not really have you. That's one situation. Then this work thing. To say work, work, and really do it. – for a while; then lapse, justifying it in one thousand ways. Then, *verdomme* – work is the thing, so go, go. But, Laura, you are spending too much time on the ultimate goals, all the abstracts of career and desire for respect and me. For I am not the most exciting, I am not the most beautiful, I am not the most of anything. But apart from me, the other things are worth thinking about, and setting aim for. You should write the papers and letters you need to. But plans? And much of your requirement for self-esteem will be fulfilled without me, when you get the job – and you'll get it."

Willem: "Deserve me? God, what am I offering you?... God, you will, in the end, make me feel guilty.

"I wish I could make my letters crackle with great local and social happenings, but *niks*, nothing. Nothing except for thoughts, thoughts, thoughts of you, you, you.

"I've got to divert myself with work, otherwise I find that I'm doing nothing but looking at your picture and thinking of you all day and night. At work I'm only reasonably successful, but it's better than abject resignation to an as yet unattainable ideal. You should think of what I said when we parted, that you have to do what you want... Now I'm letting my fantasies transport me away from reality, like it's too long before we can meet, and by then you'll be in Chile. I selfishly hope you'll get so involved with work looking for that 300-year-old man that you can't get away from Spain for months!

"Laura, is it inevitable that I cause you unhappiness? For me, memory and anticipation are diversions enough, but you... I have fantasies of meeting in Sevilla, and then up into the mountains!"

Willem: "Since our experiences way back in July, August, September, my feelings for you have intensified, until by September I was no longer concerned with presenting just that part of me that appealed. Together, we have had to cope with 'all elements or none' in each other's characters. But through it all, doesn't the constancy of the one real emotion show itself to you?"

Laura: "A couple of jobs have shown up: a crummy one at Cornell, a temporary one at Tulane. I've heard things are going slowly for everyone. I'll apply, as usual, but getting weary."

In January, she wrote "Marilu has learned that my name is no longer on the *persona non grata* list. Charlotte and I can now return to the Philippines. we'll fly from Santiago to Manila International Airport on 1/7/73. May I ask you to check to see if my name ever got onto a POLRI list in Indonesia?"

Back in Ternate, Laura wrote late in the evenings under a kerosene lantern She sat at a little *lauan* wood desk with a *katol* coil under her chair to discourage the several mosquitos buzzing in her room. Now and then she glanced over to the net-draped bed to be assured that her little daughter was sleeping soundly and safely. And later she climbed into the mosquito-net-canopied bed over the thin kapok-filled mattress next to her daughter.

She wrote about the vegetable garden she had started after cleaning out a trash heap at the back garden of the house where she and Charlotte were guests. This garden Laura was contributing for the house owners. "The okra plants are now six feet tall. They look like trees, and the fruits are also very big (ca. 1 x 8") though tasty. Also germinated so far: bean stalk and ginger root. Now the neighbors are asking for seeds, and a happy consequence is how a beautiful, large vegetable garden has appeared across the street, in what used to be a vacant lot. The owner of this garden told me I should have "castrated" the plants (*mag kapon*) when they were small in order that the energy would have been concentrated on fruits not bush. I watched him, and he meant that I should pinch off some branches while still very small."

Laura wrote again, "I hadn't made a compost pile, so I'm just putting more horse manure on the garden. Now people across the street have two big gardens, much nicer than mine, but stimulated by mine, they said. I expect more to crop up, since part of the martial law edict is to clean up everything, including keeping pigs tied up, so people now don't have their threat to dig up gardens.

"Charlotte is outside this window pouring water on a pig, who seems quite content."

PHILIPPINES, 1973

45. Lotsa Traffic

"Laura, you're scaring me!"

"Gotta drive like this to survive, Willem!"

"But you're going to kill us! Look out! That car almost crashed into us! ... Now how'd you dare go first?"

When on her frequent but short visits to Manila, Laura stayed at Marilu's house in Magallanes Village, a gated, patrolled compound with enormous mansions and beautifully manicured gardens. Marilu always made a car available to her, and Laura always turned down the kind offer of a chauffeur.

Willem had stopped by the Philippines on his way back to Ternate, Indonesia, for his next two years of research. Laura had gone in to Manila to meet him. And here they were in super busy downtown.

What a challenge to brave driving here! Anarchic! she thought. *I do see a traffic cop once in a while, but these drivers don't worry about them.*

A thousand new cars a month were being imported to Manila, even though 100% duty was added to the American and Japanese car prices. *Mainly these drivers are all new drivers! They're mostly young, and they're crazy!*

When she first arrived in the Philippines five years earlier, and before she herself braved driving, she noticed patterns, and she felt comforted that she could begin to predict other drivers' behaviors.

- On the few expressways in the city, lanes marked on the road were hardly adhered to. A road marked for two lanes each way was frequently made into three or even four chaotic lanes. Lane changing was frequent and aggressive.

- On roads with sidewalks, that is, within shopping or fancy residential areas, sidewalks were frequently used as "passing lanes."

- During monsoon season in Manila, May through December, many roads flooded, usually up to thigh high if you were walking. Some roads had a sewer system under the middle of the road, and manhole covers were frequently "taken," that is, missing.

- Nevertheless, drivers routinely used these flooded roads, even though the open sewer holes were completely invisible when the streets were flooded. Now and then a car wheel would get stuck in such a hole, with the rear end of the car sticking up helplessly above the water. Taxi drivers knew where to drive in order to avoid the manholes, covered or not, and so other drivers followed taxis through flooded streets. Laura learned to do the same.

- In the city and out in the country, most roads were single lane two-way or even one-way. Oncoming traffic was sometimes handled with polite gestures of agreement on who would do the pulling to the side and who would do the passing. Usually, though, the confrontation was treated like a game of chicken: who will give up?

- This kind of confrontation was encountered most frequently at intersections. The "zipper" informal rule of taking turns that Laura had learned while driving in California didn't work here at all. Instead, all drivers were ready to gun the engine and quickly squeeze into a perceived potential open space ahead.

- Laura noticed she was relieved to see that *all* the drivers were alert. She could count on them noticing her when she made a move. This was quite in contrast with her earlier experiences in California. Twice she'd been a passenger in an accident there, and each time the other driver apologized, saying, "I'm so sorry, I just didn't see your car." Here in Manila, almost all of the drivers were young men. Perhaps a third of them drove solo in their cars, but the majority appeared to be chauffeurs, because she saw people in the back seat. *They're young, they're alert, they drive like we're playing in bumper cars!*

She continued her report to Willem. "I kind of like driving here, now that I've gotten accustomed to the local rules!"

"Rules?" Willem asked.

"Well, 'local behavior,'" she said. "Anyway, people drive like this as well in Jakarta, right?"

"Well, in Jakarta we still have so many *betjaks* and pedicabs, and the roads have even more ruts and pedestrians and bicyclists and ducks than here, so it's much harder for a car to travel with any speed. (Looks like you have chickens on roads here, not ducks.) And out in Ternate, we have mostly *betjaks*, very few four-wheel motor vehicles yet. So I haven't really experienced this. How do you dare? I mean, you're pretty aggressive out here on the road!"

"Well, look at the drivers inside these cars. We all look at each other; we're not anonymous like in California. We're all looking to see who dares to go first, or, alternatively, who can be intimidated to wait. And whereas as a woman if out on a football field, say, I'd be at a disadvantage confronting a young man. But in contrast, here on the road, my motor is just as strong as theirs. They know that I can accelerate and go as fast as they can. I let them see from my face that I'm not intimidated, and I intend to shove through. Oh, I'll be polite if I have the opportunity to move along, but only then. Sometimes I generously offer the right of way to another, but then I make a show of it on my face."

"Isn't there a middle path, somehow?"

"I don't think so. It's either jump into the fray or sit helplessly in traffic with cars swarming around on all sides. Even more dangerous."

"God."

"Yeah. It's kinda fun, but I do like walking in the *boondocks* a lot better. What you in Indonesia call the *rimbu*, right?"

46. Traffic Ticket

Laura told him about a recent traffic danger she had experienced. "I had another big reminder last week that foreigners have special challenges, including in traffic."

On the afternoon of January 14th she accepted the loan of Marilu's second car, a small light green Toyota Corolla, to check on her mail and to keep an appointment at Ateneo de Manila University. She had driven it before, with gratitude, because it could cut an hour off her travel time each way.

At the major intersection of Highway Epifanio de los Santos and Cubao Boulevard, the yellow light before her changed to red, so she stopped. In the next lane, two cars went through the red light. And then in what seemed like slo-mo in her rear-view mirror, she saw a car behind her, coming, coming, and *Oh, no, they wouldn't would they?!* – crashed, rear-ended. Looking into her rear-view mirror and still in disbelief, she saw inside that car that the driver and the passenger maneuvered themselves into switching places.

Hmm, I wonder why?

She jumped out of her car, and the driver and passenger did the same from their car.

Then Laura noticed a traffic policeman approaching them from his station, a tiny turret at the side of this enormous intersection: white, round, raised maybe 1-1/2 meters above the roads, with a red conical roof. The traffic cop had blown his whistle to stop all traffic. Dozens, and shortly, hundreds of cars all halted. "No room to move around us."

The passenger, formerly driver, approached the traffic cop and quietly spoke to him in urgent tones. The traffic cop approached Laura and asked for her driver's license.

She responded, in English, "I cannot carry it; it's as big as a magazine! I will just bring it to you. I'd like you to know that I had stopped at the red light when this car rear-ended me." The "driver," formerly passenger, said, "Not true; it was yellow light, and her car just stopped without warning."

The policeman looked at the other's driver's license, noted it down, and told him he was released. The two men drove away. To Laura he said, "No driver's license? Then you must follow me to the police station."

The bumpers of the two cars were damaged but apparently not the structures of either car, and Laura had no trouble driving hers. She followed the policeman on his motorcycle. She filled out a form with her name, age, and local address, and checked the box for her promise to appear the next day with her driver's license.

It took her an hour to reach Marilu's house on the opposite side of Manila. Marilu ran out to the driveway to announce that a policeman had come and had left a warrant for her arrest!

"Arrest?! I just signed a promise to bring my driver's license to the police station tomorrow!"

She paused and then asked, "This warrant is in English?!"

"Yes, it says that you are arrested for reckless driving and driving without a license. If you do not surrender yourself by tomorrow morning, then you will be booked and incarcerated."

"What?! Let me see it." And she read. "Says here that I am to appear in court tomorrow morning at 10:00. Very fast. Marilu, can you find out how I should pay *tong* (bribe) and how much? Do I put 100 pesos inside of my driver's license papers? Or what?"

"Oh, and of course, Marilu, I'll pay for the damage to your car and drive it to and from the repair shop."

Marilu went to her phone to find an informant for this business of *tong*.

Next morning, Laura drove the bumper-damaged Toyota Corolla to the courthouse in Cubao City. Hers would be the third case. She waited; she was called up to the judge, who told her that the arresting policeman had not shown up, and so the case was dismissed. She hadn't even had to show her driver's license (or pay *tong*).

Willem said, "Oh, I'm sorry this happened to you, Laura."

"Well, it's one more example of our challenge as foreigners. I mean the other drivers and the police expected that I didn't have a local person of power to back me up. We Americans are demi-gods, living close to paradise in America, but then if we get into trouble, the moment might be seen as an opportunity for revenge for all these years of colonization."

"*Ja*, similar for Dutch in Indonesia."

Laura said, "Probably. Probably you've had such experiences there too. I was frequently implored, kind of jokingly, 'Please marry me so I can go to the U.S.' Or, 'Please adopt my child so he can get a U.S. education, and then send him back home to me.' And 'Please sponsor me for an immigration visa.'"

"*Ja*. But usually I could just say, "I'm married; I already have a wife and children."

Laura said, "How many times did I hear from older Filipinos that "American soldiers rescued us from the Spanish occupiers, and then again from the Japanese occupiers, and we'll be forever grateful?" I have always answered, 'Never mind Spain and Japan. We also are colonizers. You deserve more self-respect.' And I thought to myself, 'I'll even help remind you of your history with my *magnum opus* on one of your languages, Chabacano.'"

Willem gave a kind response. "Sometimes words can change the world."

"But you do see, Willem, that this was an opportunity to seek revenge on us colonials. I was in a position of very little power, kind of helpless. I think I told you already, didn't I? that shortly after President Marcos declared martial law, my fellow American and historian, Dr. Henry Scott, was arrested and has been in prison now for five months now, allegedly for inciting his adopted sons to protest martial law."

"So you could be in danger again as well. The authorities could somehow get reminded of your articles criticizing the Indonesian government for allowing Americans to exploit lumber, and the Philippine government for allowing Americans to bomb Basilan in order to exploit oil. In other words, you could be seen as a whistle blower and trouble-maker."

"Yeah, that's a risk. Foreigners need to be especially careful. The traffic incident reminded me of one time when I re-entered the Philippines from Hong Kong, on the last flight, arriving after ten p.m. In Customs, I was informed that my re-entry visa had expired. Before I had left the Philippines, those exit and re-entry visas had taken me two full days to get, including waiting in hours in lines while dripping with sweat. When I arrived with a recently expired re-entry permit, I was informed that I'd be deported on the next flight out. But the next flight wasn't until 9:00 the next morning. I hadn't noticed that my visa had expired three days earlier. I had had a sudden serious three-day delay in California."

Willem said, "What a frustration: just three days..."

"Yeah, it would have been so easy to re-do the re-entry visa, because it was handwritten, and mine was a carbon copy. I could have changed the date from 8/11 to 8/14 just by putting in a piece of carbon paper and then drawing to make a 4 out of the 1. But I hadn't noticed."

Willem asked, "So did you sleep that night arriving from Hong Kong?"

Laura responded, "Well, I could only wonder what to do. Then I thought of Corazon Aquino, whom I had met, the wife of Benigno Aquino, a national senator. I called her at night! Her person informed her who informed someone, and that person called me back to say that the deportation was called off."

"Wow, Laura. You've had more experiences like this than I have had in Indonesia. But I agree, a foreigner, even of exalted prestige if not status, like an academic, is vulnerable."

"Yes. And forget about supporting yourself in this country on a local academic salary. I know two American academics who have spent their entire careers in the Philippines. One of them has lived on U.S. research grants, and the other is a missionary, paid by tithes from back home."

"Well, but you have a grant from the U.S., right?"

"Yes. I have given serious thought about staying on in the Philippines, but financially I'd have a third world income. I started teaching this semester at Ateneo de Manila University. Not that it pays living expenses! My pay at the university *almost* pays for my transportation costs from Ternate, two bus rides and two hours away."

Willem said, "*Ja*, same for local academics in Indonesia. They frequently take two full time positions at different universities in order to support themselves and their families.

"Hard to manage in a developing country, hmm. But hey, do you have to come clear into the city to get your mail?"

"Yes, it's about getting a job. During my entire time here, each time I've come into the city, I come to get my APO mail at the embassy, because I'm looking for job openings in the States. Colleagues send me notices, my university department sends out a monthly notice, and I receive *The Chronicle of Higher Education*, which has job notices. And usually while still in the city, I write up and send off more applications to universities in California and the rest of the U.S., even internationally. I carry my little portable typewriter back and forth, and paper and carbon paper and envelopes. I buy U.S. stamps at the APO office.'"

"And still no bites yet?"

"Only one, at ANU, in Canberra, Australia, and I've made it to second base."

"Australia!"

She responded, "But to be truthful, these brushes with the law here have intensified my longing for home, where I could be an ordinary person."

"That's hard here, isn't it? Of course you're always noticed here."

"You can hear that I'm wondering whether this is the place for me – and Charlotte - long term. Perhaps the greatest difficulty as a foreigner is not having a lifetime buildup of family and other protectors. At least in Spain and Chile I looked a little like locals, with similar skin colors and features. But even though I could speak Spanish, I was a foreigner culturally and with accent. Here I also get tired of being noticed even before I talk."

"Your blond and blue colors..."

"And by the way, you can see that I'm taller than even most men here. Just ordinary height in the U.S.

"But now my feelings are changing from, say, a year ago. I love this country: the people, the weather, the warm air and warm water, the beautiful trees, flowers, tasty tropical fruits and vegetables, the volcanic peaks, the coral atolls. But I'm getting tired of being a foreigner. I can't get a long-term job here, and I miss home."

She turned to him. "Hey, Willem, you wrote that you were very lonely even at home, and you told me that you've overcome most of it. How have you handled it?"

Willem answered "*Ja*, I had to overcome it as well."

Laura waited. They were both quiet for a while.

He finally replied, "With time, I guess."

47. Special Garden for Laura

Laura invited Willem to her field site, "her" Ternate. She took a risk because she was behaving very differently than the women did in the small town. There, no woman traveled with an unrelated man if not accompanied by other adults. Now Laura did have the company of her daughter, but the four-year-old could hardly be considered a chaperone. In Ternate, if a man and woman traveled alone together, they were considered as "eloping" and that they would stay together in the future.

A year earlier, settling into the village, she had decided to lie.

"Where's your husband, her father?" she was asked, in Chabacano.

"*Oh, está dehando in Manila porké necesita trabahar.*" (Oh, he stayed in Manila because he must work), she responded in Spanish. Of course she was there to start learning Chabacano, and with its around 80% vocabulary from Spanish, she hoped she would be understood. Maybe her host family really did understand her speech; maybe their frowns were about her message, that she had traveled away from her husband to come to their town.

And now she was bringing another man! She had warned Willem in advance, "Now, behave, please! Don't touch me, don't walk very close to me, don't smile at me in a romantic way. In other words, please don't blow my cover."

"Blow your cover?"

"I mean, please let them think that you are just a business acquaintance. Think you can manage that?"

"Of course, but it'll be hard."

"And I'll ask Gabriel's brother and his family to put you up. These are one-room houses, and I don't want any talk going around the village about night time. Okay?"

"Yes, m'dear, but what if your little Charlotte wants to hold my hand? She already has now and then, you know."

Laura pondered. "Well, I'll have a little talk with her as well."

At Manila's bus station, Laura asked around for the next regional bus out to Ternate. The three of them squeezed into a seat toward the back, Laura first, and she put little Charlotte in her lap. Willem's long legs stuck out into the aisle, and he had to stand up many times to let other passengers pass farther to the back. He carried a big sack which he put on his lap. The driver started up the noisy engine, and then honking all the while, drove around the big earth parking lot several times. Not having quite enough customers, he broadened his loops to several nearby streets before finally starting the two-hour drive to Ternate.

The bus driver was a young Cavite man, his left arm very brown from the sun, his hair matted down with coconut oil, with a large bandana on his head that he occasionally poured water onto from a recycled coke bottle. He wore a ragged white t-shirt with an *Aji no Moto* (M.S.G. – monosodium glutamate) logo on the front, and faded navy polyester pants.

In Ternate, Laura showed Willem all around and introduced him to people. Their evening and night went smoothly. On the second day, Willem said, "Laura, would you like me to add to your vegetable garden? I brought some seeds and even some seedlings and small orchid plants."

"Oh, is *that* what's in your bag? I'd be delighted!"

Gabriel and his wife, Corazon, appeared happy as well, and they promised to water the garden regularly when Laura was away in Manila, so Willem got to work with Laura's and even little Charlotte's help. "Let's put the beans here, and the parsley there. Where do you think we should put these orchids? Gabriel suggested a more prominent place in the front of the house and brought a stack of clay pots for the orchids. Willem, Laura, and Charlotte lovingly placed one orchid in each of eight pots, tamped earth around the small plants, placed them carefully in front of the house, and then watered all the plantings.

Next morning Laura decided to take Willem out to a rocky peninsula a quarter hour's walk from town. Charlotte begged to stay behind to continue to play with a neighbor girl, Alyssa. The two girls looked for small seashells that would fit into slightly larger shells. Laura got the parents' agreement, so Laura and Willem ventured out without Charlotte.

"I can't believe you enhanced our garden for us." Laura admired the handiwork as they passed "her" house.

"I loved doing it. Legacy from my father. When I was a child and we visited relatives, he'd work in their garden or even make a new one for them. House gift, and he escaped sitting inside talking with them."

"Ha! Well, we'll have this little garden to remember you by long after you go back to *your* Ternate."

The coconut palms shaded the sandy path leading them away from Ternate's little delta. Soon they left the shade to make their way over to a point with a jumble of large white broken coral rocks. A few short forest trees struggled their way up through the rocks, so short that they offered no respite from the late morning sun. It shone indirectly as well with reflection from the sea beside them.

Willem said, "Trees... maybe 5-6 years old. Do you know why these rocks are piled here?"

"To make a deeper passage to shore. Several of the young men in town now have inboard motors. Their boats sit lower in the water, so they dynamited some of the table corals, and they threw the pieces up here."

"And hey," Willem pointed. "Cloth strips tied to some trees, fluttering. Do you know why?"

"That's what I wanted to show you. I clearly still have plenty to learn about the language and customs, so I'll be here for many more months. Antero told me that people who are sick or have other problems come out here, murmur incantations, and tie strips of old t-shirts to bushes and trees. These people are Christians, but they still have plenty of pre-Christian beliefs."

They sat on the rocks for a while, looking out at the peaceful, almost glassy sea. The horizon shimmered a watery mirage, disguising the line separating water from sky. Laura looked around to see if they had been followed, perhaps by pesky little boys, but even looking carefully into the shade of the trees, she could see no one.

Willem saw an opportunity. "Laura, please come to Indonesia again. Now is the time, don't you think? I've checked with POLRI, and you're not on a 'no entry' list. And this time bring your daughter. We need more time together."

She was quiet for some time. She reflected on the recent months away from him, when, during her *persona non grata* status in the Philippines, she had traveled to two distant countries to learn more about Chabacano. *If I went to Indonesia now, I'd have a different perspective, kind of like when you first hear about a person, having difficulty remembering the new information. But then, after meeting the person, one's memory is much sharper about the face, the name, their history. So on my next visit I'd see the Spice Islands with a deeper, more historical, perspective.*

She had another reason to go: she and Willem needed to talk about their future - that is, if they would have a future together. And she hadn't forgotten her contemplative experience with the clove tree back in June, when she reflected on her new excitement of meeting Willem. She wanted to visit that clove tree again.

She turned to him. "Okay, I'll come. But first, let's go, just the two of us, down to Zamboanga for two days. I want to show Zamboanga to you. We can stay in a special retreat by ourselves, and we can talk."

"Okay my dear, of course I can find two more days here with you!"

But she worried. "Now, let's go back. Charlotte's familiar here, but I don't want to leave her too long."

Under trees again, they soon returned to houses on the sea edge of the village. Under her neighbor's house, Laura could just manage to see Charlotte still playing with Alyssa.

Coming to Gabriel and Corazon's house, Willem pointed. "But hey, where are the orchids?" The orchid pots were gone from the new garden in front of the house, and the indentation the pots had made in the soil had been smoothed over. "Couldn't have been animals."

"Charlotte," Laura called as she neared the girls, "do you know what happened to the flowers we planted yesterday?"

Charlotte unfolded her crossed legs, walked close to her mother, and softly said, "I saw that Alyssa didn't have any flowers, so I thought we should share with her. We have so many vegetable seeds and plants."

"But why didn't you ask me?"

"Well, you were gone, and I felt so sorry for Alyssa. She looked up at Willem and then back to her mother. "You aren't mad at me, are you?"

Laura said, "I don't know what to think. I'm astounded. I'll think. In the meantime, you can go back to play."

Charlotte ran back to sit with Alyssa under her house, and Laura and Willem noticed the same row of orchids, now in front of Alyssa's house.

Laura and Willem sat on the ground under "her" house, out of earshot of the girls.

"I'm so sorry, Willem. She certainly doesn't seem respectful of your gifts for our garden."

"Laura, you have a very clever daughter. Of course she doesn't like us together. I'm intruding on her relationship with you. And instead of having a tantrum over my presence, she took, to her, seemingly justifiable but subtle action against me. Super clever. I'm not at all mad at her. I kind of admire her!"

48. Could This Be Real Love?

Charlotte was asleep upstairs, the whole community appeared to have retired, and Willem and Laura went out to the front of Gabriel and Corazon's house, sitting discreetly apart, on a horizontal log, but delighted that they were alone.

"No one is around; no one can hear us. Laura, let's talk about our love."

"Good idea! Look, the stars are out tonight, and we can see the Southern Cross. Are we just starry eyed?" She looked at him, and smiled. He did too, but she noticed in that smile a hint of seriousness. *Why'd he bring this up? We both know that this can't last. Maybe he's going to call the finish?*

But then he said, "I'm serious. We're not just 25-year-olds, falling in love, oblivious to rational decisions. But like a young man, I've fallen for you, I've never met anyone like you, and I just want to be with you. I miss you terribly when we're not together. I want for us to stay together."

"Mm, I've fallen for you as well, and I also think about you constantly when we're not together." She paused. "But let's try to be rational: first and most of all, you're married."

"Yes. But, do you think you can manage to talk about us for a moment as if I were not married?"

She asked, "You mean, otherwise, are we meant for one another? Or, another way of considering, are we good for one another?"

"Oh, yes! For instance, do we really love one another, or is our attraction mainly carnal? Out here in Southeast Asia, away from home, perhaps a little lonely, both foreigners?"

Laura considered. "Maybe. Or, clinging together during our traumatic situation, our 'rumble in the jungle' for two plus months!"

"Yes, all that. But I think it's bigger. It's a miracle that we've found one another."

Laura questioned him. "We've fallen in love, but will it last? I mean, they say that when falling in love, everyone puts on rosy colored glasses. But when, inevitably, the glasses come off, could we stand the test of time?"

Willem answered, "I'd do anything to be with you, for the rest of our lives."

"Willem, you're older than I am, more settled in your career. But did you have any failed romances in your past? I mean, before you met and married, did you fall for someone else, think she was the most wonderful person in the world, and later fall out of love?"

"Well, not really, I mean, only in high school. We grew apart, and I wondered what I had seen in her."

"Hmm. Willem, I'm younger, but maybe I've traveled this road more. No relationship stays in the "falling in love" stage, and at least in modern days, most relationships cannot successfully transition - the inevitable transition - after those rosy colored glasses fall off."

"I won't find fault in you, Laura."

"Time would tell."

He laughed as he stretched out to reach her hand, and said, "Come on now, what faults do you find in me? – I mean, besides being married?"

She laughed. "Let's see. You like to puff on your pipe, several times a day, now that we're out of the forest. It doesn't bother me much now, but it could. I always said I wouldn't be attracted to a smoker."

"Dear Laura, for you, I'd even consider giving up my pipe." He smiled and sat back on his seat on the log.

He added, "I don't have much experience with falling in love that maybe wouldn't last, but I do know a poem to share with you. It's in Dutch; indulge me, and I'll translate."

> De Zee zingt haar lied
> Over Wind, Regen, de Golven
> Deinend in het ritme
> Zingt ze over Jou
>
> Ze fluistert zacht je naam
> Nog net kan ik het horen
> Als een zilte fluisterstem
> Golvend in mijn oren
>
> Dan ebt ze plotseling weg
> De melodie versterft
> Een vloed van Gevoelens
> Voor altijd in mijn hart gekerfd...

"It's by Peter Alting."

"And in English?"

"Yes, but my translation is primitive."

> Sea sings her song
> About Rain, Wind, Waves
> Swaying in rhythm
> She sings about you.
>
> She whispers softly your name
> I just cannot hear it
> When a salty wave whispers

Billowing in my ears

Then she suddenly fades away
The melody dies
A flood of Emotions
Are forever carved into my heart...

In spite of doing his best to honor Laura's request to behave like a business acquaintance, he reached out again for her hand and gently pressed it. They searched each other's eyes.

Laura broke their reverie. "In the poem, they no longer see one another, but we don't know for what reason. Hmm... Willem, could, would we transition to real loving? For instance, do we really want the best for each other?"

Willem sighed. "I suppose I'd have to admit that the best for you is not to get hooked up with a married man. In your thirties, you're in the prime of your life. And if you're ever to have another child, now is the time."

She looked away from him. "Yeah."

Willem grabbed her hand again and held it tightly. "God, I'd love to have children with you!" and he squeezed her hand again.

After a short time, she pulled away and looked at him, returning to her earlier question. "Willem, do you really want the best for me? I wonder, I ponder. You urge me to stay with linguistics, with contact languages, because I have a long investment in these topics; I know a lot. But is your view short sighted? Might you see your own continued success in academia and just expect that stability would be good for me too? I'm not sure there's a position for me in a university. There's only a very outside chance that my specialized research topic, a contact language, will be my ticket to a university position. There's no job open in my field. Maybe I'll have to broaden my search."

"Laura, I want to be with you for the rest of our lives. I've been thinking about this a lot over the months we were apart. I want to marry you."

They held their outstretched hands tightly and looked at one another. But Laura said nothing.

49. Tree House

"Let's stay at one of my favorite places here in Zamboanga," Laura said. "I've learned how to rent the Tree House! We can stay there both nights."

Marilu had offered to take Charlotte and her two children on a two-day trip to her parents so that Laura and Willem could "talk it out." They fly down to Zamboanga on Mindanao Island. Even though 600 miles to the south, the flights would take only two hours each way, and Zamboanga was very special to her. She wanted to offer Willem the opportunity to experience being there.

In Zamboanga, the first public transportation to come along was the most usual in the city, a horse-drawn *calesa*.
"I always feel a little guilty having such a small horse pull me, the driver, and the tall *calesa*, especially up this big hill," she said. "But let's go."

Rolling gradually and slowly upward, both Willem and Laura admired neat gardens surrounding small rural houses. Bougainvillea plants of many colors: dark pink, light pink, peach, yellow, maroon, lavender, and white, grew profusely out of small cans placed in rows around modest corrugated tin-roof houses, houses that were held high on ten-foot stilts. Cans showed "Peel Gas" in yellow and red. A soft breeze caressed their arms; fragrant aromas of *plumeria* (frangipani) and *sampaguita* (Philippine jasmine) flowers kissed their noses.

The Tree House was attached to the base of a tall forest tree. Its approach was eight stone steps, not a ladder, and the interior was large enough for a double bed and even a small separate bathroom. Wide windows on three sides opened to a grand vista of a big "natural" pool below them. Beyond the pool they saw the city far below, and farther out, the azure

Sulu Sea glistening, and white sand-rimmed, forested islands in the distance.

Laura paid the *calesa* driver; his little horse clop-clopped him and his cart back down the hill.

"Let's swim first of all!" Laura offered, and quickly opened her satchel to pull out a suit.

"Is the pool nice?" Willem asked. He looked for his suit. "It looks more like a small lake down there, with its shallow edges and trees hanging over."

"You'll love it. Though the water is a little cool, the pool is quite clean. Sometimes families are there swimming, but I don't see anyone down there now, do you?"

They walked into the pool, they ducked under the water to get accustomed to its coolness, and they each swam to the far side and back. They looked for one another, they glanced around to be sure they were alone, and they then entangled their slippery limbs. They kissed long, and then again; they pulled their bodies closer together. Laura ducked under and came up with her head facing the sky to clear her hair from her face. With wet faces, they kissed again.

She pulled away. "Beat you to the other side!" and she swam away. He followed; they turned at the same time, and he was back on the near side standing in waist high water when she returned.

"Laura, I'm overwhelmed; we're in heaven." He couldn't say more; he couldn't even tease her that he had swum faster. He pulled her toward him for another long kiss, refreshing water dripping from both of them.

"Let's swim a few more laps and then go bathe," he said.

"Okay. There's a shower right down here; see?"

They walked up the little hill to their treehouse, entered, and closed the curtains.

.....

Sometime later, they sat on rattan lounges on their balcony, resting, awestruck by beauty, soft breeze, sweet smells, quiet. Oh, they heard a few bird songs and now and then a katydid buzzed. Laura closed her eyes, smiled, inhaled and exhaled, and then said, "What a dream. I'm so grateful to the City of Zamboanga for making this Tree House Park. I feel real peace. How about you, Willem?"

"Mmm-hmm." He smiled, he reached for her hand and held it for some time.

She returned his smile and took his offer.

"Laura, I want to marry you, and I have thought of a way."

She quickly searched into his eyes, concerned, but saying nothing.

He reached out his hands and gently pulled her into his chest and wrapped both of his arms around her back.
She responded with her arms.

"Laura, I want to have a baby with you. A little brother or sister for your Charlotte."

She pulled back in wonder and uncertainty to look into his eyes. "Why? Why, Willem?"

He said, "We'd make such a beautiful new creature, wouldn't we? Each of us, blended together."

They held one another tightly. And then Laura pulled away again to look at him. "Marriage?! A baby?! You can't do that, Willem!"

"Marrying, we'd give public notice that we're serious about one another. And a baby, would give notice that we intend to stay together for the rest of our lives."

"I don't know what to say." she said.

He continued. "A branch of the WOTRO, our governmental tropical research organization in the Netherlands, has cultural exchange teaching jobs that pay Dutch salaries. It's possible to hold such a position for an indefinite period of time. I would teach in Bali but also continue my research there and in "my" Ternate and Halmahera. I would – I will – divorce and then invite you to marry me and come here to live with me."

She slowly looked away. She took her hand from his, and she exhaled deeply. She brought her eyes back to his. "Phew. You surprise me. You overwhelm me, Willem! Until three days ago, I hadn't known you were thinking about this."

"Laura, we have the romance of the century! I've never met a woman like you before. We fit together like ideal mates, in Dante's concept. I've never felt like this before. We have only one lifetime, and our coming together is too important to pass up."

INDONESIA, 1973

50. Laura Takes Charlotte to Ternate

In Manado, Sulawesi, Laura and Charlotte deplaned from their four-hour flight out of Jakarta after their earlier four-hour flight from Manila and two hour flight from Singapore to Jakarta. Down at the harbor, Laura found a small inboard motor cargo boat that would be leaving that afternoon for Ternate Island. It would take 18 hours, and she and Charlotte would have a little sleeping berth on deck. They'd also be served a hot dinner.

They embarked around four o'clock, the afternoon's rain already finished. Just they and the two-person crew were already on board, and the two men would be sleeping below deck.

"Mom, we have two curtains, look!" Charlotte was delighted to inspect their quarters, and she didn't seem to mind the prevailing smell of diesel or the smudges of oil on the curtains.

What an ideal travel companion! Laura thought, as she tried her best to match Charlotte's enthusiasm.

Soon it wasn't hard for her to exult in their journey. *I'm finally taking Charlotte to Ternate! And we're on the last leg!* Under way, after a half hour, a glorious sunset completely enveloped them: soft gray-blue water below, with small, smooth, unbroken rolls, white narrow lines of the boat's wake spreading out diagonally behind them. The entire western sky – even the clouds behind them in the east - displayed a magnificent parade of colors: light copper oranges, becoming brilliant flaming oranges, then reds, crimsons and finally fading to deep purples and dark indigo.

They remained watching on deck, continuing to experience the deepening colors of the sky and the water. Laura put her arm around her little daughter's shoulder, who then reached around her mother's waist. Laura stroked Charlotte's free arm.

"Soft night breeze here, just like in the Philippines!"

Charlotte added, "And fire in the water, like in the Philippines, look!" and she pointed to the phosphorous flickers in the emerging wake at the boat's water line.

Out on deck the next morning around ten o'clock, the captain signaled from the helm that Ternate was the island straight ahead in the distance. The two passengers quickly closed their satchels and carried them out, ready to disembark.

Laura's heart swelled with her thrill of approaching the idyllic tropical island. *In the Philippines I'm excited every time I arrive by sea at a small island, but now, to share the experience coming to Ternate, Indonesia, with my Charlotte, I'm doubly rewarded!*

Laura was curious to learn Charlotte's first observations. "Does it look like our beach on Ternate in the Philippines, darling?" she asked.

"Well, the water is darker. Oh, I see black sand! I kind of like white sand better," Charlotte responded.

Laura asked, "Do you think that the island is an atoll?"

"No, because, look, a very tall mountain in the middle, like an upside-down ice cream cone! It even has whipped cream on top."

Laura laughed.

"Upside-down whipped cream, Mama!" and they both laughed, as Charlotte pointed to the small cluster of cumulus clouds hovering over the mile-high volcanic Mount Gamalama.

Laura reminded her that a volcano had formed the little island of Ternate and of course its mountain and its black sand.

As they approached the little town on the east side, they passed some black and some white beaches along the shore of the 30 square mile island. "Look, Charlotte, some white sand. So they must have coral reefs out here."

The helmsman slowed the motor as they approached Ternate's pier.

As they came closer to shore, the smell of clean sea air gradually became infused with the rich sweet-mildew fragrance of tropical plants. And yes, she again caught the fragrance of cloves, just as she had on her first arrival here a half year before.

Laura asked, "Those little puffy clouds in the sky that we've been looking at, the 'whipped cream'?" She leaned down to Charlotte and pointed toward the mountain. "These little cumuli will fill the sky in a while, and we'll have rain this afternoon."

"How do you know?" Charlotte smiled, inquiringly.

"Because it rains here every afternoon!"

"Really?"

"That's what they say, and that's what I experienced in my two weeks here last year."

"I notice something else, Mom."

"Oh? What?"

"Only a few palm trees. Mostly darker trees with little leaves, But tall, like the palms."

"True. We don't see so many forest trees in our Ternate, do we? These are original forest trees, not brought from somewhere else like palm trees. And some of these are spice trees!"

"Spices? Like cimanon and pepper?"

"Mainly, what they have here are cloves and nutmegs."

"Oh, you put those in our pumpkin pies, hmm. And cimanon."

"Yep, and you've helped me bake them. Cinnamon."

"Cinnamon."

"Right. Cinnamon trees grow here too, but they also grow in other places, like Malaysia and India. Originally, nutmeg and clove trees grew only here, and these little islands became famous for them."

They watched as the boat was gently eased into a space at the pier.

Charlotte said, "Something else that's different here..."

"Oh?"

"Yeah. Our Ternate doesn't have roads or cars down by the beach, just sandy paths. But now I see trucks and... what are those, Mom? Little motorcycles with something hanging on them!"

"They call them *betjaks*, and they're taxis. The passengers sit in the little cars hanging onto the motorcycles."

"Can we ride in one?

"Of course, we'll catch one as soon as we walk off the pier."

51. "Oh, Just Overcome That"

Two evenings later, and after dinner, Laura and Willem, with Clifford and Charlotte, chatted outside. Soon, Laura took Charlotte inside to read to her. After she had been tucked in and was asleep, and Clifford had turned in as well, Willem and Laura sat by themselves outside on the terrace.

"Dear Laura, six months ago we sat out here several evenings on Clifford's terrace, admiring the panorama of Ternate and Tidore, our Spice Islands, and we started to fall in love." He reached for her hands and smiled into her eyes.

She returned his smile. But she was thinking about her daughter whom she had just put to sleep. "She's much better than I was about sleeping in strange places alone. I'm still not good at it."

"What do you mean? Are you afraid to be alone at night?"

"Yes, and I don't really know why. I've asked women friends, and I haven't met any others who are afraid. Maybe it's because I had – mild, mind you – sexual harassment experiences as a little child."

"*Tjonge-jonge* (Oh boy), what difficulties you've had, my dear!"

"I think those experiences of harassment led me to feel powerless and therefore to make decisions not in my own best interests. So maybe that's why, ever since early childhood, after experiencing the first sexual assaults, I haven't been able to sleep a single night in a house with no other people in it. I'm happy that in the Philippines there are always other people in the house. And as an adult, in the work setting in California, I've had several uncomfortable experiences, but I've been quiet about them. I didn't publicly call the man out. Not terrible, mind you. But I should have had more courage."

"But you're so brave! You were a marvel during that whole long experience in the forest!"

"Yeah, well…Uhm, that bravery is different, veering slightly off sexual harassment. Now I wonder whether I reached my best potential, or, on the contrary, did I cower, because of harassment by an older boy when I was a kid, or by a man later? Well, I sure cowered from my brother, who forcefully let me know that I must always be feminine. He criticized me when I got sweaty, - 'Be a girl!' - and later he hit me for wearing a slightly see-through blouse. So, in spite of math teachers' very strong encouragements to me as being especially smart, I stayed away from math, science, and thoughts of engineering, as 'masculine.'"

"Oh, so you were good in math! Well, social scientists do use statistics…"

"Of course I was growing up in the days and place when and where I had no role models for women having a career. I expected to become a full-time homemaker like my mother. My job would be support: support for the man and for the children."

"But that's not what you did. You told me that you didn't want to marry the father of your little girl."

"True, but I also couldn't imagine getting an abortion. I couldn't handle being a murderer."

"Oh, the abortion topic. In the Netherlands we kind of settled that to be the woman's choice, but I know Americans are still fussing over it."

"Yeah. About my ideas for career: actually, I started to expand my world view when I was still an undergraduate. I had women professors, women who also had husbands and children, who strongly encouraged me to go to graduate school, to become a professor myself."

"So professional women helped you overcome, then?"

"Well, first I did the only women's profession that I knew of:
I got a teaching credential and taught elementary school for a
couple of years.

"But then I applied, and I was accepted, at UC Berkeley, and
I was delighted with the study and my classmates. But
I stayed in a social science field, maybe because I thought it
was more feminine, not like natural science or math. But oh,
did I have mixed feelings! – Becoming a graduate student,
I was intruding on men's aspirations. I actually had
nightmares that I was becoming a man, real nightmares."

"Being a man, that's not so terrible!"

"I really didn't want to become a man! But then practicality
intervened."

"How?"

"Toward the end of my first fieldwork in the Philippines,
I had a boyfriend in Manila. I didn't know until I got back to
California that I had gotten pregnant, and then I had a
daughter. Therefore a professional salary became doubly
important. My very sweet, delight-of-my-life little daughter
Charlotte meant that I simply had to have a good job. But the
university teaching jobs had dried up, especially in my field."

"There weren't any anywhere?"

"Oh, I applied for the few that I learned about, positions in
the U.S., even in other countries. I got just three interviews.
They asked my "status" – it was legal to ask back then – and
I had to tell that I was single with a daughter. No offers. I've
sure wondered if my "status" might have turned decisions."

Willem crossed his legs; his upper leg now faced away from
Laura. "Oh, in the Netherlands I don't think that would have
made a difference. But I do have to admit that most
university professors there, in all fields, are men. Hey Laura,

you're making me wonder about basic relations between men and women."

"Hmm." She took a long drink of her water. "I know a lot of women who have been more courageous than I."

"Than you? I told you, you're very brave! So don't you think that you can overcome this problem, now?"

Laura continued. "For instance, I know women who have gone into what were considered masculine fields and have done well. More marketable fields."

"So, what then? Are you blaming sexual harassment for your choice of fields, and your status as a single mom for not getting a job?"

"You mean, do I blame men for my cowardice? – for not following my love of math? Well, I've been reflecting. Until now, I was fiercely denying to myself that I might be fearful about being assertive. Lately, though, I think early sexual harassment was relevant. I recognize that all my confusion has limited my scope. At puberty, how could I (or any 13-year-old girl) sort out that boys, and then men, were attracted to me as a female, but at the same time disrespected me because I was a female? My response was to be feminine, and a "good" female. Insofar as I didn't live up to standard as "good," I suffered, a lot. Like, having a child as a single mom wasn't "good." I've worked hard to overcome that obvious self-criticism.

"Yes, I can imagine."

"So, back to your earlier question, Willem: why didn't I just move on after harassment? Well, mostly I did. Only in the last couple of years have these reflections come up. Earlier, I would have dismissed them simply as self-serving excuses."

"But Laura, you did have awful experiences to overcome, you said."

"Well, I was never raped. That is, never penetrated. But Lord, how those many experiences of sexual harassment have caused me to live in fear for months, months, that I'd be bumped out of college or my job... And of course I had the usual, old-fashioned, adjunct, that maybe I was too sexy, too attractive, and shouldn't I just hide my female body in lots of clothes and cover my face with long hair? In other words, wasn't I guilty?"

"Have you been able to move on? Or in contrast, did you feel ruined?"

"'Ruined' doesn't explain my responses, starting by age two, to sexual harassment. My responses have been fear and cowardice. Lifelong. I've overcome a lot, but by now I recognize that these responses have become a deep weakness of my character."

"So, recognizing your problem now, don't you think you can just overcome it? And do you think you'll find the courage to work harder to get a good job?"

"Hey, Willem, do you think it's all my weakness, not trying hard enough, that I don't have a job?"

He doesn't understand. Oh God!

52. No Blood on My Hands

Late afternoon and after the finish of the daily downpour, Willem jumped up from his desk and walked over to Laura, who sat bent over her field notes. He gently lifted up her hair at the back of her neck and leaned down to press his lips against her slightly damp skin.

"Let's walk out to *Benteng* (Fort) Kalamata. I know that you know that it was built in 1540 by Portuguese invaders!"

She sighed, turned her head up to him, shrugged her shoulders, patted her hands on her papers, and slowly opened her eyelids with a smile.

"Okay, for a little while. I'm on to something with my notes. And I have just an hour because Charlotte will be getting out of her guest day at school. We could pass by the school for her on the way back."

Clouds quickly dissipated and the asphalt of the narrow road steamed under the re-emerging sun. The island's prominent volcanic peak, Gamalama, was already in afternoon shadow on their right as Willem and Laura walked southward. Laura noticed palm trees in neat rows heading up the mountain for a short distance, and then they were overtaken by cloves and nutmegs, and then natural forest trees, including some cloves.

Reaching the promontory overlooking the Ternate Strait and across the half mile of quiet sea to the island of Tidore, Willem led Laura to the ruins of a little stone pier leading to an arched opening in a large stone wall. The disheveled wooden pier was just strong enough for each to step onto it and jump across the water, through the arch, and into the fort.

So quiet in here! Laura noted that the interior foundation was still intact. *Doesn't look like it ever needed repair for these three hundred and more years. No roof, though.* Portuguese had built it to fight off the Spanish, but lost. Later, Spaniards fought the Dutch explorers from here, but lost. *They all came after Ternate's precious cloves and Banda Islands' nutmegs. The Dutch may have won the spice war, but this Portuguese-Spanish fort is still standing, at least the stone foundation and low walls.* On the pier side and the island side, the wall was twenty feet high and covered with clinging banyan trees, sending their branches another thirty feet into the sky. On the seaside and westward side of this four-pointed star "footprint," the wall was much lower, perhaps three feet high. At these two points, rusted cannons still stood and pointed outward, as if waiting patiently all these years for the next battle.

"No children followed us!" Laura exclaimed. "Usually we've been followed here by children as frequently as I've ever experienced in the Philippines. But school is in session now."

"I'm glad that we're by ourselves," Willem agreed.

Laura, and then Willem, lifted their feet up and over the low wall to face the sea and the islands to their south. Sitting, Laura inhaled deeply, closed her eyes, and said, "I could work fine out here."

"Yes, quiet now, but imagine how busy it must have been 300 years ago!"

Laura looked to the sea below their feet, gently lapping against the stone wall.

She sighed, slumped her shoulders, looked up to the dark sky, and then down to Willem. "It won't work out."

"What won't? Working here?"

She straightened her shoulders back in line and looked at Willem. "I mean, Lord, why did I get involved with a married man? And even if you weren't married, it wouldn't work out."

"But think of our destiny, Laura! This is much bigger than coincidence. Our work, our separately conceived passion for the Spice Islands, has brought us together! And look at the beauty!" He spread his arms out toward the sea.

"Yeah. But even more, our home base is on different continents. And your passion for the Spice Islands enhances your faculty position in the Netherlands; but mine won't get me anywhere in the States."

They looked intently at one another, taking in their difficulty.

"Hey, Laura, what do you think about coming to one of our universities? We have openings because we have a new university, and our faculty salaries are the best in the world."

Laura thought for a while. "I'd be the Other Woman."

He closed his eyes, looked down, and said, "I'm being selfish."

She turned to look at him. "Willem, you had no intention to divorce before you met me."

"No, but I was in denial about the years of problems."

"What about your children?"

"They'd likely side with their mother, and I'd lose them."

She slowly inhaled, then exhaled. "Willem, I don't want blood on my hands. Your cost, for yourself and for your family, would be too great."

"I've thought a lot about it. I think that that great cost would be worth staying together with you."

She looked out to the sea for some time, and then she turned again to Willem. "If you would divorce, I think that we should not see one another for two years during and after. In that time, you'd know if it was really right for you, even without me."

Hands still apart, and both surprised, they each looked out to the azure sea and the small volcano-peaked, forest-covered islands beyond.

"Let's go pick up Charlotte," she said.

They walked back into town just in time for the elementary school to let out. One of Clifford's staff, Hammid's wife Aisya, had loaned Charlotte one of their daughter Devi's uniforms for her visit to Devi's class. The girls all wore the uniform of a white blouse and kelly green jumper. As Willem and Laura approached the school, at first Charlotte was hard to distinguish. But as they came closer, her hair and her skin were obviously lighter, and she smiled and waved to them. The teacher, standing at the schoolroom door, was delighted to give a glowing report. Several girls lingered as well, but then they ran for home, skipping, laughing.

53. The Clove Tree Listens

The next day, Willem invited Laura to accompany him down to his storehouse of botanical collections. She replied, "You'll go again tomorrow as well? Can I go then? I'd rather wait; I have a little project here to finish. And I'll take Charlotte soon to play with Devi."

Laura felt a little silly about the importance of another experience with "her" clove tree from a half year earlier, so she didn't want anyone to know. She waited until Willem had left, and then gave their host a cheery "Bye, Clifford, I'll be back soon."

She set out for the path leading through the palm trees and the forest and then partway up the volcanic cone. *Ah, here it is, in the same place. We can all count on trees.* Sitting, she leveled her legs down on her plastic bag and, putting her arms down to her sides, rested her hands on the plastic with her palms facing upward. She silently spoke. *Dear clove tree, it's been so long since I last sat at your feet, but I haven't forgotten how important you were to me in sorting out my thoughts, all those months ago. I want to experience serenity again. You're so old, you've seen so much, I know you have memory about your forebears, and so you must be wise.*

Late morning now, the sun shone brightly into the eastern, seaward, side of the tree.

I've come to contemplate again, dear tree. My first visit, I was so excited to meet Willem! He was so kind to me, and we are both doing research on the peripheries of the Spice Trade. After my experience with you, he showed great care for me by leaving his work to hide out with me for over two months in the Philippine forest. Oh, he didn't know at the beginning what difficulty we'd get into, and neither did I, but he stuck it out. Had to. Living in and on the primeval forest, the Philippines wasn't easy for him, even though he's an expert on trees. He did manage, but with some complaining. And by the way, he is studying something about your beneficial root fungi that will help you trees, to overcome the malevolent fungi lurking down there.

Wind gently rustled the leaves. The leaves hummed a melody and danced on their thin stems and sent sun reflections in all directions. The little flashes distracted her for a moment, to a memory of six years before, when she first experienced a strobe light on a twirling mirrored ball. She and several fellow graduate students danced on the flashing lights to the incredibly loud psychedelic music of Jefferson Airplane at The Fillmore in San Francisco on April 12, 1967. But now, sitting under her clove tree in Ternate, Indonesia, she felt grateful for the quiet.

Willem's been honest with me. He let me know right away that he has a wife back in the Netherlands. Children too, but they're off in college. He's got a very stable position at his university and he has funding to come do research on you guys, hopefully to help you out, especially since you still suffer so much commercial interest in your flower buds, and consequently creating considerable disturbance to you and nutmegs.

She looked up the trunk into the tree's branches, and on up to its canopy.

You've sacrificed so much, especially when Europeans came to grab you, starting around 400 years ago. So much killing of you trees and local people! You probably weren't yet alive. But, I estimate from your size that you could be 200 years old, dear tree, and by the time of your youth, maybe 1773, medicines had become more scientific and consequently, world clamor for your medicinal properties had dwindled. Europe's first multinational monopoly had moved from here to Jakarta. Now your kind are grown on other Indonesian islands and in other countries, even as far away as Zanzibar and Grenada.

She heard sudden leaf movement. She looked up to see a big bird *(Was it a toucan?)* spring off a branch to fly out of the tree's canopy. *Oh, I startled it; it hid while I sat down and it has been hiding from me.*

So now I have three problems, maybe decisions. Can you help me?

One, there aren't any jobs in the States. I get letters and newsletters, and they all show that the university jobs in my field have dried up. I don't know what I'm going to do. I have my daughter to support, and I'm feeling desperate. I've agreed to teach a course at Ateneo de Manila University in Manila, but the pay only barely covers bus fare! But maybe it'll look good on my C.V. (Curriculum Vitae), and I'll enjoy the learning, too.

Second, should I let Migo become an active father?

And then, third, there's Willem. Our romance blossomed in spite of our best intentions because of the big danger we shared in the forest. That is, we both knew it couldn't last. And do I really have time in my life for a married man? Of course not, and besides, I don't quite approve, and I don't want to hurt his wife. I mean, she's far away, and we are not associating with any of her friends or contacts, so maybe she's not suffering about this. But still...

And now, dear Clove, he has proposed marriage to me! It's not the greatest proposal, because he's asking me to wait while he divorces.

She looked up into the tree again.

I don't want blood on my hands. He had no plan to divorce before this.

Tell me, dear clove tree.

Laura sat. She closed her eyes and listened to insects, to leaves rustling, to bird calls far away, to *betjak* put-puts farther away. She swatted a mosquito on her forearm.

She frowned. *Has he been completely honest with me, that is, about everything I should know? Tree, you're causing me to doubt my trust in him. He's married; wouldn't that be the biggest information that he would have wanted to keep from me, if he were not honest?*

She squeezed one fallen leaf, and then another.

What? She imagined she heard this:

- Forget that man: not telling you everything. He really hurt a woman.

What?? Where'd this come from? He might hold an even darker secret? ... Dear tree, I think I should think about this a lot more. A lot more. Maybe I need to meet and hear from others who have known him for a while. Clifford... Talk with him when Willem isn't around?

Tree, last time I came to sit here, I asked if I could help you, your kind. I was very happy to discover that Willem is researching how he can help you and nutmeg trees. But what can I do to help you?... You're forgotten in current history. I mean, in the States, students learn about "The Spice Islands," but only that Christopher Columbus was looking for a western route and instead bumped into the New World. Why would people today be interested in your story? Hmm... Medicine, still some relevance. Country inter-relationships, still relevant. Evolution and habits of languages, and of trees? Yes. Food? There's a lot of current interest in "learning from the ancients." Don't under-estimate the depth of human greed? Important and relevant. Hey, maybe I could tell your story!

54. His Twenty-Year Secret

When Laura returned to the house, Willem was still gone, surely down at his warehouse, and Charlotte was outside at Devi's, playing with her and her family's pet parrots. Clifford sat outside in the shade reading yesterday's *Jakarta Post* English language newspaper. His man Hammid had gotten it down at the port for him.

She sat down at a short distance from him, not wanting to disturb him.

He looked up. "Oh, hello again, Laura. Was your favorite tree happy to see you back?"

"Oh, you know. Yes, it offered me shade."

Clifford raised his hand, and Hammid appeared. "Two iced teas, please, Hammid" he said.

"So Laura, you and Willem have both come to my favorite place in the world! We're so happy to receive you here."

She told him that his place was as beautiful as the Philippines, how she loved the sounds of Indonesian languages and music, such colorful clothing, and she felt passionate about the fragrance of cloves in the air.

"And you've known Willem for a long time?" she asked.

"Oh yes, since he first came here 20 – 21 years ago during his fieldwork in the Bandas south of here, mainly with nutmeg trees back then. And I was here for a long visit, contemplating moving here."

"So, long-time friends! But that was back ...21 years... ago, in 1951, not long after Indonesia had gained independence from the Netherlands. How did you men get permission to be here?"

"In my case, because my father was born here in Ternate, and the new government was cooperating with thousands who were of mixed heritage, so I was treated like a citizen. In Willem's case, I believe his Dutch research grant included negotiations for his entrance. His botanical work was seen as potentially valuable for the export market back then."

"But he left early, he told me, before his year was up."

"Yes, he said he became homesick, in spite of becoming a sort of family member down there in the Banda island of Run."

"Hmm?"

"Oh... Well, I know this is very sensitive, Laura, but because you've become such a dear person to me, I want to tell you, confidentially: he married a local woman in the Bandas. Her family was suspicious of him, but nevertheless, through the family relationship he had better access to the local community, and he felt less lonely. People had to accept him because he moved into the village and appeared ready to stay indefinitely. But when his time was up, he decided it would be too difficult for her to live in the Netherlands. So he left by himself. And then she had a son. He had to recognize the son. He sent money, and now he's come back and has hired the son and trained him as his assistant. That's his way, he said, of handling his feeling of guilt."

"Oh! Is that the young man I saw last time I was here? Ali, I think Willem said was his name."

"Yes. But let Willem tell you the rest."

"Okay." She went into the house to wash her face and hands; they had become sweaty from her walk back to Clifford's house, and now from this report.

God, so small. He's so small to have done that. The temporary fieldwork so-called marriage! And he kept it a secret from me... Does his wife know?

Lord... But partially, I did the same! I didn't ask Migo to go with me back to the U.S, and for some of the same reasons. But then, in my case, I didn't keep the affair a secret from Willem. But is that only because I'm a woman? Because I'm the one to bear the child?

Would I have told Willem if I didn't have Charlotte? But I didn't get married! If I didn't have the child, then I wouldn't have told him. It was an affair, not a marriage.

That's a big difference. I'm disgusted with him.

She looked into the mirror in her guest bathroom, and then vigorously washed her face again.

So I'm going to confront him!

She dried her face, and then her hands.

Or, maybe not. Clifford told me confidentially. That'd make for awkward discomfort and not be fair to Clifford. And I – and Charlotte - are guests in his house.

Hmm. How about if I keep quiet while we're here with Clifford? I'll wait a while, and I'll see if Willem takes the initiative.

She hung the towel to dry and opened the restroom door to leave. *I don't need to confront him, because I've made my decision.. Looks like it took this information to knock sense into me. Anyway, my decision is firm: I've lost respect for him, so it's over.*

PHILIPPINES, 1973

55. Why Does Fely Have Blond Hair?

Laura and Charlotte returned to the Philippines, and they resumed their earlier routines. Marilu and her husband welcomed them back to their house in Makati, Manila. Charlotte continued her nursery school, and Laura's main work continued of writing up and analyzing her large accumulation of data.

She had been invited to teach a graduate class on contact languages at Ateneo de Manila University. She accepted, deciding that she could add the class, which would meet just once per week for three hours, to her weekly trip to Manila to check on her incoming mail. *I go to the city anyway.*

In their first class meeting, Professor Laura Rhodes introduced the history of the European involvement in the Spice Trade starting in the early 15th Century as the cause for the emergence of the many contact languages around the Earth's equator. Then, after introducing herself, she said, "Just ten of you; so let's go around the room to learn why you've signed up for this class."

Several were taking the class as an optional course for their field of Linguistics. Only two had had first-hand experience with Philippine Creole Spanish, and those experiences were tangential. 50+-year-old Sister Inez from the nearby Catholic K-12 Dominican Santa Catalina College, had gone to elementary school with Chabacano speakers in the southern city of Cotabato. And the student Fely reported that her maternal grandmother had told her that she had been raised in Ternate, out at the mouth of the Manila Bay, where people spoke Chabacano. Her dear grandmother could still remember words and phrases, in what she called "a bastard Spanish."

Laura wondered about Fely. After class, she saw a black
Lincoln Town Car pick Fely up, and so Laura guessed that she
came from a wealthy family. Fely had a beautifully structured
face and wore exquisite but modest clothing. She didn't carry
herself with the haughty grace of other wealthy young
women, many of whom were proud of their Spanish as well
as Philippine heritage. Fely was unpretentious, open, and
willing to initiate confrontation in class discussions. Not only
did Fely not fit the usual pattern of the young of the
Philippines' oligarchy, but Laura wondered about her hair.
It was blond, wooly blond. *How could that be? The color, the
curls look natural. I know that some people from the central
islands, and Negritos from Mountain Province, have curly hair,
but not blond, and they're not among the oligarchy! The blond
color: I've seen only occasionally, on a Badjo child in the south,
who live their whole lives on boats down there, with blond and
also wooly hair, but people have told me that their hair color is
explained by lack of healthy nutrients. They're said to have
kwashiorkor or scurvy or something.*

Laura even decided to look up about the hair. She read that
kwashiorkor developed from lack of protein, and one
symptom was lack of hair color. She wondered, Protein
deprivation *can't be it; those children eat mainly fish and
other mariscos. They're out in the sun so much; could it be just
sun bleaching? But if so, why not the adults? I never saw a
blond adult among the Badjo, or for that matter, any other
Filipinos.* She looked up scurvy and read that it developed
due to lack of plant matter, especially Vitamin C., and she
remembered hearing, back in high school history, about
scurvy among early ocean explorers. But loss of hair color
was not a symptom of scurvy. *So, it's not explained by lack of
nutrition, and besides, how would privileged Fely lack nutrition
or have heritage from those boat people?*

Fely stayed after class the next week, and the two sat on a
campus terrace with iced teas, and they talked.

Fely was excited about her professor's interest in her hair, she said, even though she was occasionally (mildly) teased as a child that "there must have been an American G.I. in the closet!"

Laura asked, "What else do you know about your genetic heritage?"

Fely responded, "Well, my *abuela* told me that Ternate nearby here – where you're working, right?! - is where my blond hair came from. She said that a few children out there have blond curly hair, but very few keep that light color by the time they're adults."

"Hmm, in America, a lot of toddlers are 'towheads' but their hair also usually turns dark by adulthood. So how did you respond to her information?"

"I protested. I said, 'But *Abuelita*, my papa says it's our Spanish heritage coming out!' And my abuela laughed. She said, 'Hmmpf; he wishes!' This is because, as you know, Professor Rhodes, Ternate is out in the boondocks, where farmers and fishermen live, and has no prestige. So I asked her, and this was when I was still a kid, 'But *Abuela*, why are those children different?' She told me, 'Our village started when Spaniards brought 200 Ternatenyos from eastern Indonesia, what used to be called 'the Spice Islands.'' So this was the first time I heard this. I said to her, 'Wow, so I might have ancestors from the Spice Islands?' She smiled and said, 'So far away and so long ago.' So I looked it up on my school atlas, and saw that they're about 1800 kilometers away."

"So since high school, you've been wondering about this part of your heritage?"

"Yes, Professor Rhodes. In biology class I learned a little about inherited traits. The teacher had us all feel our earlobes and look in a mirror to see who had attached lobes and who had detached ones. And then we were to go home to investigate our parents' lobes. And we learned about dominant and recessive traits.

"And then she wanted to talk to the class about my hair color. She asked me in advance if I'd mind. I said 'No, of course not!' But I really did. Teenager, you know. Because after that they teased me, telling me that because it was 'kinky,' it wasn't glamorous. So, Professor Rhodes, do you think that my hair color shows high class origin, or low class?"

Laura laughed, and mumbled something about the perception of others, versus Fely's own feeling about her special trait, versus inherited traits.

Fely continued. "The teacher taught us that blond hair is a recessive trait, and that a person with blond hair has to inherit the trait from both parents for it to be activated. And for each generation of no activation, the chance of activation is halved.

"And Dr. Rhodes, then the teacher probed further. She asked me, 'So Miss Fely, have any of your ancestors had blond hair? From your mother's, *and* from your father's side?"
I answered – and I was just fifteen years old then – 'Teacher, I don't know anyone else in my family with blond hair.
We have photos of my grandparents and even a couple of great-grandparents – black and white photos, of course – and they all have dark hair, or they're old enough to have gray hair. I don't even see any children in the photos with light hair. I'm the family mystery!' The students laughed, though kind of politely, because they were sort of kind to me."

"So you learned a lot about your hair, something that most people didn't know, back when you were fifteen!"

"Yes. I've learned that, as I said, chances are cut by half each generation. Hmm, 1662 to now... no, when I was born, in 1952. That'd be... let's see, if I calculate one generation as ... 25 years, then that'd be... almost 12 generations! Our teacher said traits very, very rarely show up after five generations."

"I don't know about heritable traits, but I'm sure interested."

"And then there's my father's side... Haven't heard of any blonds. He did say that unlike most Filipinos with Spanish surnames, who were assigned them from the 1870 Cordoba, Spain census, my father said that we had a real Spanish ancestor, Señor Juan Esquivel, who was sent by the King of Spain in 1605 to lead 600 soldiers to battle against the Portuguese in ... the Spice Islands!

"Oh, a possible connection with Ternate, Indonesia, then?"

"I've been wondering ever since learning this. So did that eight times great grandfather contribute blond hair from Spain, or did he marry or "marry" a woman from Ternate, Indonesia?"

Laura went to the Ateneo University library to learn more. She found the latest archaeological evidence of the first migration of humans to the Spice Islands. No proto-humans had ever gotten there as they had to Java in the west, because those new, eastern volcanic islands never had a land bridge. Around 3200 years ago, Melanesians from New Guinea were able to use dugout canoes to cross about 300 kilometers of open sea to reach Halmahera and then the islands to its west, including Ternate and Tidore.

Continuing her reading, Laura discovered that Melanesians are the only dark-skinned people in the world to have blond hair, and then only a tiny minority, around six percent, and mainly only as children. Those blonds all have wooly hair as well.

Like blonds in Europe, most Melanesian blond hair turns dark by adulthood. But another important difference is that European blonds tend to have straight or wavy, but not wooly hair. (Of course there's variability.) And, most notable of all, the recessive gene for Melanesian blond hair is a quite different gene than the gene for European blond hair.

The next week after class, Laura and Fely talked again, and
Laura told her of her reading.

Fely was intensely interested. "It must mean, then", she
mused, "that it wouldn't help for these two different
recessive genes for blond hair to get together! I mean,
offspring of two such people wouldn't lead to a manifestation
of blond hair! Do you agree, Professor Rhodes?"

"I think you're right."

"So I must have a low-class heritage from both sides of my
family. Oh, *Dios*, how am I going to handle this?"

She paused to think, and then she said, "At least I can forget
looking for the Spaniard or the American in my heritage,
except for my Spanish surnme. Oh, my papa will be ashamed.
He never teased me. He always said that I was showing our
Spanish heritage. But now I want to know, who were these
people, my blond ancestors?"

"What a mystery, Fely! And it sounds like it'll be difficult for
your father."

"Yes, I'm worrying about him. He always protected me, and
he told me he was proud of my hair, that it was an important
sign of our Spanish heritage."

Laura patted Fely's forearm sympathetically.

Fely sat quietly for some time, and then almost jumped out of
her chair. "Hey, Dr. Rhodes, I just got an idea that would
preserve my father's pride! I'll show him that our blond
ancestors were among the people who discovered those
miraculous spices! You've shown me that Melanesians
migrated to Ternate, and there, that they learned how to use
the spices for food and medicine. And the whole world took
notice, even the Spaniards, and that's why they came to the
Philippines! Hey, I'm a descendant of people who changed
the world!"

56. The Sister Stole?!

During the following summer, Laura stopped by the university bookstore to look for Dr. William Henry Scott's history of the Mountain Province, *On the Cordillera*. Walking past the 'New Publications by our Faculty and Students" section, her eye caught a glimpse of a book spine with "Chabacano" in the title. *What's this? Something new about my people! A history?!* She backed up and eagerly picked up the book, a paperback with a simple white, glossy background and bold black letters, showing" "Chabacano: Our Own Philippine Contact Spanish." *What's this? Who wrote it? No author on the cover!* She turned to the spine, and there it was: Sister Inez Ruiz. *My student in last semester's class! Oh!...She borrowed, for just the weekend, my vocabulary cards!*

Laura leafed through the book, some 450 pages. She read one after another vocabulary entry. Each entry included a text using the entry word. *God, she even used all my texts that I had recorded while interviewing people, for more than a year!* Laura found a chair and sat down to read a page more carefully. She opened the book to the middle, and on that page found two entries with the Cotabato Chabacano variation included, the regional dialect that Sister Inez had told the class that she had learned from classmates in elementary school down in Cotabato.

I'm going to have to buy it. But then what? Laura paid the 28 pesos price, put it into her tote bag, walked to the bus stop, and waited and pondered.

Now what? I can't believe that my two years of work has been pirated and plagiarized! And by a nun, that is, a Sister. Adds irony to the frustration. Maybe she thought she could get away with it because she's a person of the church?

Laura looked for the bus. She and a few students waited. Now and then another student arrived and joined the standing cluster.

Antero, my typist Evelyn, and I have been working full time on this dictionary for more than a year, and I already have the contract with De La Salle University to publish it! And who published this one? She pulled it out of her tote and read "Augustinian Order of the Catholic Church Publishing, Quezon City, Philippines."

Here I thought I was going to do a good turn for Filipinos by having the dictionary published in this country... Oh, and it'd also be my ticket into a linguistics department in an American university, because it'd be a strong contribution. But the readers would most of all be Filipinos.... Now what? I suppose they can read this one!

She pushed the book into its plastic bag and shoved it back into her tote. *Now what? What should I do about this? Should I expose her? And what about my contract with De La Salle?*

Her bus arrived, and she and a few of the students slowly made their way to the few empty seats in the back, where she sat in the middle of a seat with her tote on her lap and her elbows tightly at her sides. *No reading here.*

The bus headed into heavy stop-and-go traffic and pulled over to the side now and then for passengers along Epifanio de los Santos Boulevard, slowly wending its way over to Makati and Laura's room in Marilu's house.

I know: I'll start out by asking Brother Ramirez how I should proceed. I signed the contract with him. Brother Ramirez was the President of De La Salle University, the respected Jesuit university on Taft Avenue in Manila. He had been delighted to learn that Laura would be working on this language, one that had been ignored, so far, by both Filipino and foreign linguists. He knew that contact languages were finally getting attention globally in the field of linguistics, and that the language deserved respect rather than the disdain with which it was treated. Brother Ramirez was not only President, but he was also editor of the quarterly *Philippine Journal of Linguistics*.

From Marilu's house she called down to Brother Ramirez' office and made an appointment for the next morning.

.....

Graciously ushered into his office, he stood to greet her warmly and motioned for her to sit at one of two chairs in front of his desk, and he took the other. "Brother Ramirez, I found this yesterday, in the Ateneo de Manila bookstore." She pulled the dictionary out of her tote and handed it to him. Very soon his face expressed dismayed surprise. He looked at the cover, repeated Laura's perusal of the previous day, and then handed it back to her.

"Oh, Laura, what a problem we have. She was your student last semester?"

"Yes."

"Have you decided what to do about this?"

"Brother Ramirez, I am coming to you for advice."

"Hmm. We must think hard." He looked to Laura and gazed away for a short time. Back to Laura, he said, "I know Sister Inez. We are of different orders, but we are both linguists, and we are a small, exclusive club here in Manila. Hard to believe she did this. How did she get your data, by the way?"

Laura explained that in the previous semester, when Sister Inez was a student in Laura's class at Ateneo, she had asked to borrow Laura's boxes of vocabulary cards for just a weekend in order to see in more detail Laura's sophisticated entries: pronunciation, etymology, part of speech, and quotation in an utterance by a speaker in Ternate.

"Let's talk about the options," Brother Ramirez said. "And by the way, I keep telling you to call me "Alberto.""

"I'll continue to try, ... Alberto!"

"Good. Now, the options: first, it's already published, but I want you to see an intellectual property attorney."

"Oh! My thinking hasn't gone this far."

"Well! I can recommend one to you, and he might consider your case as a charity to our university. Part of the question is whether you can retrieve any credit for all your work. Another is whether the Sister should get away with this. ... You said that she speaks a regional dialect of Chabacano?"

"She said that she learned it as a second language, playing with classmates in elementary school."

"Not her first language, then. Still, she might resent you as a foreigner coming in with American money to study 'her' language. She might even feel that she deserves to be the author, and that justifies the pirating and plagiarizing."

"Maybe. I did experience resentment by another of your linguistic colleagues, at the University of the Philippines, when I visited him to ask if he had ever considered studying Chabacano, or encouraging a graduate student to do it. He told me 'You people still try to colonize our country, and now you take our data for your own aggrandizement!'"

"Oh, who was that?"

"He'd better remain anonymous," Laura said.

"But I think I know."

"Hmm. Back to options. I will accompany you to the intellectual property attorney."

57. She Owns It Now

Brother Alberto, in his role as her publisher, accompanied Laura to the attorney. Their efforts were to no avail, because Sister Inez's publisher was not only legitimate, but the work had been copyrighted in the Philippines.

Laura glumly settled into the back seat of the chauffeured "De La Salle University" car with Brother Ramirez. The black Toyota Crown sedan quietly hummed its powerful air conditioner, and Laura felt her body cooling down from the heat and dust they had just escaped. She turned to her companion. "Now what?" she asked. "Should I just leave it?"

"Looks like a second legal opinion wouldn't help," he replied. "This is a great loss for you, Laura. Even publishing internationally, that is, in America, you would violate our international copyright agreement. For us Filipinos, you have done fine work for our people, and we would have been proud to publish it here in our country."

Laura smoothed out the white denim car seat cover that had been starched and pressed. "Thank you, Brother Rami... Alberto. An important part of my motivation has been to help Filipinos cast off the inferiority complex that seems to have developed being colonized, not only by three hundred years under the Spaniards, but also the last seventy years under the Americans. "

Brother Alberto searched her eyes. "You mean through your study of this language?"

The driver, meanwhile, drove slowly through side streets in order to avoid heavy traffic. He carefully skirted around deep potholes and slowed down for the occasional group of playing children, even for a hen that dashed out into the road.

Laura responded, "Yes. You know as well, people here are always referring to it as 'a bastard Spanish, with no grammar.' It's been so important to me to show its speakers, and their neighbors as well, that it does have a grammar, and it's a legitimate language in its own right."

He looked out his side window and then back to Laura. "I'm very disappointed that we at De La Salle cannot now help you deliver that message. We Filipinos need to improve our self-esteem."

"I sure agree. Surrounding countries – China, India, Indonesia, all cast off their colonizers by revolt, and they have been proud of their successes. Filipinos were too hospitable."

"Oh, but Magellan was killed here! On April 27, 1521, by a poison arrow, on Mactan."

"Yes, but then the Spaniards did later take over the country, right?"

"Yes, all except the Moros in the south. I mean the Muslims."

"And then the Americans by 1902, and the Japanese occupied during World War II, and then the Americans were back here...And now, you're suggesting, are you, that Sister Inez might think she can justify her plagiarizing by considering me a colonizer whom she has cast off?"

"Could be, but I'm just guessing. Hmm, maybe I will ask her. Maybe I will pay her a visit and invite her to accompany me when I visit her bishop."

"Oh, you might go there? And even tell her bishop?"

"Yes, I will go, and I will report to you how her supervisors react. But my visit won't rectify her theft. Even if she published a profound confession and apology in *The Manila Times,* the damage has already been done to your work."

"I know, especially after learning from your attorney."

He put his hands together emphatically and then looked up to her. "My dear child, I know you have been counting on this pioneering research on our creole Spanish to be your key to a faculty position in an American university."

"Yes, Brother Alberto."

"Have you already thought of alternatives?"

"No. It's all too new to me. I'm overwhelmed."

58. How Can I Provide For Us?

Laura walked between errands in Manila.

Alternatives for career?! I've already tried that... Tried going to medical school; that advisor at Loma Linda University talked me out of it. They said that at age 23 I was too old for any medical school to accept me. They all want them young and malleable to AMA (American Medical Association) philosophy.

She shuffled her feet on the sidewalk with disappointment on leaving Manila's USIS office where she had looked for her APO mail from the U.S. *"Still no new linguistics jobs."*

Why oh why did I go into this field? She kicked an empty coke can to the side of the road and continued her slow walk to the bus stop for return to Marilu's luxurious walled compound. *Why didn't I choose a marketable field? Why was I so naïve to think that it could be as good for me as for our faculty? When I was in graduate school, they all lived in nice houses. Had wives who took care of their children, full time. When we were undergraduates, university career advisors all said, 'Follow your passion.' So I listened, I fell in love with the science of language structure and language change, and then discovered contact languages. Even more exciting.*

The "Makati" bus arrived. She squeezed through the narrow aisle to a rear, rare, open seat. As the bus started up again, she looked out the window at people. Most walked and carried plastic bags. Here was a woman holding the hands of two children. Now, she saw several waiting at another bus and jeepney stop. Now she saw a couple at a stand apparently buying lanzones, those little unassuming yellow-gray fruit, ripe in October, that held inside a surprisingly delightfully intense sweet-tart smooth pulp.

I've loved coming to Southeast Asia. Troubles at first, but I've met some big challenges. Visa, eviction threat, custody battle over my dear daughter, 'wantid,' forest survival, traffic ticket, and, oh God, failed romance.

The bus swerved to the side of the road. Two men carried boxes up the bus's outside ladder. The whole bus swayed back and forth. Laura heard several soft thuds and assumed that the boxes were being tied onto the roof rack. Meanwhile, several new riders entered and stood in the aisle of the by-now-full bus.

Thought I was heading for a fine career: research out here in these incredibly beautiful tropics and then research and teaching in a university back home. I'd have enough income to manage well for Charlotte and me. Buy a house. Maybe have to live in another country, but that'd be okay too. Charlotte would learn another language starting at an early age. – Quite an advantage! I didn't start learning until my teenage years, much harder.

The pace of the bus picked up as it passed between tall modern commercial buildings of downtown Makati. But then it deviated from its usual route to take one after another small side roads into a rundown residential area.
It screeched to a halt in front of a *sari-sari* store. Two men jumped down from the bus and up the side ladder. Laura again felt jostling, heard more thumps, and then saw boxes on the ground at the side of the bus. Two women squeezed through the crowded aisle to exit. They joined the men and boxes. Another man banged on the back of the bus with his open palm and shouted "Roll!" to the driver, who started up, then drove over bumps and ruts back to the main street and toward the elegant gated "villages" of Makati.

Now it was Laura's turn to push through the crowd to the exit. Letting her out, the driver then lurched the bus back to the street, and Laura walked slowly toward Marilu's house.

The school bus will bring Charlotte back in two hours. Gotta get cheerful, somehow.

She looked for something to kick; couldn't find any debris here, no empty coke cans. *So many kalachuchi petals here covering the road; beautiful but not for kicking.* She picked up a fully formed flower under its tree and deeply inhaled its sweet fragrance. *Plumerias in Hawaii, main flower of their leis. With this flower I'm infused with the full beauty of the tropics... Oh, Lord, what can I do?*

She stopped to look up into the tree, one of a long row of tidy umbrella-shaped canopies lining both sides of the entrance drive into Magallanes Village.

No university jobs. No other kind of work for linguists. People ask me, 'how about translator?' But no, no jobs there. I've worried so long about this! No backup plan! But how can you have an alternative plan while going into such a specialized field? So I have to look elsewhere. I'd have to start over on training. I already tried medicine. And if I went back to school for another degree, how could I provide for little Charlotte? She'll be ready for kindergarten next September, and I've got to find a place to live and stay in one place for her schooling. And what field could I go into? Next time, one that's marketable! Engineering? That'd take several full-time years. Nowhere to turn.

Bag lady, that's my biggest fear. I do have my trusty Toyota Corona stored in my sister's garage. Will that car become our new bedroom?

59. Can't Go Home Empty-Handed!

Laura accepted her friend Becca's standing offer to visit her in Mountain Province. Charlotte by now was content to remain with Marilu and her children and their nursery school. She had again learned to trust that her mother would return.

Laura sent a telegram; Becca replied, "Come!" Becca was an anthropology student from the University of Chicago and had almost completed her fieldwork.

Laura flew to Baguio and then caught a bus for Barlig, Bontoc. The bus ride took one full day. Laura bought a bunch of bananas for her day's nourishment.

Next morning the two women sat outside of Becca's house on the terraced hillside above the little town of Barlig.

"I need to decide what to do about the theft; maybe I should just leave it? But maybe that's wimpy."

Becca held her teacup with both hands to keep her fingers warm, sitting on a log outside her Mountain Province house, elbows on her knees, and looked up to Laura.

"Do you think maybe it'd be wise?"

"Wise, or wimpy?" Laura responded. They both laughed.

Laura continued. "Well, some expats here say we need to atone for our countries' sins, colonizing. Like what Malcolm X said, who famously insisted, you'll recall, that every white American should kneel down in front of every black person and beg forgiveness. White people might say, 'why me? Slavery took place before I was born!' But Malcolm X responded that white people are still living on the spoils." Laura took a big gulp of her tea, it having cooled a little by now, and looked back to Becca for her response.

"Gotta think about that one; hadn't heard it before."

The women were silent, inhaling the steam and aroma rising from their teacups.

Becca resumed. "We have treated Filipinos as our 'little brown brothers,' like the book title of the early 1900's. But do we also 'colonize' with our academic research?"

Laura said, "Well, we've taken data back home. Several Americans over the 20th century, ever since 1898-1902 when we won occupation of the Philippines from the Spaniards, have written dissertations after their field work here, and have gotten fine jobs in American universities."

They sat quietly again. Becca went into her kitchen for the teapot, and returning, poured refills for each.

Laura looked up into a conifer tree above them. "The birds here are so different from the lowlands. You have temperate birds! That one sounds like a jay!"

"It is a jay, and he's here every day. We have so many birds, so many songs."

"Their world up there in the air, oh, to know more about them, their colors, their food, their songs... Kinda like the world under the surface of the sea, a whole world we tend not to learn about."

"Yeah."

Laura continued. "This woman, this nun, or Sister, she must have been indignant that I came in with enough money to pay my expenses and to hire an assistant researcher and a typist, and maybe felt that I was taking Filipino data out of the country for my own aggrandizement."

"How did she know you, anyway?" asked Becca.

"I was invited to teach a course to graduate linguistics students at the Ateneo de Manila University. The campus was reachable from my field site, which is the main original village of Philippine Creole Spanish, settled in 1662. Ateneo paid me the regular Philippine salary, which just covered my bus expense to get there and back."

They both laughed.

"Go on."

"So I had ten students, all with some experience with or interest in Chabacano. One of them was Sister Inez, who lived in a convent with an elementary and high school near our university, which is, by the way, also a Catholic university and funded largely by the church. The students all started the semester intrigued that research attention was being paid to this 'corrupt dialect.'"

"You convinced them otherwise, surely."

"Yes, they quickly became passionate about the language."

"They wanted to collect their own data?"

"Yes. One of them said her grandmother still lived in the Ermita district of Manila and spoke Chabacano as her first language, but her grandmother didn't know of any other living speakers. Sister Inez said that she was from Cotabato in the south and knew some of that dialect of Chabacano. By the middle of our semester, she announced that she had asked permission of her bishop to go down there for field work, and that she was excited to learn how to go about it in this seminar with me."

"You were honored, then?"

"She was bright and diligent, liked by the other students, and I liked her as well. The other students treated her even more respectfully than they did each other, probably because she was a little older and a Sister. She wore a habit. She is a little older than I, maybe by eight or so years."

Becca smiled and waved to two women passing by on the trail near her house, and Laura followed her example. The two women called a greeting, and continuing on their way, looked at each other, put their hands to their mouths, and giggled.

"That's about me, your visitor, I suppose," said Laura.

"Of course! They usually take that path farther down" and Becca pointed, "but they had heard that I have a visitor, and they wanted to take a look."

They were silent again for a few moments.

Becca resumed the topic. "So how'd she plagiarize?"

"In my weekly classes I brought information about Chabacano. Some items I had already published, including *Sound Changes in Chabacano* and *Relexification Processes in Philippine Creole Spanish* in a respected linguistics journal from another Manila university and a respected U.S. academic volume. Other data was raw. I even brought in one of my drawers of vocabulary cards, 3x5's."

"You wrote words on 3x5's?"

"Yes, and more extensive information on each entry than you usually see in a dictionary. Except for function words, that is, grammatical markers, I had a quotation for each word from a text. And the text came from tape recordings I had been making this past year. That's why I had a full-time research assistant, a local man who transcribed those recordings. That's laborious work, you know, 5-7 minutes of writing for each minute of recording. I was very happy to have found this man, Antero Icasiano, who speaks Chabacano as his first language, and he's quite competent. And then I hired a young woman who typed up all of his hand-written transcripts, also time-consuming work. So I was able to concentrate on interviewing people on a large variety of topics, like night fishing, and evil spirits at dusk, and why pigs seem to know when they'll be slaughtered. And I could take the time to plan who with and where to make the recordings. I went out into fields to follow farmers around as they talked about their crops. A midwife allowed me to accompany her to a birth, and she talked with the mother while she worked. One night I went out into the Manila Bay with night fishermen, but there I worried about keeping my recorder dry."

"Exciting recordings, then?"

"A lot of them, for this very full year and more. And another kind of work I did for each word: etymological search. I had dictionaries: an etymological Spanish one, and a Portuguese, and dictionaries of Sanskrit and Arabic loans coming in the past into Philippine languages. And Tagalog, of course, because, as you know, that's the language spoken by people in all the neighboring villages and in Manila."

"So you've been preparing a very deeply researched dictionary, then!"

"Yes, and I've been trying to capture *all* the vocabulary. No dictionary has been written for Chabacano, and I've been looking forward to making this contribution to Filipinos, to show them how rich this language is. It's not a corrupt language, but a heritage they can be proud of."

"They can sure use the boost. You and I have talked before about Filipinos' lack of self-esteem, that their belief that their culture is not as good as, in particular, America's."

"Yes, and likely because they never fought off the colonials. We've both heard many times, 'Americans rescued us from Spanish occupation [around 1902] and then Japanese occupation [1940-45] and we'll be forever grateful.'"

"Yeah, the Asian countries that did fight for independence don't suffer from this humility."

"So you have been planning to offer years of data and analysis to show Filipinos they can be proud of their heritage, right?"

"Yep, that's been a big motivator for me, even as big as getting a university position back home."

"But of course you really need a job, as well."

"Yeah, I really don't want to be a bag lady."

"But then, this Sister."

"Yeah, I've just learned that she published a Chabacano dictionary and 97 percent of all the material she stole from me!"

"You let her borrow all of your data?"

"Yes, for the weekend. We researchers like to help each other, don't we?"

"Um hmm, but weren't you even just a little suspicious?"

"Actually, no, I wasn't. In that class I felt that we had a good spirit of cooperation. I had had a confrontation with a professor at UP – University of the Philippines – in Manila, earlier. I had made an appointment with him to ask about the history of the Chabacano speakers that I heard he was working on. He had found some 17th century Spanish documents, I had heard. He expressed his annoyance at 'You Americans. Get your own data!'"

"Yes, Filipinos are usually so respectful to us, way too respectful, I think."

"I agree. But every once in a while, we experience a crack in the respect, hmm." Laura continued. "Like remember that time when I got in trouble over a car accident?"

"When that guy rear-ended you?"

"Yes, you remember."

"So you trusted this Sister."

"Yes. And then she published all of my vocabulary words, with each one used in a recorded utterance, and she published all this as the dialect of her area, Cotabato Chabacano, in her dictionary, and made no mention of my work."

"God. So what're you gonna do?"

"Becca, now I've come to ask your opinion."

"Let's see, what are your options, Laura? You could just leave it, never publish your years of data collection and analysis. Two, you could just proceed with your own publication."

"But I'd have to cite hers, somehow!"

"Hmm. Three, you could expose her. Write to her bishop, her dissertation advisor – she got her Ph.D. out of this, you said?"

"Yep."

"Or even a Manila newspaper article?"

"Not attractive to me."

"Or, four, you could write her a private letter. Wouldn't get you anywhere academically, but might help you feel a little vindicated?"

"Maybe. Get this: she has risen in the Catholic ranks. She is now a frequent substitute speaker for the Bishop of the Philippines, Cardinal Sin - hard to believe his name, isn't it! -

who we hear is on a short list to be the next Pope! She's a good public speaker."

"So, it'd be hard for people to believe that she could be such a cheater, then. So my advice is to write her a letter. Maybe cc. it to her bishop."

"Hmm. I'll think about this. Wise to remain silent? Or, wise to expose her, publicly or perhaps just privately?"

"Hey, want me to help you write *the* letter? I see it in big letters: 'I'm disappointed in you.' Or, 'You've disappointed me. You cheated, a person of God!'"

Laura laughed, and said, "Thanks for your offer, and I'll think about it."

60. Now What Can I Do?

A week after return to Ternate, Laura made her weekly trip to Manila to check on her mail. On this day, Marilu drove her downtown. Along with letters from her mother and from her sister, Laura received several thin letters from American universities and one British university.

Marilu waited for her in the car. "Any good news?"

Laura used her finger to rip open each envelope. "Rejections."

"Oh, I'm sorry." Marilu started up the car. "Remind me, Laura: when is your research grant finished?"

"I'm paid for eight more months. I can do the writing up either here or back in California. And by then, I need to have a job."

"You've got more applications out?"

"Yeah. But with my year and a half of data stolen, and not many openings anyway, I have slim chances for a university position."

They sat in heavy traffic, and the car's air conditioner dripped cold water on Laura's sandaled feet. Marilu said, "You have so much investment in your career!

"No jobs. You know, Marilu, I need to earn enough to survive plus be able to come here to the Philippines sometimes. I had been counting on a university job that would pay me for doing research here. I've always wanted to make a contribution, like my current goal, to make and write about a discovery that would help other people."

Traffic started moving, and they weren't far from Marilu's home. She asked, "Could linguistic research help other people?"

"I thought so. It's been an important part of my passion to study contact languages. Most people in the world are loyal to their own language, sometimes even fiercely so. Think of recent wars over languages in India, even Belgium! But with contact languages, the speakers are ashamed of them. They all know that the vocabulary came from a major language in the world, the language of the colonizers. I've been on a mission to show these people that even though it is quite different than the grammar of Spanish, Chabacano definitely has a real grammar, and it shares grammatical similarities with other contact languages all over the world. And furthermore, these contact languages developed right on the forefront of European exploration and discovery, starting in the late 15th century, that have greatly expanded our knowledge of the world. I've been planning to show Chabacano speakers that their heritage came right on the crest of great discoveries of the world."

A guard opened the compound's security gate to the "village", and at Marilu's house, the gardener opened up the garage door. Marilu slowly pulled in, stopped the car, and turned to Laura.

"Hey, Laura, I want you to meet some friends tomorrow. They're four filmmakers, and they just got a windfall, a big grant from one of our oligarchs, whose daughter wants to 'make a serious film', a documentary. I told them about you, and they want to meet you."

"Uh, okay, but I don't know anything about filmmaking." *Oh, so this is why she was asking these questions about my job prospects!*

Marilu invited the film friends for *merienda cena* [afternoon snacks], the next day. Three young men and one woman had recently completed their study in the best film school in the country, Ateneo de Manila University in Quezon City, the university where Laura was also teaching! And Laura was surprised and delighted to find her former student Fely, who had graduated in linguistics, greeting her.

"We want to show our countrymen and women that we can be proud of ourselves," Berto said.

"We thought of showing that we live in one of the most beautiful places on earth," added Nanoy.

"And then concentrate on our excellent educational system. Nationally, almost 100% high school graduation, and we supply nurses to the whole world!" Ligaya added.

And finally Fely spoke. "I asked these fellow graduates to join me because I heard that they are the very best in filmmaking. My dad offered to fund our first film."

Berto spoke again. "When Marilu and Fely told us about your Spice Islands project, we all wanted to hear more.

"About Chabacano?" Laura asked. "I'm surprised, because it has such low status, and here in Manila, the only speakers are seniors in their seventies and eighties."

"Fely told us that you said it developed because Spaniards came eastward to beat the Arabs at the Spice Trade, and they hired local people, and they developed this strange new language as they learned to communicate with each other."

"Something like that, yes," Laura said.

"And some people wondered if Chabacano might even show us how human languages first evolved!" Fely said. "And you people who study languages had already decided that how babies learn to talk doesn't show us the missing link."

"But what about other Chabacanos? Where else in the world are they? Were they also in places where Spaniards explored?" Stefano asked.

They talked until late evening, their excitement building with each new discovery about their shared interests. Marilu furiously took notes. By the end of the evening they had a story of grand scope starting with the first historical evidence of trees that evolved only in eastern Indonesia and that had medicinal and aesthetic value; how Arab traders introduced spices from these trees to Europeans; how Europeans built ocean-worthy ships and explored ways to reach Southeast Asia via the east and the west; how they discovered and colonized as they competed with one another for the Spice Trade; and how all this had ramifications up to the present time.

The following Monday they met to drive to the estate of the potential donor in the most prestigious Manila district, Forbes Park. Laura and the three young men and young woman crowded into a little Toyota Corona taxi for the trip. They waited at the compound entrance for the guards to call to Mr. Esquivel's house for clearance. At his estate gate, they waited again for clearance. After the enormous metal gate was rolled back for their little car, they drove through hectares of the bright green and brilliantly blooming garden, pinks of striped lilies and *bougainvillea's*, vivid blue of *Clitoria Ternatea*, white and yellow of plumeria and spiral ginger. The curving cobblestone driveway was shaded by overhanging tropical forest trees.

The taxi driver pulled to a stop at the entrance to a wide two story, light gray stone house. As a uniformed staff member approached the car, Fely ran out toward the guests, springing down the steps, laughing, welcoming them. "My father can't wait to hear about your story."

They talked into the night and then again the next day, and Laura agreed to a new work adventure in the Philippines, with a three-year contract.

61. Adapt!

Becca came down to Manila now and then from her Mountain Province field site to pick up her mail. This time she stopped in to see Laura and Marilu just after Laura had signed up for the documentary.

They sat as usual in the cool shade of Marilu's terrace. Becca asked after Marilu's husband. "I see his car in the driveway, so he's here?"

"Oh, he came home for some documents, but he'll go back to the office soon."

Becca turned to Laura. "Looks like you're starting over, Laura. So how does the film industry look?"

"Daunting. I really don't know a lot about it yet. I don't know what value this work here would have in the States for continuing work in this field. But I'm invited here to learn from the four filmmakers who have been hired to work with us. I'll have new skills to take back to the States, but... I don't know! I've gotten a three-year job offer, with a U.S. level salary, so I'm going with it."

"How can you be the leader of a group in such a new field for you?"

"Well, we've agreed that I'll lead the team like a teacher, a professor, a skill in which I have experience. Our first big task at the start is to identify research fields. We'll do that by brainstorming and asking experts in each of those fields. Then I'll help the students – I mean the new graduates whom we're hiring – and they'll work in singles or pairs to research topics. We'll come together from time to time to hear working reports, and then after critiquing, they'll go back for more research. I'll help them to identify sources, that is, people and material, and I'll ask questions as well."

"How about the story?"

"That's another kind of brainstorming, and we'll have the help of a fantastic Filipino screenwriter. But first we're going to gather a lot of research data on different topics to bring into those conversations."

Marilu sat back in her chair, quietly listening, not adding any details, but preparing to take notes.

Becca asked further. "So what kinds of research will you go out for?"

"Yes, 'out.' We'll probably be sending at least a couple of our people to other countries. Our budget is generous. Here are some of our topics", and she handed Becca her copy of notes from the recent negotiations and brainstorming.

- Geology of the Spice Islands
- First peopling of the Moluccas
- First discovery of the spices
- First foreigner discovery, first trade, of the spices
- History of Chinese traders in the Moluccas
- History of Arabs in the Moluccas
- Relation of Spice Trade to the Silk Road
- Relation of the Spice Trade to the spread of Islam
- Relation of the Spice Trade to the Crusades
- Importance of spices in medicine, food, prestige
- Development of pidgins/creoles along the routes of European explorations and trade
- Europeans compete: Portuguese, (Vasco da Gama, Columbus, Magellan) Spanish, Dutch, English, French
- Relation of the Dutch East Indies Company to the Spice Trade
- Manhattan traded for Run, one of the Bandas, in 1667 (in the Treaty of Breda)
- Collapse of spice prices in the 19th century as medicine advanced into science
- Spread of cultural behaviors with the Spice Trade

"Exciting, and I envy you!" Becca said. "Sounds like you've found a fantastic alternative to a drying up field in a university."

Laura said, "I guess I've learned a lot this year. I've learned more about leading a student group, and I did teach elementary school a long time ago, but this project does not take place in a university. I should have had better foresight about choosing a career, and when the jobs started evaporating, I stuck with this field too stubbornly. A job is even more urgent now that I'm responsible for two, not just for myself. I learned that I shouldn't look for or count on a man to take care of me, of us. I've got more fortitude than I knew. Friends are valuable. And now I'll learn if I can meet this new challenge."

62. A New Job

Fely and her father, Francisco Esquivel, invited Laura to his office downtown to formally offer her the position of director and producer of a documentary on the Spice Trade.
Mr. Esquivel called the working title "the role of the Philippines in the great Spice Trade that started more than five thousand years ago and changed the world."

"Now, what are your salary and benefit requirements, Dr. Rhodes, and length of contract? Let's sign you up first and then deal with details, including budget. I have full confidence in my daughter, who has convinced me of your full capability to handle this job."

The three worked all afternoon on the start of their business plan, and then they drove to the Esquivel house in Forbes Park for dinner.

By the time Laura returned home, Charlotte had already been put to bed and was sleeping.

Next morning, Saturday, they laid in bed talking. Charlotte told her mom that at yesterday's birthday party she had ridden in a *calesa*, "and after, the driver let me feed a carrot to his horse! But first he had to take the... the thing ... out of the horse's mouth..."

"The bit?"

"Yeah. And he gave me a carrot and he said, 'hold your hand open, like this,' and the horse nibbled it out of my hand!"

"The horse was gentle?"

"Yes, tall, but big teeth, a little scary, but he didn't hurt me."

"Oh, what fun for you!" and she hugged her daughter.

"Hey, Charlotte, what do you think about staying here in the Philippines longer?"

Charlotte looked into her mother's eyes, waiting for more.

"I got a job offer yesterday. That's where I was last night. You remember Fely?"

"In your class?"

"Yes. Well, last night she and her father offered me a job that'd be for three years, maybe more. And they would pay tuition for you to attend the International School, because as you know next fall you'll get to go to kindergarten."

Charlotte was silent.

"What do you think, my dear?"

"Kindergarten! Will I get to wear a uniform?"

"You already know that they have uniforms?"

"All the big kids, the school kids, wear uniforms, don't they! White blouse, green skirt with little straps. Like I wore in Indonesia! I want to wear like that!"

63. The Spice Islands Rose Out of the Sea

Laura facilitated their brainstorming. She had asked the small assembled crew, "Can you think of questions you'd like to be answered about spices and The Spice Trade?"

Berto asked, "Why would we want to make a movie about the Spice Islands, Laura? The Philippines are not, "the Spice Islands," you've let us know."

Nanoy added, "Yes, you're right, Berto. I mean, I've heard "the Spice Islands," but I don't even know where they are, just that they're not ours. What are the spices, even? Like are both chili and salt spices?"

Laura looked around at each of them and waited for Marilu's maid to pour another round into their glasses. "This country has had great, direct consequences of the search for spices, for more than 5,000 years. And consequences not only this country, but every other country on earth."

Ligaya asked, "Even our small 7,000 islands?"

Fely wrote questions on a big blackboard as the "crew" brainstormed questions.

Fely turned to the group to say, "Here's a question I'd like to be answered: 'How could the whole world change because people were looking for something they didn't need? – incense, spices, and perfume? I mean, they're luxuries, aren't they?"

And Berto asked, "Why didn't the Portuguese just plant those trees in other places? Why go to war over some little, out-of-the-way islands?"

Nanoy asked, "Is it true that the Dutch traded Manhattan Island in the U.S. for that tiny spice island, Run?"

Fely asked, "Is it true that Spaniards came to the Philippines mainly because of their interest in the spices? And if so, why come to some islands that did not have spices?"

More questions included the following:

- Why did people pay so much for frankincense and myrrh?

- Why did those governments go after the spices?

- How did Portuguese develop those boats? How did they navigate?

- What have been consequences for us by now, the 20th century?

- How did power shift from Arabs to Europeans?

- What role did weapons have in the competition for the spices? No guns back then, right?

- Were spices carried along the Silk Road? Or were there separate routes?

- If the Spice Trade has been so important to world history, then why haven't we heard much about it?

- What languages did sellers, traders, buyers use? And did our Chabacano really evolve as a part of the Spice Trade?

Laura concluded their meeting with her invitation to them to come to tomorrow's meeting with more questions for all to consider, and as a second step they would brainstorm the feasibility and relevance of each idea. From the surviving questions she proposed that they would start to construct their story arc.

64. Migo Visits

Migo visited as usual by now on Friday afternoons, just as the nursery school bus dropped the three children (Marilu's two and Charlotte) off at Marilu's. They politely greeted Laura and Migo on their way toward the kitchen.

Laura and Migo sat on the terrace. Marilu was downtown. Laura and Migo had just finished snacks when Charlotte came in with a drawing she had made at school this day for Migo, a *bahay kubo* (nipa hut on stilts) with a girl on the steps leading up to it. "For you," she held it out to him. "That's me" she pointed.

"Oh, *salamat po!*" and he smiled as he took it with two hands. She smiled, and then ran back to the other children in the kitchen.

"Oh, very dear of her." Migo showed the drawing to Laura, who smiled with pride and returned it to him.

"Did you learn in your U.S. mail this week of any job openings?"

So Laura told him about the Sister's plagiarizing and publication of Laura's field data on Chabacano.

"What a story!" he exclaimed. "What are you going to do about it?"

"Too late to do anything. It's already published, with her name."

"I wonder... I wonder what the publishers would do if they knew about it? ... Which publisher, did you say?"

She told him.

"Hmm.. Laura, would you mind if I investigate?"

"Well I guess I wouldn't mind. But could you please tell me before you publish anything?"

"Sure. I'll even offer you last editing rights."

....

Migo wrote a feature article which appeared in the front section of *The Manila Times*. He had interviewed the publisher and also Brother Alberto at De La Salle University. He had requested an interview with the Sister, but she refused.

At Migo's next visit to Laura and Charlotte, Laura said, "But you're making it more possible for me to return to the U.S. even if later. If I could get my own dictionary published, it'd be a major contribution , though in a very specialized field. It would enhance my chances of getting a university position in the U.S. You'd see less of Charlotte!"

He responded, "I really want what's best for you and Charlotte, Laura."

Laura asked Marilu that evening, "Is this man really so magnanimous, so selfless?"

65. Migo, Journalist

Here are excerpts of Migo's article.

The *Manila Times*

October 3, 1973
by Miguel Montemayor
Staff Journalist

"She's a foreigner, but she was doing more for our country than the Filipina Sister who stole her years of carefully collected data.*

"Dr. Laura Rhodes planned to show Filipinos that we can be proud of our heritage, and she would show us new historical evidence. The thief, in contrast, published just the vocabulary, without any valuable analysis."

The long article listed Dr. Rhodes' bonafides including her research on the Spanish contact language Chabacano in Cavite Province and several other locations in the Philippines. And, during this year how she has taught a graduate linguistics seminar at Ateneo de Manila University on contact languages, especially Chabacano.

"Dr. Rhodes had investigated but found no Filipino with plans to conduct research on the language. Filipinos have shown little respect for the language, saying 'it has no grammar.' Dr. Rhodes has planned to publish her analysis that the language deserves respect. Furthermore, its evolution is directly related to the millennia-long great Spice Trade, which was the main reason Spaniards came to the Philippines. 'This language,' she wrote, 'shows how important for centuries people in the Philippines have been to world history.'

"Among her students in the seminar was a Dominican Sister from Santa Catalina College who apparently in good faith asked to borrow all of Dr. Rhodes' by-now 15,000 vocabulary cards – in ten boxes - for a weekend.

"Imagine Dr. Rhodes' astonishment when she discovered last month that Sister Inez has just published a Chabacano dictionary! It was published by our venerable Augustinian Order of the Catholic Church Publishing in Quezon City. No mention of sources. Dr. Rhodes' careful examination reveals that more than 98% of this volume has been taken from those vocabulary cards that she had "borrowed" six months ago from Dr. Rhodes.

"What, if anything, can be done? Is there any way that Dr. Rhodes can reclaim her rightful ownership? After all, she did want to publish in the Philippines – 'for Filipinos.' She had already taken a contract with De La Salle University Publishing, and she had even gotten a copyright in this country and in the U.S. Her title for the Philippines? *Filipinos Can Be Proud of Chabacano.*

"When this journalist learned of the theft, a story was envisioned for the public. Plagiarism is not a legal theft, but it's a moral transgression that affects not only the real author, but also the readers. And of course it harshly reflects on the character of the perpetrator.

"This journalist interviewed Dr. Rhodes. Her data and even copies of many notes were examined. These and a copy of the plagiarized dictionary were taken to linguists at two of our universities. After learning of the dating of theses compared with those in the published book, they agreed that the data had been stolen. One of these linguists admitted that he was reluctant to offer his analysis, because "These rich foreigners come here with their tape recorders and their money to hire local helpers, and they just take our national treasures. But she – Dr. Rhodes – looks like she's the one who got there first and gathered all the data. And her analysis is completely credible."

"We contacted the Sister again, who again declined our request for interview.

"We presented evidence to the Philippine copyright authorities, who investigated and proclaimed that the published dictionary infringed on Dr. Rhodes' prior copyright.

"We contacted the Augustinian Publishing House, who immediately stopped sales, requested return of copies they had sent out to universities, and requested that Sister Inez return her monetary advance.

"With these actions, Dr. Rhodes will be able to reclaim her ownership of the data she had so diligently gathered, together with the cooperation of many native speakers of this unusual and intriguing language.

We contacted the rector of Santa Catalina College of the Dominican Order where Sister Inez is an established member; they have confronted her, they are considering several actions, and they will report results to this journalist.

"And we of the *Manila Times* newspaper expect and will publish a profound apology from the plagiarist."

———

*Dr. Rhodes of course still has her hundreds of tape recordings and her draft manuscript.

66. Maybe We Could Go Home, After All!

Letters to the editor poured in (pro, con, mixed) in response to the *Manila Times* article.

Laura was astounded. "Marilu, he's made it possible for me to get a job back in the States! But why would he do that? He surely knows that I'd be taking Charlotte, and he'd therefore see much less of her. He wouldn't have secret plans of trying to keep her here, would he?"

"No, I don't think so. Now that we've gotten to know him, seeing him every week, he doesn't seem devious at all. Maybe he thinks that your Charlotte would get a better education in the States. You know that many Filipinos would love to live in the States if they could! And by now he knows you're not going to rekindle that long-ago romance."

"Well, Marilu, it does seem like he's making a big sacrifice. He wouldn't see much of Charlotte, after all his effort to see her in the first place, and his faithful visits with her every week. Even with a good salary, it'd be a challenge for him to afford an international ticket to visit her in the U.S."

"I wonder, Laura, if he really might have your best interests at heart. From all you've told me, and from what we've learned with his visits, he might be a real good person."

Laura sat silently for some time before she said, "You know, Marilu, It's hard for me to trust that he – or any man – could be so generous."

She sat silently again. And then said, "Marilu, he really *has* been generous, making it possible for me to reclaim all my data. And that he even followed through with the publisher and all to stop the theft!"

"So what are you going to do for your thank you, my dear?"

"What? Oh... I'm thinking, Marilu. I haven't gotten that far in my thinking."

Marilu smiled quietly.

Laura said, "Well, I still haven't seen any job opportunities in the States, so in the meantime I'll continue working on the Spice Trade documentary here. That means we'll be here for a while, so he can continue to see Charlotte."

"And then?"

"And then... if... I mean *when* I get a job in the States, I suppose I could send him a plane ticket to visit after we get settled."

"Good thinking, Laura! You know what? I can imagine that he'd love to write a strong review of your Spice Trades documentary. Everyone in the Philippines would learn about this important part of our history."

FIN

APPENDIX

The Spice Islands Chronology

Homo erectus walked to Java, Indonesia, across a land bridge almost 2 million years ago. Homo sapiens, in contrast, didn't get anywhere by sea crossings until sometime between 53 to 65K years ago, that is, until after they made boats. Probably the first boats were dugout canoes. In the Moluccan islands, including the Spice Islands, there never were land bridges; these new islands emerged from the sea as volcanoes long after the big land masses had broken up. On these virgin islands, small numbers of flora and fauna developed, some of them unique, including the clove and nutmeg trees. That's why the Moluccas' miraculous trees were found nowhere else.

As early as 60,000 and as late as 45,000 years ago, early Homo sapiens walked by a land bridge and settled in Indonesia west of the Moluccas (that is, west of the Wallace Line). The island of Flores became an archaeological hot spot 30 years ago with the discovery of "island dwarfism." Remains were found of people who had stood 3 feet tall, and also found were associated dwarf flora and fauna.

- These dates compare with analysis of H.s. remains in Australia showing that they first settled there around 50,000 years ago. And those people arrived by sea.

- 43,000 BCE, analysis shows that Homo sapiens on Java already had high level maritime skills; sites show remains of deep sea tuna. They came in what is known as "the Neolithic Expansion."

-By 9,000 BCE, in South Asia, Indians had agriculture. Later, they were the first to have started exporting spices. They first traveled over land (on "the incense route"), with their cinnamon and black pepper to the Mediterranean, mainly to

Romans. They also exported to Indonesia and all of Southeast Asia.

- By 9,000 BCE (< D. Yen, personal communication), as well, archaeological sites show that lowland New Guinea Melanesians (Homo sapiens) had agriculture, and were cultivating, harvesting, and eating yams and taro. So surely later, when people migrated from Melanesia to the Moluccas, their people had been cultivating crops for 5-6 thousand years and brought agriculture with them. They hunted deer, (that they had brought with them to propagate in the new terrain), they made sago palm starch, and maybe they brought bananas.

- Around 3,200 BCE was when the first people migrated to the North Moluccas, including Ternate and Tidore, they arrived in boats, having crossed 200 miles of open sea.

Because they had traveled across open sea, they undoubtedly ate fish. One archaeologist, T. Flannery, showed sites dating from 1400 BCE to 250 CE that pigs and dogs were introduced into Halmahera, the larger island next to Ternate and Tidore. They were brought from New Guinea so that pigs would reproduce for food, and dogs were not eaten but were used for hunting. The humans hunted and fought with bow and arrow.

These islands formed on still active volcanoes. They're still very steep and forested with just a fringe of relatively flat sandy perimeter. So the migrants would have settled along the shores.

They probably immediately started using cloves and nutmegs, because these spices are easily available, aromatic, and tasty.

Early users of the spices disguised tainted meat, but the spices, especially cloves, prevented spoilage as well. And in the process of eating, they surely discovered the pain-killing property of cloves. They also used the spices in preserving the burial of their dead.

2,700 BCE is the date archaeologists have determined of Egyptian mummies embalmed with nutmeg.

Around 2,000 BCE, The Austronesian language family evolved in Taiwan. Austronesian speakers arrived from Taiwan into Malaysia, Indonesia and the Philippines. Speakers of these languages came to settle on land around one third of the earth's circumference! In doing so, the language family spread out more than any other language family, that is, before the European expansion starting in 1492.

Also ca. 2000 BCE, North Africans traded frankincense and myrrh to West Africa. The transport was by camel caravans across the Sahara.

1700 BCE is the date archaeologists determined for cloves found in a site in Tel Ashara, Syria. This site is 6,000 miles away from the Spice Islands, and traders likely passed through Cochin in India and overland through Mesopotamia. At each port and trade of hands, the value was multiplied. In Europe, the value was thousands of times more than in the Moluccas.

By 1,000 BCE, Arabs were getting spices from India. Early on, they first carried the spices over land.

By 100 BCE, Egyptians were the first to record their trading around the Red Sea of Indonesian spices. By then, Arabs and others (Chinese, Siamese) were trading spices, and they traveled by land and sea.

Also by 100 BCE, Indonesians were trading in spices (mainly cinnamon and cassia) with E Africa using catamaran boats. And by then, wet rice agriculture had started and made possible the development of small towns.

Human passion for spices and the subsequent Spice Trade funded explorations, expansions and empires of the old world up to the 19th century. Passion declined when modern medicine was more effective, and guns were brought into use. Empires were funded by the sale of spices from Indonesia and India.

By late 200-100 BCE, Indians and Arabs had control over the Indian Ocean. Greeks learned from Indians how to sail; then they took control of the sea trade.

By 60 BCE, Arabs took control of the land trade of spices from South Arabia to the Mediterranean. Sea, making Arab tribes very wealthy.

In 570 CE, the Prophet Mohammed was born in Mecca. He died on June 3, the year 632, in Medina.

In 650 CE: Islam started rising. As Muslims carried their religion eastward, they returned home to the Near East with cloves and nutmeg. And then from the Near East, they used overland and sea routes westward to Mediterranean coastal ports.

647-850 CE: Chinese went to India and learned there how to refine sugar.

600-1100: The Srivijaya Empire (Hindu-Buddhists, from India) took over Indonesia including the Moluccas. They came first to trade spices with China, but then they settled in. Later, they were overtaken by Islam.

8th – 15th centuries CE: Venice, on the Mediterranean coasts, had a monopoly of the Spice Trade in Europe. City-states developed all along the routes, and became wealthy by trading silk, spices, incense, and herbs, medicines, and opium. At one point in the 14th century, a pound of nutmeg in Europe cost seven fattened oxen and was more valuable than gold.

1293 CE: Mongols from China – Muslims – invaded Java.

1300-1500 CE: The Majapahit Empire, also from India, Hindu-Buddhists, developed and had tremendous impact in Indonesia including the Moluccas and even the southern Philippines. Its boundaries actually became the modern boundaries of Indonesia in 1949. The empire was financed by wet rice agriculture in Java and by the Spice Trade.

1400 CE +: Islam came to Indonesia, fueled by Arab trading of spices. As they expanded, they converted people to Islam. (Among major religions, only Christianity and Islam actively proselytize. Now, in the 21st C, Indonesia has the world's largest Muslim population.) Arabs used a system of local controls at ports and cities along the thousands of miles of routes.

The Tordesillas Treaty of 1494 gave Ternate (and Brazil, and part of Africa) to Portugal, but the Dutch didn't honor the treaty. See below.

But by 1498, Europeans sought to bypass all the middlemen of the Spice Trade. Europeans wanted monopoly and consequently the thousands of percentage of financial markup for themselves. They got it, and their trade importantly contributed to the growing wealth of their countries.

Portuguese, captained by Vasco da Gama in 1492, were the first to successfully navigate around the Cape of Good Hope in Africa in order to reach the Indian Ocean by sea. They sailed to Cochin in Kerala, India, the Indian center of spice trade. In pioneering the maritime route, they successfully skirted around their competitors, who were using the overland trails of the Silk and Spice routes.

In 1512, Portuguese settled in Ternate, confronting the reigns of the sultans of Ternate and Tidore.

Portuguese controlled most of the Spice Trade from 1580 to1640 but they lost their battles with the Spaniards by 1640, who then lost to the Dutch by 1662.

Spaniards arrived a decade after the Portuguese. They had been slowed down for twenty years fighting Arabs at sea, and so they didn't sail into the Moluccas until 1521. Other European expeditions, all funded by ruling kings, competed: the Netherlands, England, and France. They fought against each other and against the Moluccans.

In 1521, the Spaniard Ferdinand Magellan was killed in Mactan, the Philippines, on April 27th of that year. His ships continued on, and they arrived in Tidore on November 6, 1521. There they took in an enormous amount of spices (documented by Pigafetta). Magellan's expedition became the first global circumnavigation, but only 18 of the original 240 men had survived. His single surviving ship returned to Sevilla in 1522 with 26 tons of spices, paying for the whole circumnavigation and making the king and many others even more wealthy.

In 1529 the Spaniard Ceron tried to sail eastward from Manila but couldn't find winds. Up through this time, the trade routes all went westward from the Spice Islands.

In 1565 the Spaniard Andres de Urdaneta reasoned that the winds of the Pacific might move in a gyre as Atlantic winds did. So they sailed north to the 38th parallel off the coast of Japan, and there they caught the eastward blowing winds. Their first trip eastward got them to Cape Mendocino, far north of their destination. So they followed the coast down to Acapulco, Mexico.

The role of the Philippines? Even though none of the desired spices were native, and they couldn't even be cultivated there, by 1565, Manila had become an international trade center of products from China and from the Spice Islands, carried eastward by Spanish galleons to Mexico and then from Caribbean Sea ports on to Spain.

Spain and Portugal spent much of the 16th century fighting over cloves in Ternate and Tidore while England and the Dutch dueled over nutmeg in Ambon and the Banda islands, where Portuguese also held power.

In 1605, Dutch conquered the Portuguese to take control of Ambon, but they weren't successful in chasing out the English. So, tension continued to develop between the English and the Dutch.

In 1619, King James 1st of England (who was also busy that year with the Mayflower expedition to the New World) cooperated in a treaty with the Dutch, resulting in the spice market being divided and shared. But tension remained.

In 1623, in the great massacre of Ambon, Europeans killed thousands of people in Ternate, Tidore, Ambon, and other Banda islands.

During that time, Spain allied with the sultan of Tidore, and the Portuguese allied with the sultan of Ternate.

In 1667, Dutch finally conquered all of Indonesia. Their first headquarters was the island of Ternate, and for the Spice Trade, in 1602, they had formed the Dutch East Indies Company (the VOC – Verenigde Oostindische Compagnie), the first publicly traded company in the world.

In 1687, the Dutch finally got the English out of the Moluccas by exchanging the tiny Banda island of Run, which by then had domesticated nutmegs, for the island of Manhattan in New York.

By 1800, people lost their intense passion for the spices. But by then, Europeans had eclipsed the trade power of the Arab world, and they had "discovered" the New World, brought first to European attention by Spain and Portugal. Excitement for the New World eclipsed thousands of years of passion for the Spice Islands.

In the 20th century, Portuguese and Spanish pidgins and creoles were found, and some still exist, in many of the places that Portuguese and Spaniards colonized as they moved eastward to Asia and Southeast Asia, and westward to the Caribbean and Central and South America.

During1942-45, Japan occupied Indonesia and the Philippines.

On August 17, 1945, the Moluccas became part of the new Indonesian Republic (against Dutch accord). In 1949, Indonesians successfully freed themselves of almost 300 years of Dutch colonization, and they formed their new republic.

In the 1960's, Indonesia's President Sukarno committed genocide against Indonesian Chinese, resulting in thousands killed, including those in the Moluccas.

In the late 20th century, Christians and Muslims fought there, resulting in several thousand people killed.

REFERENCES

Creoles:

Archives in Santiago, Chile: ca. 120 pp. photocopies of original documents.

"Boundaries and Bridges: Language Contact in Multilingual Ecologies" by Kofi Yakpo, U. Hong Kong, Academia.edu, 1 p.

"Creole Languages" in AWL (About World Languages.) 13 pp.

Esquivel, Don Diego de, "*Gramatica y Diccionario de los Mardikas*" of Ternate, Indonesia, 1662.

"English is Not Normal" by John McWhorter. The Week 12/29/16, 2 pp.

"Middle English Creole Hypothesis." Wikipedia, 3 pp.

Murillo Velarde, Pedro, s.j., *Historia de la provincia de Philippinas de la Compañia de Jesus.* Imprenta de la Compañia de Jesus, Tomo IV, Lib. III, Manila, 1749.

"Recent Relexification Processes in Philippine Creole Spanish," by Carol H. Molony [Pechler], 1977, in *Sociocultural Dimensions of Language Change*, edited by Ben G. Blount and Mary Sanches. Academic Press, New York.

"Sound Changes in Chabacano" by Carol H. Molony [Pechler], 1973. In *Parangal Kay Cecilio Lopez*, Linguistic Society of the Philippines, edited by Andrew B. Gonzalez, F.S.C.

"The Scarcity of Spanish-Based Creoles Explained" by John H. McWhorter. JStor Online, from *Language in Society Journal* 24:2, June 1995, pp. 213-244.

Whinnom, Keith, *Spanish Contact Vernaculars in the Philippine Islands.* Hong Kong: Hong Kong University Press, 1956.

Explorer:

"Ferdinand Magellan," Wikipedia, 11 pp.

Humors:

"Humorism" Wikipedia. 7 pp.

"What is Damp Humor?" Canadian Gynecology Institute of Chinese Medicine. 5 pp.

"The Five States of Change." Wu Xing. Kheper Home/Eastern Philosophy 4 pp.

"Valence" Google 2 pp.

Indonesia, Moluccas:

"The Spanish Presence in the Moluccas: Ternate and Tidore." Internet, 7 pp.

"Sultanate of Ternate." Wikipedia, 5 pp.

Maps, geology, geography:

"Ancient Seafarers." Special report by Peter Bellwood in Archaeology, 1997. 4 pp.

"Banda Islands." Wikipedia, 9 pp.

"Diving in the Moluccas" starfish. ch. 4 pp.

"Indonesia: Other Islands" Wikipedia.

"Maluku Geology and Ecology." Indahnesia.com, 1 p.

"Maluku Islands." Wikipedia, 8 pp.

"Marek Bialoglowy's Blog, Siau Island: North Sulawesi (Indonesia) Internet, 6 pp.

"Siau Island," Wikipedia, 1 p.

"Spice Islands (Moluccas): 250 years of Maps (1521 – 1760). 8 pp.

"Moluccas Geology", Wikipedia,9 pp.

 "Morotai Island Regency to Siau Island"; "Siau Island;" "Run Island." Google Maps

"Prehistory of the Philippines." Wikipedia, 14 pp.

"The Indonesian Archipelago: an Ancient Genetic Highway linking Asia and the Pacific." In *J. of Human Genetics* 58, 2013. 22 pp.,7 authors.

"Underwater Ternate." www.SamTernate, 5 pp.

Navigation;

"History of Navigation: Wikipedia, 3 pp.

"Trans-Pacific Passage, West to East. CruisersWiki, 6 pp.

"When was the sea route from the eastern part of Asia (Japan, Australia) to the western part of North/South America (California, British Columbia) discovered and who discovered it?" Online, 3 pp with maps.

Philippines:

In Our Image: America's Empire in the Philippines, Stanley Karnow, 1989, Random House.

"It's still genocide even if they die by starvation." Carol H. Molony (Pechler). *Stern* Magazine, Germany, July 1973

"Laguna Copperplate Inscription" Wikipedia, 8 pp.

"Libraries in the Philippines," Wikipedia, 11 pp.

Little Brown Brother: How the United States Purchased and Pacified the Philippine Islands at the Century's Turn. Leon Wolf, 1961, Doubleday.

"Manila Galleon" Wikipedia, 10 pp.

"Martial Law in the Philippines": Wiki 8 pp.

"On Father's Rights in Custody Cases" Wikipedia

"Rebels fighting in south, Marcos says." NY Times, 11/30/1972. 2 pp.

"The Spanish Period" (in the Philippines). Online Life Inspired, 4 pp.

"Traditional Filipino Nicknames." The Philippine Genealogical Society On-Line: 3 Sept. 2010. 8 pp.

Plants; Agriculture:

"Interactions of Beneficial and Detrimental Root-colonizing Filamentous Microbes with Plant Hosts." Thomas Rey and Sebastian Schornack, 2013, *Genome Biology:* 14(6): 121, 8 pp.

"Meet the biologist who says trees have their own songs. " Biologist David George Haskell, Tennessee, in CBC Radio online, "As It Happens." 4 pp.

"Plants talk to each other using an internet of fungus." Nic Fleming in BBC online, 11 November 2014, 11 pp.

"Subsistence to Commerce in Pacific Agriculture: Some Four Thousand Years of Plant Exchange" Douglas E. Yen, in *Plants for Food and Medicine*, 1998. 23 pp.

The Hidden Life of Trees: What They Feel, How They Communicate – Discoveries from a Secret World. By Peter Wohlleben, 2015. Translated by Jane Billinghurst, 2016, Greystone Books. The book quotes Suzanne Simard several times.

"The Human Consequences of Deforestation in the Moluccas." Roy Ellen, in: *Civilisations* 44, 1997. 3 pp.

"The Origins of Subsistence Agriculture in Oceania and the Potentials for Future Tropical Food Crops." Douglas E. Yen, In *Economic Botany* 47:1, 1993. 12 pp.

Spices:

"Chinese Herbs Healing" Art of herbal remedies revealed. About Nutmeg. Wikipedia, 5 pp.

"Cloves." Wikia.com/wiki, 6 pp.

"Cloves, Cinnamon, Mace and Nutmeg: the Spice Islands Spices." In Factsanddetails.com. 8 pp.

"Cloves Consumption by Country." ChartsBin, 2 pp.

"Cumin, Camels, and Caravans: A Spice Odyssey" by Gary Willem Nabhan, 4/7/14. 4 pp.

"Fresh Mace and Nutmeg" by Marketman. In *Market Manila*, 7/18/12.

"History of Cloves" Wikipedia, 5 pp.

"How to Grow Cloves" Wikipedia, 2 pp.

"Magical properties in common herbs and spices!" Andrew. 5 pp.

"Nutmeg, Wikipedia. 8 pp.

"Nutmeg and Mace." WebMD 5 pp.

"Nutmeg , Nutmeg Benefits." In "Herbwisdom.com. 7 pp.

"Sacred Spices." 3 pp.

"Spice use in Antiquity." Wiki. 8 pp "The Nutmeg" by Dr. Albert Schneider. "Birds and All Nature," April 1899. 2 pp.

"The World's History in a Clove Tree." By Amitav Ghosh, NY Times, 1/1/17 2 pp.

"The World's Top Clove Producing Countries. Cloves are grown in what countries?" Wikipedia, 4 pp.

"Two Forgotten Healing Herbs of Christmas" from Miriam. In *The Sacred Science: Healing Knowledge for the Strong of Heart.* 4 pp.

Spice Trade:

"Dutch East Indies Company" (VOC): first publicly traded, first international company. Wikipedia, 30 pp.

"English East Indies Company," Wikipedia, 2 pp.

"Fort Kochi, Kerala: Remains of a Spice Coast." LiveMint online, 5 pp.

"History of Kochi" Internet, 6 pp. + 1 map

"History of the Spice Trade." 2 pp.

"How the Spice Trade Changed the World." Livescience.com, Heather Whipps, 5/12/2008 2 pp., McGill University, Quebec, Canada.

NCDEX, Indian stock exchange, on spices. Internet.

"Spanish Galleon Trade Between the Philippines and Mexico." Online Facts and Details, Jeffrey Hayes, 2008, 9 pp.

"Spice Trade in India" by Caroline Lee Schwenz. DMS, Postcolonial Studies @ Emory, 4 pp.

"Spice Trade Route" Wiki, 16 pp.

"Spice Trade": Wiki. 7 pp.

"Spices: how the search for flavors influenced our world." YaleGlobalOnline. 5 pp.

"The Ancient Spice Trade route from Asia to Europe 1500s to 1700s that changed the world." by Luanne Teoh, 12/19/2013. Internet, 19 pp.

"The History of Cloves." InDepthInfo, 1 p.

"The History of Spice." UCLA. 8 pp. Esp. cloves

"The Manila Galleon, A Spanish trade route that connected 3 continents." Internet, Spain Naval Museum, 12 pp.

"The Spice Trade and its Importance for European Expansion." By Doz. Udo Pollmer. 15 pp. Summary of a book on this title (?)

"When and why did the Spice Trade end?" Reddit

"Why was Spice Trade so profitable in the 15th century?" from History Stack Exchange. 3 pp.

"Why were the spice islands important?" in rmg.co.ukdiscover/explore/spice islands. 4 pp.

Wallace:

- "1 July 1858: what Wallace knew; what Lyell thought he knew; what both he and Hooker took on trust; and what Charles Darwin never told them." By Roy Davies, 5/30/2013, Biological Journal of the Linnean Society, 3 pp.

"Wallace" original documents. Natural History Museum, London. His original journals, in a whole Wallace wing of the museum!

"Responses to Questions Frequently Asked About Wallace" Wallace section of the Natural History Library, London (collected in person 2016). 10 pp

"Wallace" in the Linnean Society. 4 pp.

ABOUT THE AUTHOR

Some of Carol Hodson Pechler's experiences were too good to pass up, she discovered, as she wrote this mostly fiction book about a young American woman pursuing her career in America by first seeking her fortune in the fabled Spice Islands of Southeast Asia. That is, she went to research a Spanish contact language, hoping to shed light on the mystery of how human languages first evolved. She'd bring back a treasure to launch her university faculty career.

After three years of field work in the Philippines, she stayed another year to analyze her data while teaching in a university in Manila. During the following four years, while teaching in universities in Germany, the Netherlands, and the U.S., she continued to analyze and process her Philippine data for publication. But then she discovered that her entire transcripts of recordings, and her extensive dictionary, had been stolen and published by a Filipina Catholic Sister.

Previous books by the author:

Run, Rima! – 2015, Menlo Publishing Company, Menlo Park, California

Deutsch im Kontakt mit anderen Sprachen; German in Contact with other Languages. Edited by Carol Molony [Pechler], Helmut Zobl, and Wilfried Stoelting. 1977, Scriptor Verlag, Kronberg/Ts., Germany.

MAP OF THE PHILIPPINES
AND INDONESIA

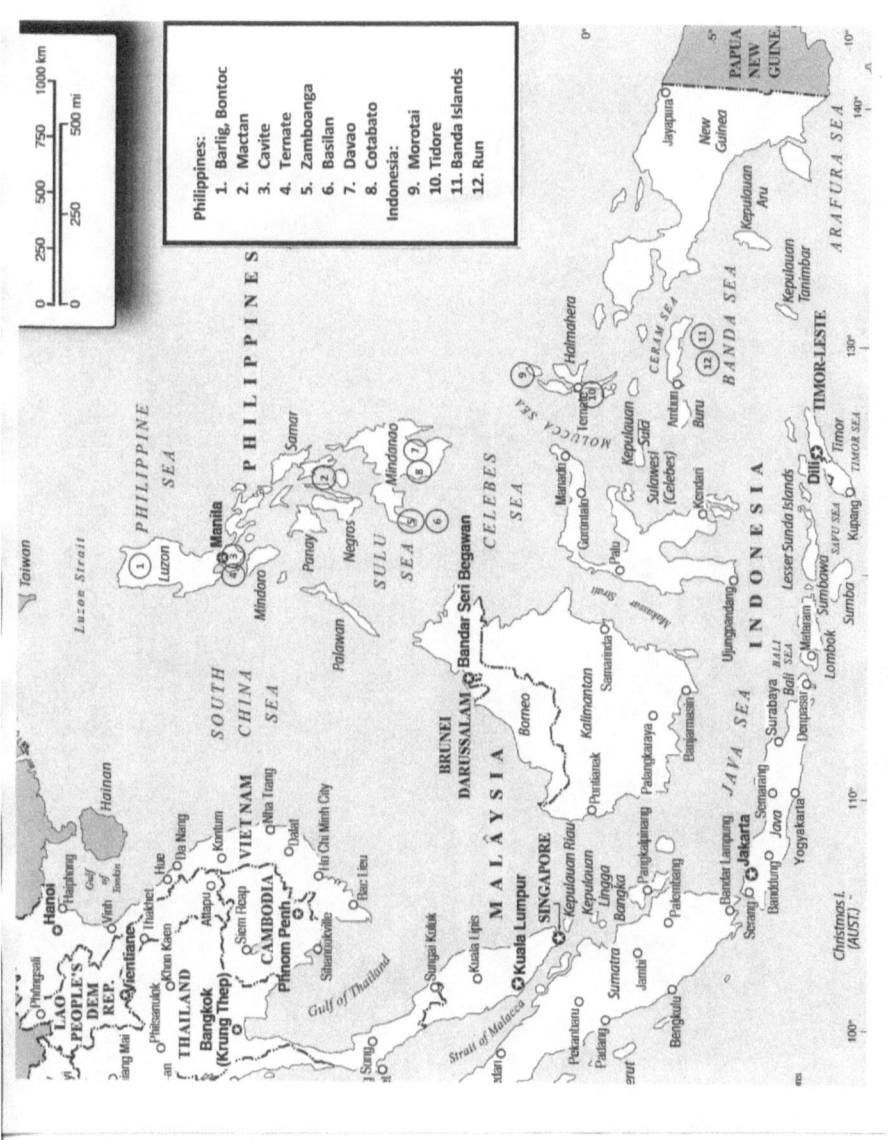

www.ingramcontent.com/pod-product-compliance
Lightning Source LLC
Chambersburg PA
CBHW030633260626
47157CB00007B/2315